CALLING OUT FOR YOU!

Karin Fossum

CALLING OUT FOR YOU!

Translated from the Norwegian by
Charlotte Barslund

THE HARVILL PRESS
LONDON

Published by The Harvill Press, 2005

2 4 6 8 10 9 7 5 3

First published with the title *Elskede Poona*
by J.W. Cappelens Forlag A.S., 2001

First published in Great Britain in 2005 by
The Harvill Press
Random House, 20 Vauxhall Bridge Road
London SW1V 2SA

Random House Australia (Pty) Limited
20 Alfred Street, Milsons Point, Sydney,
New South Wales 2061, Australia

Random House New Zealand Limited
18 Poland Road, Glenfield,
Auckland 10, New Zealand

Random House South Africa (Pty) Limited
Endulini, 5A Jubilee Road, Parktown 2193, South Africa

The Random House Group Limited Reg. No. 954009
www.randomhouse.co.uk

A CIP catalogue record for this book is available from the British Library

This edition was published with the financial assistance of NORLA

ISBN 1 84343 213 7

Papers used by Random House are natural, recyclable products made from wood
grown in sustainable forests; the manufacturing processes conform
to the environmental regulations of the country of origin

Typeset by SX Composing DTP, Rayleigh, Essex
Printed and bound in Great Britain by
Mackays of Chatham Plc, Chatham, Kent

With thanks to Finn Skårderud

CHAPTER 1

The silence is shattered by the barking of a dog. The mother looks up from the sink and stares out of the window. The barking comes from deep in the dog's throat. All of its black, muscular body quivers with excitement.

Then she sees her son. He gets out of the red Golf and lets a blue bag fall to the ground. He glances towards the window, registering the faint outline of his mother. He goes to the dog and releases it from its chain. The animal throws itself at him. They roll on the ground, sending the dirt flying. The dog growls and her son shouts affectionate curses in its ears. Sometimes he yells at the top of his lungs and smacks the Rottweiler hard across its snout. At last it stays down. Slowly he gets to his feet. Brushes the dust and dirt from his trousers. Glances once more at the window. The dog gets up hesitantly and cowers in front of him, its head down, until he allows it to come and lick the corners of his mouth, submissively. Then he walks to the house and comes into the kitchen.

"Good God, look at the state of you!"

The blue T-shirt is bloodstained. His hands are covered in cuts. The dog has scratched his face, too.

"Never seen anything like it," she says and sniffs angrily. "Leave the bag. I'm doing a load of washing later."

He folds his scratched arms across his chest. They are powerful like the rest of him. Close to 100 kilos and not a hint of fat. The muscles have just been used and they are warm.

"Calm down," he tells her. "I'll do it."

She can't believe her ears. Him, wash his own clothes?

"Where have you been?" she says. "Surely you don't work out from six to eleven?"

Her son mumbles something. He has his back to her.

"With Ulla. We were babysitting."

She looks at the broad back. His hair is very blond and stands upright like a brush. Thin stripes have been dyed scarlet. It's as if he were on fire. He disappears down the basement stairs. She hears the old washing machine start up. She lets the water out of the sink and stares into the yard. The dog has lain down with its head on its paws. The last remnant of light is disappearing. Her son is back, says he's going to take a shower.

"A shower at this hour? You've just come from the gym?"

He doesn't reply. Later she hears him in the bathroom, sounding hollow in the tiled space. He's singing. The door to the medicine cupboard slams. He's probably looking for a plaster, silly boy.

His mother smiles. All of this violence is only to be expected. He is a man, after all. Later, she would never forget this. The last moment when life was good.

It began with Gunder Jomann's journey. Gunder went all the way to India to find himself a wife. When people asked, he did not say that that was why he had gone. He hardly admitted it to himself. It was a journey to see a bit of the world, he explained when his colleagues asked. What an outrageous extravagance! He never spent anything on himself. Hardly ever went out, never accepted invitations to Christmas parties, kept himself busy either with his house or his garden or his car. Had never had a woman either, so far as anyone knew. Gunder was not troubled by the gossip. He was in fact a determined man. Slow – it was undeniable – but he got where he wanted without making waves. He had time on his side. In the evenings when he was in his fifty-first year he sat leafing through a book – a present from his younger sister, Marie – *People of All Nations*. Since he never went anywhere except to and from his workplace, a small, solid business that sold agricultural machinery, she could make sure that at least he had the chance to see pictures of what went on in the great wide world. Gunder read the book and leafed through the illustrations. He was most fascinated by India. The beautiful women with the red dots on their foreheads. Their painted eyes, their flirtatious smiles. One of them looked back at him from the book and he was soon lost in sweet dreams. No-one could dream like Gunder. He closed his eyes and flew away. She was as light as a feather in her red costume. Her eyes were so deep and dark, like black glass. Her hair was hidden under a scarf with golden frills. He had been gazing at the photograph for months. It was clear to him that he wanted an Indian wife. Not because he wanted a subservient and self-sacrificing woman, but because he wanted someone he could cherish and adore. Norwegian women didn't want to be adored. Actually he had never understood them, never understood what they wanted. Because he lacked nothing, as far as he could see. He had a house, a garden, a car, a job, and his kitchen was well equipped. There was under-floor heating in the bathroom, and he had a television and a video recorder, a washing machine, a tumble-dryer, a microwave, a willing heart and money in the bank. Gunder understood that there were other, more abstract factors, which determined whether you were lucky in love – he wasn't an imbecile. However, it was not much use to him unless it was something which could be learned or bought. Your time will come, his mother used to say as she lay dying in the big hospital bed. His father had passed away years before. Gunder had grown up with these two women, his mother and his sister, Marie. When his mother was seventy she developed a brain tumour and for long periods she was not herself. He would wait patiently for her to once more become the person he knew and loved. Your time will come. You're a good boy, you are, Gunder. One fine day a woman will come your way, you'll see.

But he did not see anyone coming his way. So he booked a flight to India. He knew it was a poor country. Perhaps he might find a woman there who could not afford to turn down his offer of following him all the way to Norway, to this pretty house, which belonged to him. He would pay for her family to come and visit, if they wanted to. He did not wish to separate anyone. And if she had some complicated faith, then he certainly would not stop her from observing it. There were few people as patient as Gunder. If only he could find a wife!

There were other options. But he did not have the courage to get on the bus to Poland with others, strangers. And he did not want to jump on a plane to Thailand. There were so many rumours about what went on there. He wanted to find a woman all by himself. Everything should be down to him. The thought of sitting down browsing through catalogues with photographs and descriptions of different women or staring at a TV screen where they offered themselves one after the other – that was unthinkable to Gunder. He would never be able to make up his mind.

The light from the reading lamp warmed his balding head. On a map of the world he found India and her principal cities: Madras, Bombay, New Delhi. He favoured a city by the sea. Many Indians spoke English and he felt reassured by that. Some were even Christians according to *People of All Nations*. It would be the most happy coincidence if he were to meet a woman who was perhaps a Christian and spoke English well. It mattered less whether she was twenty or fifty. He did not expect to have children, he was not over-ambitious, but if she had one, he would accept that as part of the deal. He might have to bargain. There were many customs in other countries so different to the ones here at home; he would pay handsomely if it was a question of money. His inheritance after his mother died was considerable.

First of all he needed to find a travel agency. There were four to choose from. One in the shopping centre, consisting only of a counter which you stood leaning against while going through some brochures. Gunder preferred to sit. This was an important decision, not something you did standing up, in a hurry. He would have to go into town; there were three travel agencies there. He looked through the telephone directory. Then he remembered that Marie had once left a holiday brochure in his house to tempt him. So like Marie, he thought, and looked in the index under "I". Ialyssos. Ibiza. Ireland. Were there no holidays in India? He found Bali under the Indonesian islands, but dismissed the thought. It was India or nothing. He would just have to ring the airport directly and book. He would manage as always, he always had, and in a big city they would be used to travellers. However, it was evening now and too

4

late to call. Instead he turned the pages of *People of All Nations* once more. For a long time he sat gazing at the Indian beauty. Imagine that a woman could be so wondrously pretty, so golden and smooth, so exquisitely delicate. She had gathered her shawl beneath her chin with a slender hand. She wore jewellery on her wrists. Her iris was practically black with a flash of light, from the sun perhaps, and she stared straight at Gunder. Into his longing eyes. They were large and blue and he closed them now. She followed him into his dream. He dozed in his chair and floated away with the golden beauty. She was weightless. Her blood-red costume fluttered against his face.

He decided to telephone from work during his lunch break. He went into the empty office they hardly ever used. It had been turned into a storeroom. Boxes of ring binders and files were stacked against the walls. A colourful poster on one wall showed a rugged man sitting on a tractor in a field. The field was so large that it disappeared, like the sea, into a blurred, blue horizon. *No farmer, no Norway*, it said on the poster. Gunder dialled the number. "Press 2 if you are travelling abroad," a voice said. He pressed 2 and waited. Then a new voice came on. "You are now number 19 in the queue. Please hold." The message was repeated at intervals. He doodled on the pad next to him. Tried drawing an Indian dragon. Through the window he saw a car pull in. "You are now number 16 in the queue . . . number 10 . . . number 8." He felt that he was being counted down towards something very decisive. His heart beat faster, and he drew his clumsy dragon even more enthusiastically. Then he saw Svarstad, a farmer, emerging from his black Ford. He was a good customer and always asked for Gunder; he also hated to be kept waiting. It was getting more urgent. Music began to flow through the handset and a voice announced that he would soon be connected to an available travel consultant. Just then Bjørnsson, one of the young salesmen, burst into the room.

"Svarstad," he said. "He's asking for you. What are you doing sitting in here anyway?" he added.

"I'll be right there. You'll have to keep him busy with small talk for a little while. Talk about the weather, it's been very fine recently." He listened to the receiver. A female voice came through.

"He just ignores me and tells me to get lost," said Bjørnsson. Gunder motioned him away. Eventually Bjørnsson took the hint and disappeared. Svarstad's disgruntled face could be seen through the window. The quick glance at his watch indicated that he didn't have all the time in the world and was irritated that they did not all come running at once.

"Well, it's like this," Gunder said. "I want to go to Bombay. In India. In a fortnight."

"From Gardermoen airport?" asked the voice.

"Yes. Leaving Friday in a fortnight's time."

He heard how her fingers swept across her keyboard and marvelled at how rapid they were.

"You need to fly to Frankfurt, departing at 10.15," she said. "From Frankfurt there is a flight at 13.10. It lands at 00.40, local time."

"The local time is?" Gunder said. He was scribbling like mad.

"The time difference is three hours and 30 minutes," she said.

"Very well. I would like to book the ticket then. How much is it?"

"Return flight?"

He hesitated. What if there were two of them flying back? That was what he was hoping for, dreaming of and wishing for.

"Can I change the ticket later on?"

"Yes, that's possible."

"Then I'll take the return flight."

"That will be 6,900 kroner. You can collect your ticket at the airport, or we can post it to you. Which would you prefer?"

"Post it," he said. And gave her his name and address and credit card number. "Blindveien, number 2."

"Just one small thing," the woman said when the booking was done. "It is no longer called Bombay."

"It isn't?" Gunder said, surprised.

"The city is called Mumbai. Since 1995."

"I'll remember that," said Gunder earnestly.

"SAS wishes you a pleasant flight."

He put the receiver down. At that moment Svarstad tore open the door to the office and gave him an angry look. He was looking to buy a harvester and had clearly decided to terrorise Gunder to the limit. The acquisition made him sweat all over. He clung grimly to his family farm and no-one dared to buy a new machine jointly with Svarstad. He was utterly impossible to work with.

"Svarstad," said Gunder and leapt to his feet. Everything that had happened had made his cheeks go scarlet. "Let's get started."

In the days that followed Gunder was unsettled. His concentration was poor and he was wide awake. It was difficult to fall asleep at night. He lay thinking of the long journey and the woman he might meet. Among all of Bombay's – he corrected himself – among all of Mumbai's twelve million people there had to be one for him. She was living her life there and suspected nothing. He wanted to buy her a little present. Something from Norway that she had never seen before. A Norwegian filigree brooch, perhaps, for her red costume. Or the blue or the green costume. Anyway, a brooch was what it would be. The next day he would drive into town and find one. Nothing big or ostentatious, rather something small and neat. Something to fasten her shawl with, if she wore shawls. But perhaps she wore trousers and sweaters, what did he know? His imagination went wild and he was still wide awake. Did she have a red dot on her forehead? In his mind he put his finger on it and in his mind she smiled shyly at him. "Very nice," said Gunder in English into the darkness. He had to practise his English. "Thank you very much. See you later." He did know a little.

Svarstad had as good as made up his mind. It was to be a Dominator from Claes, a 58S.

Gunder agreed. "Only the best is good enough," he smiled, bubbling over with his Indian secret. "Six-cylinder Perkins engine with 100 horsepower. Three-stage mechanical gearbox with hydraulic speed variator. Cutting board of three metres, 60."

"And the price?" said Svarstad glumly, although he knew perfectly

7

well that the cost of this marvel was 570,000 kroner. Gunder folded his arms across his chest.

"You need a new baling press, too. Make a proper investment for once and get yourself a Quadrant with it. You don't have much storage space."

"I need to have round bales," Svarstad said. "I can't handle big bales."

"That's just giving in to a habit," said Gunder unperturbed. "If you have the proper tools, you can reduce the number of seasonal workers. They cost money, too, the Poles, don't they? With a new Dominator and a new press you can do the job without them. I'll give you an unbeatable price as well. Trust me."

Svarstad chewed on a straw. He had a furrow in his weather-beaten brow and sadness in his deep-set eyes, which gave way slowly to a radiant dream. No other salesman would have tried selling one more piece of machinery to a man who could barely afford a harvester, but Gunder had gambled and as usual he had won.

"Consider it an investment in the future," he said. "You're still a young man. Why settle for second best? You're working yourself to death. Let the Quadrant make big bales, they stack easily and take up less room. No-one else in the area has dared to try big bales. Soon they'll every one of them come running to have a look."

That did it. Svarstad was delighted at the prospect, a small group of neighbours poking their noses into his yard. But he needed to make a call. Gunder showed him into the empty office. Meanwhile he went away to draw up the contract, the sale was practically in the bag. It could not have worked out better. A substantial sale before the long journey. He would be able to make his journey with a clear conscience.

Svarstad reappeared. "Green light from the bank," he said. He was lobster red, but his eyes shone beneath the bushy brows.

"Excellent," Gunder said.

After work he went into town and found a jewellery shop. He stared at the glass counter containing rings, only rings. He asked to be shown the national costume silver and the assistant asked him what kind.

8

Gunder shrugged. "Well, anything. A brooch, I think. It's a present. But she doesn't have a Norwegian national costume."

"You only wear filigree brooches with a national costume," pronounced the woman in a schoolmistressy tone.

"But it has to be something from Norway," Gunder said. "Something essentially Norwegian."

"For a foreign lady?" the assistant wanted to know.

"Yes. I was thinking she would wear it with her own national costume."

"And what sort of costume is that?" she asked, her curiosity increasing.

"An Indian sari," said Gunder proudly.

Silence behind the counter. The assistant was evidently torn as to what she should do. She was not unaffected by Gunder's charming stubbornness and she could hardly refuse to sell him what he wanted to buy. On the other hand the Norwegian Craft Council did have rules as to what was permissible. However, if a woman wanted to wander about in India wearing a filigree brooch on a bright orange sari, then the Craft Council would be none the wiser. So she got out the tray with the national costume silver and selected a medium-sized filigree brooch, wondering if the strangely self-possessed customer was aware of how much it was going to cost.

"How much is that one?" Gunder said.

"Fourteen hundred kroner. To give you an idea, I can show you this one from Hardanger. We have bigger brooches than this one and smaller ones, too. However, there is often quite a lot of gold in those saris, so I suppose it ought to be plain – if it's to have the desired effect."

Here her voice took on an ironic twist, but she suppressed it when she saw Gunder. He took the spiralling brooch from the velvet and held it in his rough hands. Held it up to the light. His face took on a dreamy expression. She softened. There was something about this man, this heavy, slow, shy man, that she warmed to in spite of everything. He was courting.

Gunder did not want to look at any other brooches. He would only begin to have doubts. So he bought the first one, which was

9

anyway the best, and had it wrapped. He planned to unwrap it when he got home and admire it again. In the car on his way back he drummed on the wheel as he imagined her brown fingers opening the package. The paper was black with tiny specks of gold. The ribbon around the box was blood red. It lay on the seat next to him. Perhaps he needed to get some pills for the trip. For his stomach. All that foreign food, he thought. Rice and curry. Spicy and hot as hell. And Indian currency. Was his passport valid? He was going to be busy. He had better call Marie.

The village where Gunder lived was called Elvestad. It had 2,347 inhabitants. A wooden church from the Middle Ages, restored in 1970. A petrol station, a school, a post office and a roadside café. The café was an ugly cross between a hut and a raised storehouse; it stood on pillars and steep steps led up to the entrance. On entering you immediately faced a jukebox, a Wurlitzer which was still in use. On the roof was a red and white sign with the words EINAR'S CAFÉ. At night Einar switched on the light in the sign.

Einar Sunde had run the café for seventeen years. He had a wife and children and was in debt up to his eyeballs because of his grandiose chalet-style villa just outside the village. A licence to sell beer had meant that he was at last able to meet his mortgage payments. For this simple reason there were always people in the café. He knew the villagers and ran the place with an iron hand. He pretty soon found out which year most of the young people were born in and would put his hand over the beer tap if they tried it on when they were still underage. There was also a village hall, where weddings and confirmations were celebrated. Most of the villagers were farmers. Added to that were quite a few newcomers, people who had fled the city having entertained a romantic notion of a quieter life in the country. This they had got. The sea was only half an hour away, but the salty air did not reach the village; it smelled of onions and leeks, or the rank smell of manure in the spring and the sweet smell of apples in the autumn. Einar was from the capital, but he had no longing to go back. He was the sole proprietor of the café.

As long as he had the café there wasn't a living soul who would dare try setting up within miles. He would run this café until they carried him out in a box. Because he managed to prevent excessive drinking and fights, everyone felt comfortable going in there. Women for coffee and pastries, kids for frankfurters and Coke, young people for a beer. He aired the place properly, emptied the ashtrays and replaced the nightlights whenever they burned down, kept it impeccably clean. His wife washed the red and white chequered tablecloths in the machine at home. True, the place lacked style, but he had drawn the line at actual kitsch. There were no plastic flowers. He had recently invested in a bigger dishwasher to save him having to wash the glasses by hand. The health inspector was welcome to visit his kitchen, it was fit for use as far as the equipment and cleanliness went.

It was here, in Einar's Café, that people kept abreast of what was going on in the village. Who was seeing whom, who was in the process of getting a divorce and which farmer might any second now have to sell up. A single minicab was at the villagers' disposal. Kalle Moe drove a white Mercedes and could be contacted by landline or mobile, always sober and always available. If he wasn't, he would get you a minicab from town. As long as Kalle Moe operated his minicab service in the village, there was no room for any other licence. He was past sixty and there were many waiting in the wings.

Einar Sunde was at his café six days a week till 10 o'clock in the evening on weekdays. On Saturdays he stayed open until midnight, on Sundays the café was closed. He was a hard worker, moved quickly, a beanpole of a man with reddish hair and long thin arms. A tea towel was tucked into his waistband; it was replaced the moment it was stained. His wife, Lillian, who hardly ever saw him except at night, lived her own life and they had nothing in common any more. They couldn't even be bothered to argue. Einar didn't have time to dream of something better, he was too busy working. The chalet-style villa was worth 1.6 million kroner and had a sauna and a gym, which he never had the time to use.

All or part of the village's hard core hung out at the café. It consisted mostly of young men aged between eighteen and thirty,

11

with or without girlfriends. Because Einar had a licence to sell beer, they never went into town to meet girls from further away. You could walk home from the café, the village was no bigger than that. They would rather have a few more beers than pay for an expensive minicab from town. So they married local girls and stayed here. However, before it got to that, the girls were passed around. It created a peculiar solidarity, with many unwritten rules.

Following a great deal of debate in the local council, Elvestad had acquired a shopping centre, as a result of which the local shop, Gunwald's one-stop shop, was languishing next to the Shell petrol station. Within the shopping centre some brave soul had set up shop with two sun beds, another had opened a florist's and a third a small perfumery. On the floors above were surgeries for the doctor and the dentist, and Anne's hair dressing salon. None of the young people from the village went there. Their hair had to be cut in town. Studs and rings in belly buttons and noses were also taken care of in town. Anne knew their parents and had been known to refuse. The older people, however, loyally shopped at Gunwald's. They came with their granny trolleys and ancient grey rucksacks and bought hashed lung and blood pudding and soft, sharp cheese. It was a good business for Ole Gunwald. He had paid off his mortgage ages ago.

Gunder never went to the café, but Einar knew very well who he was. On rare occasions he would stop and buy a Krone strawberry ice cream, which if the weather was good he ate outside sitting by a plastic table. Einar knew Gunder's house, knew that it was about four kilometres from the centre of the village toward Randskog. Besides, all the farmers in the village bought their machinery from Gunder. He was just coming through the door now, his hand already in his inside pocket.

"Just wanted to know," he said self-consciously, and rather hurriedly considering this was Gunder, "how long would it take to get from here to the airport by car?"

"Gardermoen airport?" said Einar. "I'd say an hour and a half. If you're going abroad you need to be there one hour before departure. And if I were you I'd throw in another half-hour to be on the safe side."

He kept on rubbing a triangular ashtray.

"Morning flight?" he asked, curious.

Gunder picked out an ice cream from the freezer.

"10.15."

"You'll have to get up early then."

Einar turned his back and carried on working. He was neither friendly nor smiling, he looked like a much-misunderstood man and did not meet Gunder's gaze. "If I were you I'd leave by 7.00."

Gunder nodded and paid. Asking Einar was preferable to revealing his ignorance to the woman from SAS. Einar knew who Gunder was and would not want to embarrass him. On the other hand, everyone in the village would know about his journey this very same evening.

"You going far?" Einar asked, casually, wiping another ashtray.

"Very, very far," said Gunder lightly. He tore the wrapper off the ice cream and left. Ate it as he drove the last few kilometres home. That would have given Einar something to think about. That was quite all right with Gunder.

Marie was really excited. She wanted to jump into her car right away and come over. Her husband, Karsten, was away on business, and she was bored and wanted to hear everything. Gunder was reluctant because Marie was sharp and he did not like the thought of being found out. But she was unstoppable. An hour later she was on his doorstep. Gunder was busy tidying up. If he were to bring someone back with him the house had to be spotless.

Marie made coffee for them and heated waffles in the oven. She had bought *crème fraîche* and jam in a Tupperware box. Gunder was touched. They were close, but they never let on. He did not know if she was happy with Karsten, she never mentioned him: it was as though he did not exist. They had never had children. All the same, she was attractive. Dark and neat, as their mother had been. Small and round, but gentle and bright. Gunder believed she could have had anyone at all, but she had settled for Karsten. She found the book *People of All Nations* on the table and put it on her lap. It

13

opened automatically on the picture of the Indian beauty. She looked up at her brother and laughed.

"Well . . . now I know why you want to go to India, Gunder. But this is an old book. I imagine she'll be around fifty now, probably wrinkled and ugly. Did you know that Indian women look fifteen till they're thirty? Then suddenly they grow old. It's the sun. Perhaps you ought to find yourself one who has been through the process already. Then you know what you're letting yourself in for."

She laughed so merrily that Gunder had to join in. He was not scared of wrinkles, even if Marie was. She had not a single one although she was forty-eight. He put *crème fraîche* on a waffle.

"I am mostly interested in the food and the culture," he said. "Culture. Music. That sort of thing."

"Yes, I believe it," Marie laughed. "When I next come to dinner I shall expect a casserole to make my eyes water. And there will be dragons all over the walls."

"I can't promise you that there won't be," he smiled. Then they were silent for a long time eating their waffles and drinking their coffee.

"Don't go round when you get there with your wallet sticking out of your back pocket," she said after a long pause. "Buy one of those little money belts. No, don't buy one, you can borrow one from me. It's quite plain, not in the least feminine."

"I can't walk around with a bag," Gunder said.

"Yes, you'll have to. A big city like that is teeming with pick-pockets. Imagine a peasant like you alone in a city with twelve million people."

"I am not a peasant," said Gunder, hurt.

"Of course you're a peasant," Marie said. "You're a peasant if ever anyone was. And what's more, it shows. When you're out walking you can't just stroll around."

"Not stroll around?" He was baffled.

"You have to stride, as though you were going to an important meeting, and look preoccupied. You're a businessman on an important trip and, most importantly, you know Bombay like the back of your hand."

"Mumbai," he corrected her. "Mumbai like the back of my hand."

"You look people straight in the eye when they come towards you on the pavement. You walk straight, taking determined steps, and button your jacket so the money belt doesn't show."

"Can't wear a jacket there," he said. "It's 40°C at this time of year."

"You have to," Marie said. "You have to keep out of the sun." She licked a blob of *crème fraîche* from the corner of her mouth. "Otherwise you'll have to get yourself a tunic."

"A tunic?" Gunder chuckled.

"Where are you staying?" his sister went on.

"At a hotel, of course."

"Yes, but what type?"

"A nice one."

"But what's it called?"

"No idea," Gunder said. "I'll work it out when I get there."

Her eyes widened. "You haven't booked your hotel?"

"I know what to say," he said, a little offended now. He looked quickly at her, at her white forehead and the narrow brows, which she darkened with a brush.

"Tell me," she said, lapping up her coffee. "Tell me exactly what you're going to say. You come out of this vast, complex, sweltering, chaotic airport teeming with people and you look around for a taxi stand. Then some stranger comes up to you, grabs your shirt and babbles something incomprehensible while taking hold of your suitcase and heads off in the direction of a dodgy vehicle. And you are so worn out and sweaty and confused that you can hardly remember your own name, plus your watch is several hours behind the time. You are desperate for a cool shower. Tell me what you're going to say, Gunder. To this small, dark stranger."

He put his waffle down, speechless. Was she joking? Then he pulled himself together and, looking straight at his sister, said: "Would you please take me to a decent hotel?"

Marie nodded. "Very well! But before that. What do you do before that?"

"I've no idea," Gunder said.

"You find out how much it costs! Don't get into a taxi without negotiating the price beforehand. Ask inside the airport. Perhaps Lufthansa has an information desk there, they'll be on your side."

He shook his head and reasoned that in all likelihood she was just jealous. She had never been to India. Only Lanzarote and Crete, places like that. That was where all Norwegians and Swedes went and the waiters called out "Hey, Swedish girl" after her and she didn't like it. No, India was something else.

"What about a malaria vaccine?" she said. "Do you need one of those?"

"Don't know," he said.

"You have to call the doctor. You're not coming back here with malaria or TB or hepatitis or anything like that, I can tell you. And don't drink the tap water. Don't drink juice or eat fruit. Make sure the meat is thoroughly cooked. Stay away from ice cream, too, you who are so fond of ice cream, and that's fine, but just don't eat the ice cream in India."

"Am I allowed alcohol?" he said snappily.

"I suppose you are. But for God's sake don't get too drunk. Then you'd be in real trouble."

"I never get drunk," Gunder said. "I haven't been drunk for fifteen years."

"I know. And you will call home, won't you? I need to know that you've arrived safely. I can collect your post. And water your flowers. I suppose the lawn will need mowing once or twice during those two weeks. You can drive the safe over to our place, can't you? Then it won't be here to tempt people. Are you parking at the airport? I expect it costs an arm and a leg."

"Not sure," he said.

"You're not sure? You have to book long-term parking in advance," she told him. "You'll have to phone tomorrow. You can't drive to Gardermoen and park just anywhere."

"No, I don't suppose I can," he said. It was a good thing that she had come over. He was quite dizzy under all this withering criticism and went resolutely to fetch a bottle of cognac. Yes, by God, he deserved a drink.

Marie was wiping her mouth and smiling. "This is so exciting,

Gunder. Imagine everything you will have to tell us when you come back. Have you got film for your camera? Have you got cancellation insurance? Have you made a list of everything you need to remember?"

"No," he said, sipping his cognac. "Would you do it for me, please, Marie?"

Then she relented and hurried off in search of pen and paper. While Gunder savoured the cognac in his mouth, Marie wrote a "To Do" list. He watched her secretly. She sucked on the pen, tapped it lightly against her teeth to focus her thoughts. Her shoulders were so round and neat. He was lucky to have Marie. There was nothing unresolved between them.

Whatever happened, he would always have Marie.

CHAPTER 2

This is how Gunder looked as he sat in the plane: His back straight like a schoolboy. He wore a short-sleeved shirt from Dressmann, dark blue blazer and khaki trousers. He had not flown many times in his life and was very impressed by everything around him. In the overhead locker he had a black bag and in the inside pocket, zipped up, was the filigree brooch in its small box. In his wallet he had Indian rupees, German marks and Sterling. He closed his eyes now. Did not like the violent feeling of suction as the plane took off.

"My name is Gunder," he said to himself in English. "How do you do?"

The man next to him looked at him.

"Your soul remains at Gardermoen. That's good to know, don't you think?"

Gunder didn't understand.

"When you travel as fast as we do today the soul stays behind. Somewhere in the airport. It's probably in a pub somewhere, at the bottom of a glass. I had a whisky before we left."

Gunder tried to imagine whisky in the morning. He couldn't. He had bought himself a cup of coffee and had stood by the long counter watching people rush by. Then he had wandered slowly around, browsing, noiseless in his new sandals. His soul was in its place under his blazer, he was quite sure of that.

"You should swap that whisky for a coffee," he said simply.

The man looked at Gunder and laughed. Then he said, "What are you selling?"

"Is it that obvious?"

"Yes."

"I sell agricultural machinery."

"And now you're going to a trade fair in Frankfurt?"

"No, no. This time I'm a tourist."

"Who goes on holiday in Frankfurt?" the man wondered.

"I'm going further than that," said Gunder happily. "All the way to Mumbai."

"And where is that?"

"India. Formerly Bombay, if that means anything to you." Gunder smiled importantly. "The city has been renamed Mumbai since 1995."

The man signalled to a passing air hostess and ordered whisky on the rocks. Gunder asked for orange juice and reclined his seat and closed his eyes. He did not want to talk. He had so many thoughts to think. What should he say about Norway? About Elvestad. What the Norwegians were like. What *were* they like? And the food, what was there to say about that? Rissoles. Fish pie and brown cheese. Ice-skating. Very cold. Down to –40°C sometimes. Norwegian oil. His juice arrived and he drank it slowly. Sat sucking an ice cube. Squeezed the plastic cup into the little net at the back of the seat in front of him. Outside he saw the clouds drift by like candyfloss. Perhaps he would fail to find a wife on his trip to India. If he could not find one at home why would he be able to find one in a foreign country? But *something* was happening. He was on his way towards something new. No-one in Elvestad had been to India, as far as he knew. Gunder Jomann. A well-travelled man. He remembered that he had forgotten to check the batteries in his camera. But they would surely sell them at the airport. After all he wasn't going to another planet. What were Indian women called? If he met one with a totally impossible name perhaps he could make up an affectionate diminutive. Indira, he remembered. Gandhi. It wasn't hard at all. Sounded like Elvira. Human beings everywhere have so much in common, he persuaded himself. At last he fell asleep. Immediately she appeared in his dreams. Black eyes sparkling.

Marie went to Gunder's house every day. She checked the doors and the windows. Picked up his post and put it on the kitchen table. Stuck a finger in all the potted plants one after the other. Always stayed a few minutes to worry about him. He was so trusting, like a child, and now he was milling around over there in the heat among twelve million people. They spoke languages he did not understand. Mind you, he was dependable. Never impulsive and certainly not liable to over-indulge. She looked at the photographs on the wall of their mother and of herself as a five-year-old with round cheeks and chubby knees. One photograph of Gunder in his national service uniform. One of their parents standing together in front of the house. He also had a wretched painting of a winter landscape, bought at an auction in the community hall. She looked at the furniture. Sturdy and reliable. Clean windows. If he ever found himself a wife, she thought, he would treat her like a princess. But he was going downhill a bit. He was still a fine man, but everything was beginning to sag. His stomach. His jowls. His hairline was receding slowly but surely. His hands were big and rough as their father's had been. What a father he would have made. She felt sad. Perhaps he would grow old alone. What was he doing in India? Was he trying to find himself a wife? The idea had crossed her mind. What would people say? For herself she would say nothing at all except to be friendly. But the others, anyone who wasn't as fond of him as she was? Did he really know what he was doing? Presumably. His voice down the phone, all the long way from India, crackling and hissing. Excited. I'm here now, Marie. The heat is like a wall. My back was wet before I was down the steps out of the plane. I've found a hotel. They speak English everywhere. There was no problem with the waitress. I said "chicken" and she brought me a chicken such as I've never seen the like of. You haven't tasted chicken until you've been to India, he said eagerly. And it's cheap too. When I returned the next day, she came to the table and asked if I wanted chicken again. So now I eat there every day. Every time there is a different sauce: red, green or yellow. No reason to look any further now that I have found this place. It is called Tandel's Tandoori. The service is very good.

The waitress, Marie supposed, and smiled resignedly. Probably she was the first person he had met and on top of it she was nice to him. That was probably enough for Gunder. Now he would sit in this Tandel's Tandoori for a fortnight and not contrive to see anything else. She told him that everything at home was fine. But was he aware that one of the hibiscus plants had greenfly? For a moment Gunder's voice took on a hint of anxiety. Then he composed himself. "I have an insecticide in the basement. It'll just have to stay alive until I get home. Or it'll die. It's as simple as that."

Marie sighed. It was unlike her brother to speak about his plants so casually. When they died he took it for a personal insult.

The book she had once given him was there on the shelf. She noticed it because it stood out a little from the other spines. She took it down and once more it opened automatically to the same page. She studied the Indian woman for a while. Imagined her brother studying the beautiful picture. What would Indian women think of Gunder? In a way there was something impressive about him. He was tall and immensely broad-shouldered for a start. And his teeth were nice; he took good care of them. His clothes were clean, if old-fashioned. And he had this trustworthy character. The fact that he was slow, perhaps they wouldn't notice that if they were busy working out what he was saying. Maybe for that reason they might be able to see him for what he really was: decent and good as gold. Not so quick off the mark, but honest. Unhurried, but industrious. Concerned, but focused. His eyes were nice. The beauty in the photograph had nice eyes, too, they were almost black. Looking into Gunder's large blue eyes was probably exotic and different for an Indian woman. Then he had this big, heavy body. Indians were delicate, slender people, she believed, though she didn't know very much about them. She was just about to put the book back on the shelf when a scrap of paper fell out. A receipt from a jeweller's. Astonished, she stood and stared. A filigree brooch. 1,400 kroner. What did that mean? It was not for her; she had no national costume. Clearly there was more going on here than she had suspected. She put the receipt back in the book and left the house. Turned one last time and stared at the windows. Then she drove to the village. Marie was, according to Gunder and her husband Karsten, a terrible driver. Her entire concentration was directed at the road in front of the car. She never looked in the mirror, but held tight to the steering wheel and focused on 70 kilometres in all areas. She had never used the fifth gear in her car. It was not that she was better at everything, though of the two of them she was the one who took charge whenever anything needed doing. However, she knew her brother. Now she was sure. He *had* gone to India to find a wife. And given his tenacity and patience it would not surprise her if he turned up in a fortnight's time with a dark woman on his arm, a filigree brooch on her dress. God help us, she thought, and went straight over a pedestrian crossing, giving a woman with a pram the fright of her life. What would people say?

She stopped at the café to buy cigarettes. Einar was polishing the jukebox. First he sprayed it with polish then he rubbed it with a tea towel. It was still the school holidays. Two girls sat at one of the tables. Marie knew them, Linda and Karen. Linda was a skinny girl with a shrill, almost manic laugh. She had very blonde frizzy hair, a gaunt face and pointy white teeth. Whenever Marie looked at the girl she immediately thought that here was someone who would turn out bad. She did not know why she thought this, but there was something about the girl's personality, the almost unnaturally sparkling eyes, the frantic movements and the shrill laughter, which made Marie think that she was the type who wanted too much. She stood out like a lamp with too strong a bulb. One day something would sweep her away. The other one, Karen, dark and calmer, sat there more subdued. Spoke with a lowered voice, kept herself to herself. Einar picked out a packet of John Player's and Marie paid. She did not like Einar. He was polite, but he always walked around as though he was hiding an unpleasant secret. His face was not open and broad like Gunder's. It was tight, gaunt. It bore evidence of ill will. Gunder did not like him either. Not that he had ever said as much, because he never spoke ill of people. If he did not have anything pleasant to say, he simply kept his mouth shut. Like the time she had asked about the new chap at work, young Bjørnsson. He had looked up from his paper and said, "Bjørnsson is doing fine". Then he went back to his paper and said no more. She knew at that moment that he did not like him. He could, however, talk about the village taxi driver for ages. Kalle Moe has bought car wax by mail order, he might say. Six hundred kroner for two tiny boxes. That man is unbelievable. I think the car has done half a million kilometres. But you would never know. I think he sings it to sleep at night. Gunder would laugh, and Marie would know that he liked Kalle. And Ole Gunwald in the one-stop shop. He suffers from migraines. Poor Gunwald. While she was contemplating these things she heard Linda's laughter once more and she saw Einar glance quickly at the two girls. At least he had something to look at while standing there rubbing his jukebox.

"So Jomann has ventured out into the big wide world?" Einar said all of a sudden. Marie nodded.

"To India. On holiday."

"India? Bless me. Oh well, if he comes back with an Indian wife I'll be green with envy," he laughed. Marie laughed. Was everyone thinking the same as she was? She left the café and drove home at an average speed of 68 kilometres an hour. A light flashed red on the dashboard. She must remember to tell Karsten.

Gunder was sweating, but it did not matter. In fact his shirt was wet, and he did not care. He sat quite still at the table and looked at the Indian woman. She was so nimble and light and smiled so pleasantly. She wore a money belt quite like his own around her waist, where she kept her change. She had on a floral dress, her arms were bare and she had gold rings in her ears. Long blue-black hair, which was plaited and coiled up at the back of her head. He sat there wondering how long it was. Perhaps all the way to her bottom. She was younger than he was. Maybe forty, and her face was marked by the sun. Her teeth showed when she smiled. Indeed her front teeth stuck out prominently. Her vanity resulted in frequent attempts to suppress the smile, but she had to give up. Smiling came easily to her. She is pretty when she closes her mouth, Gunder thought, and you can fix the teeth. He sat there observing her while drinking the strange, exotic coffee with cinnamon and sugar and he felt that she had noticed it and perhaps even liked it. He had eaten in this restaurant six days in a row. She had served him every time. He wanted to say something to her, but was fearful of making a *faux pas.* Perhaps she was not allowed to talk to the customers. He did not know the ways of this country and it inhibited him. He could stay here one evening till they shut and then follow her. No, no, of course he couldn't! He held up his hand. She came over immediately.

"One more coffee," said Gunder nervously. He was building up to something. The tension made his face look serious and she did notice that. She nodded without a word and fetched the coffee, came back very quickly.

"Very good coffee," he said and fixed his blue gaze on her so that she would remain standing there.

"My name is Gunder," he said eventually. "From Norway."

She gave him a brilliant smile. The large teeth showed.

"Ah! From Norway. Ice and snow," she laughed.

He laughed too and thought that she probably had a husband and a child, possibly a whole flock of them. And elderly parents in need of help. That it would never cross her mind to follow him anywhere at all. He felt sad, but she stayed at his table.

"Have you seen the city?" she said.

He stared at the table, embarrassed. For days he had wandered aimlessly, watching the people. There were crowds everywhere. Sleeping in the street, eating in the street, selling their wares on the pavement. The streets served as market, playground, meeting place, everything but a traffic artery. He had not visited places of interest. He had just been looking for her.

"No," he confessed. "Only people. Very beautiful people," he added.

Then she blushed and stared at the floor. It looked to him as if she was waiting for something more. She lingered by the table a little longer. Gunder felt brave. He was constrained by the lack of time, impelled by the resulting urgency; he was also a long way from home. The overpowering heat, the feeling of unreality. And his actual purpose. He looked into her black eyes and said, "I came to find a wife."

She did not laugh. She only nodded, slowly, as if she understood everything. The fact that he kept coming back. To this very place. To her. She had felt his gaze, and thought about him after work, this mountain of a man with blue eyes. The calm which surrounded him. The dignity. So exotic and so different. She had wondered what he wanted. Obviously he was a tourist and yet he was something other.

"I show you the city?" she said cautiously. She was not smiling now, and there was no sign of her protruding teeth.

"Yes. Please! I wait here," he said, slapping the tabletop. "You work. I wait here."

She nodded, but stayed a while longer. The room was very quiet. Only a low hum from the other tables.

"*Mira nam Poona he,*" she said.

"What?" Gunder said.

"Poona. My name is Poona Bai."

She held out a brown hand.

"Gunder," he said. "Gunder Jomann."

"Welcome to Bollywood," she laughed.

He did not understand what she meant, but he heard his own heart beat softly and hopefully. Then he bowed to her and at last she collected herself and disappeared out to the kitchen.

That evening he called Marie. He sounded excited.

"Did you know that they call this city Bollywood?" he laughed down the other end; she could almost hear how hot he was. "They are the world's biggest film producers. I've learned a little Indian, by the way. *Tan je vad*, it means thank you. There are more than a billion people living in India, Marie, imagine."

"Yes," she said. "Soon there'll be so many of us on this planet that we'll eat one another."

Gunder chuckled at the other end of the line.

"Have you met someone?" she asked, unbearably curious.

Yes, of course he had met people, how could she suppose otherwise, one billion, you couldn't walk down the streets without all the time bumping into people. "There's air conditioning in the hotel," he went on. "When I go out of the door, the heat hits me. That's the worst time."

"Are you taking care of your tummy?" she said.

Oh yes, he was taking care of his tummy, he took his tablets and

25

felt fine, but the heat meant that everything had to happen in slow motion. Marie visualised a slow Gunder, walking down the streets of Mumbai in slow motion.

"I expect you're looking forward to coming back?" she said, because that was what she wanted to hear. She did not like it that her slow brother had all of a sudden become a well-travelled man, and she did not like his superior tone.

"It'll be great to come home," he reassured her. "And I've bought you a present. Something really Indian."

"What is it?" she wanted to know.

"No, no. It's a secret."

"I cut the grass today. There's a lot of moss. Did you know that?"

Gunder laughed. "We'll get rid of that," he said. "We can't have moss in the lawn."

We? He seemed strangely elated. Marie hardly recognised her brother. She clutched the phone and felt that she wanted him to come back. She could not take care of him when he was so far away.

"It's hot here too," she said importantly. "It was 29°C in Nesbyen yesterday."

"Well, well, 29°C? Here we have 42°C, Marie. Yesterday it was hotter still. And when I ask the Indians if they're used to it – after all, they've lived with it for years – they say no, it is just as bad for us. Strange, don't you think?"

"Yes. If they came over here to our minus 20°C they would probably turn into ice," she said impatiently.

"I don't think so," Gunder told her. "The Indians work hard, and would keep warm regardless. It's that simple. But luckily I am on holiday. I just stroll around the streets with my arms sticking out."

"Sticking out?"

"Can't bear to have them touching my body," he said. "Have to spread my fingers, too. But there is air conditioning at the hotel," he repeated.

"You mentioned that," she said.

Then they were both silent. Marie sighed the way a sister sighs over an impossible brother.

"I have to go now," Gunder said. "I'm meeting someone."

"Oh?"

"We are going out for dinner. I'll call in a day or two."

She heard the click as he hung up. Saw her brother in her mind, gliding around with his fingers spread and his arms sticking out. In the shimmering heat. She could not understand why he was so happy.

CHAPTER 3

Gunder and Poona were married on August 4th, at noon precisely. In the City Court House, as Poona called it. Gunder had obtained the necessary paperwork and the Norwegian Foreign Office had sent a fax to confirm his status in Norway as a bachelor. It was a simple, but very solemn ceremony.

Gunder stood up straight like a soldier, listening and hoping that he answered in the right places. Poona shone. Her plait was coiled at the nape of her neck, like a huge pretzel. She did not even try to hide her teeth, but smiled joyfully at everything that happened. Gunder's English was getting better. They conversed in short sentences, helped by gestures and smiles, and understood one another very well. Often when Gunder was halfway through a sentence she would complete it exactly as he had imagined it himself. It was so easy. He explained to her about Norwegian citizenship. It could take a few years. Becoming Norwegian was certainly not straightforward, he thought. After the ceremony they walked down the streets as husband and wife. She wore gold sandals and a turquoise sari with the pretty filigree brooch at her throat. He wore a new white shirt, dark trousers and newly polished shoes. His arm was around her waist. She looked up at Gunder's face, the broad face with the strong neck. He was a sturdy and solid man and yet so humble. Sometimes he would blush and yet he possessed a peculiar confidence and was so unaffected by all the people around him. He had eyes only for her. She saw his suppressed joy and the broad smile around his mouth. She thought that this man had his own world, which he controlled. And how good that was.

It was not that she thought he was rich. He had told her so: I'm not rich at all. But I do have a house and a job. A nice garden. A good car. And a kind sister. She'll make you feel welcome. We live near a small village. It's quiet there, not much traffic. You can walk along the road all on your own and not meet a living soul."

This seemed strange to Poona. Such a huge silence, devoid of people. She knew only crowds in the city. She had only seen silence in photographs.

"I'd prefer to work," she said firmly.

"Of course you can. But then you may have to go into town. There is nothing in Elvestad. If you get a job in town, then I can give you a lift."

"I'm a hard worker," she went on. "I don't tire easily. I'm not big, but I'm tough. You won't need to provide for me."

"No, no," said Gunder then. "It's fine if you get a job. Then you'll learn Norwegian more quickly. It's going to be so good, Poona, I promise you. Norwegians are friendly. A little shy, perhaps, and very proud, but friendly."

Poona's only family was an older brother who lived in New Delhi. She wanted to write to him and tell him about her marriage. And in addition she needed to tie up the loose ends of her life in the Indian city before travelling to Norway. She would need about a fortnight. Gunder booked and paid for her ticket. Explained to her about transfers and Gardermoen airport. He gave her money so that she would not be short of anything. Wrote down his address and telephone number in neat numbers and letters.

"Will your brother be hurt when you tell him this?" he asked anxiously.

"No, no," said Poona, sure of herself. "We hardly ever see each other. Shiraz lives his own life. Has a wife and four children. I like cooking," she said. "I'll make chicken curry for you and your sister when I get to Norway."

"And I'll make Norwegian lamb stew," Gunder told her happily. "Mutton and cabbage."

"Is it spicy?" she said.

"We don't have spicy food in Norway. Bring lots of spices with you, Poona. Then we'll make Marie and Karsten sweat a bit."

She pondered this for a while. "What will your sister say once she meets me?"

"She'll be pleased," Gunder said. "Alarmed at first, but then she'll be pleased. She doesn't like me living on my own. She's always telling me that I ought to travel a bit. Now I'm bringing the whole world back with me." He laughed, and hugged her tightly. He couldn't stop himself from touching the plait at the nape of her neck with his hand. It was hard and tight and shiny like silk. When she tore the band off, the hair unravelled and became unimaginably full. How many women in Elvestad had hair like this? None! She only lets it down at night. Only for him. In the night her eyes shone white in the darkness. She held his heavy body carefully in her slender arms. Gunder stroked her softly across her back with large, hesitant hands. Poona was happy. A tall and handsome man with blue eyes had picked her from the hot restaurant kitchen; he would take her away from the burning hot city, from the sea of people and the crowds, from the tiny room with a toilet in the corridor. Gunder had his own bathroom with a bathtub and swans on the walls. She could hardly believe it. From the first time they looked at each other, they both knew that they were going the same way. The first time he leaned forward and held the slender body and he saw the big eyes grow moist and then cloud over before finally they closed and she relaxed into his broad chest, they knew it. No words were exchanged during that first night, only the beating of their hearts. His firm and heavy, hers light and quick. They were not scared at all, not yet. Poona would leave her job and clear out the tiny room where she lived. Gunder would return home and prepare the house and the garden. At the hotel someone helped them take a photograph. They stood up straight side by side, formal from the pact they had just entered into. She in the turquoise sari, he in the snow-white shirt. He had two copies made and gave her one of them.

Because of her work she could not come with him to the plane. They parted on the pavement outside the hotel and for a moment he forgot his shyness and hugged her tightly and fiercely. At that very moment a crack appeared under his shirt. Because he had finally found her and now he had to travel so far away. He was worried about everything that could happen to her. She raised a finger and caressed his nose. Then she was gone. On slender brown legs she disappeared around the corner. Later he sat in the confined space of his aeroplane seat holding the photograph in his hand. He felt his heart swell in his chest, pumping more blood than usual. He was far too hot. Poona had touched him everywhere. Even inside his ears where he had never put anything except a cotton wool bud. He felt his fingers and toes, his lips tremble when he so much as thought of her. It was as if everything inside him pulsated and he felt that everyone could see it. Gunder was a loved man. A man who loved. He was almost on fire. He looked at the other passengers, but could see only Poona. How had he actually spent his own life so far? For fifty years he had been on his own wandering around looking after himself and on rare occasions his sister. The remainder of his life would be lived for Poona. They would share everything. If she was tired or worn out, she would rest. If she longed for home, she would go there on holiday and if he was able to go with her then that would be fine, but if she wanted time to herself then she would have it. He would listen when she spoke and never interrupt. There was much for her to go through and she would need understanding and support, especially during the first year. He was already looking forward to Christmas, to showing her the Christmas tree and the elves and the angels. And to the springtime when the first shoots would force their way up through the snow. For her it must all seem like a miracle. So it would be for him, too. From now on everything would be new and wonderful.

Marie gazed at the photograph in amazement. Then up at her brother's proud face and down again at the Indian woman, Poona Bai Jomann. With a filigree brooch on her chest. For a long time she was speechless. Her brother had quite simply found himself a wife in India. Walked into a tandoori restaurant and then won her in the space of a few hours. What kind of secret weapon did her brother possess that she had never seen? It was as though she had been waiting for him, in Bombay with its millions of people.

31

"Mumbai," Gunder reminded her. "Well, this is how it happened. She was living her life there just waiting for me. She'll be arriving on the 20th; I'm picking her up from Gardermoen. Look. The marriage certificate," he said proudly.

"You're a great catch for her," said Marie. "I don't suppose there are many men in India with an income like yours."

"She knows I'm not rich," Gunder said.

"Nonsense! You're loaded," said Marie mercilessly. "She's worked that out."

He looked at her hurt, but she didn't notice it because she was still staring at the photograph.

"Karsten will have a heart attack," she said. "You'll have to be prepared for gossip."

However, she was also touched. A sister-in-law! She would never have believed it.

"I'm not bothered about gossip," said Gunder. That she already knew. As happy as her brother was now, nothing could hurt him.

"You'll help her settle in, won't you?" he asked his sister. "You women need to get together and chat like women do. Spend some time together. You'll find her gentle and kind."

"I do wonder what Karsten will say," Marie repeated, obviously worried.

"Surely you're not going to be put off by that?" Gunder said.

"I don't know," she said and shrugged. "I suppose he'll be shocked, at first. I do hope people will be friendly towards her."

"They will be," said Gunder rather airily. "Why wouldn't they be?"

"I was thinking of the young people. They are cruel."

"She's not bothered about young people," said Gunder. "She's thirty-eight years old."

"Very well. I'm just a bit stunned by everything that's happened. But she's very nice-looking. What did her family say?"

"All she has left of her family is an older brother who lives in New Delhi. They aren't close."

"But will she settle here? In this ice-cold country?"

"It's only cold during winter," he said quickly. "Living with the heat isn't easy either. It is fresher here. I told her so. Our air is drier. The humidity in India is so high that you're soaked the moment you step on to the street. She wants to try and find a job. She is capable and willing to learn. She'd prefer waitressing. We'll find something."

Marie sighed. She sat stroking the beautiful ivory elephant which Gunder had brought back for her. Her brother's optimism was so great and so strong that she didn't have the heart to tear it apart. But she did have her doubts. Mostly she was thinking of the Indian woman who was coming to this tiny spot, a remote corner of the world, peopled by farmers and callous teenagers. There were disdainful people in every single house. Gunder would probably cope, but how much could this woman put up with before she would begin to miss her own people?

Gunder pinned his wedding day photograph on to a notice board above his desk at home. He had to move a photograph of Karsten and Marie, but his wife should have prime position. Every time he looked up at the photograph a powerful sensation welled up in him – it was as though a fountain had sprung deep inside him. This is my wife, he said to himself. Come and meet my wife. Her name is Poona. Then he set eagerly about his work.

New linen for the double bed. With lace trimmings on the pillowcases. New tablecloth for the dining room. Four new towels for the bathroom. Took down the curtains – they needed washing and ironing. Marie helped him. The silver needed polishing – their mother had left him a great deal of silverware. The windows needed cleaning, they had to sparkle so brightly that Poona could look out into the pretty garden with its roses and peonies. The water in the birdbath needed replacing. There was no drain, so he emptied it using a bucket. Then he washed it with soapy water and refilled it. He tidied all the rubbish, pulled up weeds and raked the gravel drive. All the time he could hear Poona's voice in his head and catch her scent in the air. He saw her face when he lay down at night. Remembered the gentle touch of her finger on his nose.

At work everyone was very curious to hear about his trip. He was tanned and jolly and told them what they wanted to hear, but he did not mention Poona. He wanted to keep her to himself a little while longer. They would soon enough hear, soon enough to begin their whispering.

"You've been a lot in the sun," Bjørnsson said, and nodded approvingly.

Gunder's balding head glowed like a red bulb.

"Not for a moment," Gunder said. "Can't sit in the sun there. I've only been in the shade."

"Good God," Bjørnsson said.

Nevertheless his colleagues secretly suspected that something was going on. He made more calls than usual. Kept going into the empty office and motioned away anyone who appeared in the doorway. He often went shopping in his lunch break. They noticed carrier bags from the china shop and from the home furnishing place that sold textiles and bed linen.

Poona called collect. Her brother was not happy about the marriage, but she was not much concerned about that. "He's just jealous," she said. "He is very, very poor, you see."

"We'll invite him to Norway, when everything is sorted out. He should see how nicely you'll be living. I'll pay for his flight."

"There's no need for you to do that," Poona said. "He doesn't deserve it seeing how grumpy he's being."

"He'll calm down eventually. We'll take photographs and send them to him. Photographs of you in front of the house. And in the kitchen. Then he can see that you're not lacking for anything."

August 20th was approaching. Marie called to let him know that Karsten was going on a business trip to Hamburg and would not be back on the day Poona arrived. The two of them probably wanted to be alone on the first day, she said. "And I won't come rushing over at once. Why don't you come to dinner on the 21st. I'll do venison. And it's Karsten's birthday on the 24th. That way she'll meet him, too. He'll just have to make an effort and be sociable for once."

"He's not sociable?" Gunder said, taken aback.

"You know what he's like," she said.

"We'll take the time we need together," said Gunder. "Poona will need it more. She's the one leaving behind everything and everyone for something completely new."

"I'll go out and get some flowers for tomorrow. I've still got your key," Marie said happily. "I'll put them in the living room with a card for her from Karsten and me. Then she'll feel welcome. When are you leaving?"

"In plenty of time," Gunder said. "The plane lands at 18.00. She changed flights in Frankfurt yesterday and spent the night there. She wanted to do some shopping there first. I mean to be there an hour early, to find a parking space and all that."

"You'll call when you get back, won't you? Just so that I know you found each other."

"Found each other? Why wouldn't we?"

"Well, she's coming ever such a long way. Sometimes there are delays and things like that."

"Of course we'll find each other," Gunder said. And it struck his sister that it had never occurred to him that she would not arrive as anticipated. That she might have cried off at the last minute had never crossed his mind. But it had just crossed hers. He had given her money and bought her a ticket, which she might have been able to cash in. A fortune for a poor woman. Besides it was absolutely impossible to imagine an Indian woman in a turquoise sari in Gunder's kitchen. She didn't say this. She told her brother to drive carefully the long way up the E6.

"Traffic's terrible," she said. "Tomorrow's not a good day for you to have an accident. That would be bad timing."

"It would indeed," Gunder said.

CHAPTER 4

August 20th. He had taken the day off work. He got up at 7.00 and drew the curtains. The weather had been fine for a long time, but today the sky was heavy and black and it annoyed him. However, there was some wind too, perhaps it would brighten up later. Gunder was optimistic. He took a long and thorough shower and made himself a hearty breakfast. Pottered about the house. Studied the photograph of Poona and himself on the wall above his desk. Checked the sky to see if anything was happening. At about 2 p.m. he saw a blue crack. Soon afterwards the sun broke through with twinkling rays. Gunder took this as a sign. The rays were for Poona. In his mind he saw her all the time even as he assumed that she saw him, meeting her gaze in rapid glimpses. Then he could not see her any more. So he had to find something to do with himself – such as fetch the post. Look through the paper. Another hour and a half, he thought, and then I'll be on my way. But why not now? There will be less traffic if I go now. He folded the newspaper carefully and got swiftly to his feet. Left a window ajar and was just about to get the keys from the hook on the wall when the telephone rang. Ominously. No doubt someone from work. They never could manage on their own. That was why he was irritated when he answered. It was a woman's voice, not a voice he knew, but he heard the words clearly down the phone. The Central Hospital. Marie Jomann Dahl, was she a relative of his? Gunder's breath caught in his throat.

"Yes, my sister. What's happened?"

"A road accident," the woman replied.

He looked at the clock, confused. What had she got up to now?

"Is it serious?" he said.

"I have only been asked to contact the nearest relatives," she said, avoiding his question. "Are you able to come to the hospital?"

"Of course," Gunder said. "I'll leave right away. I should be there in half an hour."

He felt a nasty tightening in his chest. Not that he thought it was something life-threatening, she didn't drive fast enough to seriously hurt herself, but he had to go and meet Poona. Of course he would still make it, Marie would understand that it was important. He grabbed the keys and ran from the house. Drove without concentrating towards the town, checking his watch every few minutes. He imagined an arm in plaster and perhaps some stitches. There goes the venison you promised, he thought. There could be something wrong with her car and she might need a lift home. And *she* had told *him* to drive safely! He breathed through his nose to calm himself. Made his way to the hospital. Searched frantically for a parking space.

"Tenth floor. Neurology," said the woman in reception.

"Neurology?" he said, short of breath again. And went into the lift. Stood in it with his heart pounding. Poona's on the plane, he thought, she knows I am coming to get her. This won't take long. A sense of guilt consumed him; that bloody Karsten who was never there when you needed him! He started to sweat. The lift stopped. A doctor was waiting outside.

"Jomann?"

"Yes! How is she?"

The doctor was finding this difficult. Gunder could see that instantly.

"At the moment we're not exactly sure," he said. The words came in cautious fragments.

Gunder was amazed. Surely they knew what her condition was?

"I'm afraid she has been seriously injured," he went on and looked at Gunder sadly. "She has suffered severe head injuries. For the present she's in a coma."

Gunder leaned heavily against a wall.

"We've put her on a respirator. One lung is perforated. We're hoping she'll regain consciousness in the course of the evening and then we'll know a bit more. In addition she has several fractures—"

"Several fractures?" Gunder felt dizzy. At the same time he looked at his watch.

37

"What can I do?" he said desperately.

The doctor had no means of knowing Gunder's dilemma. He shook his head slowly. "It would be best for your sister if you could sit by her bed. And talk to her. Even though she may not hear you. We will of course provide you with a bed for the night should you wish it."

Gunder thought, I can't stay here. Poona is going to be waiting. He felt torn. But there was only one of him and he couldn't divide himself in two. He stopped because the doctor had stopped.

"Her chest has been crushed. All of her ribs are broken. One knee is badly damaged too. If we get her back on her feet again, I'm afraid that that knee will not work perfectly again."

If we get her back on her feet? I feel sick, Gunder thought. His breakfast churned in his stomach. A wide door opened into a small room. He saw something dark against the white pillow, but couldn't see how that could really be his sister, Marie. He stood in front of the bed, shaking.

"We have to find Karsten," he stuttered. "Her husband. He's in Hamburg."

"I'm glad we were able to get hold of you," the doctor said. He helped Gunder into a chair. Marie was white, almost blue below the eyes. A tube was taped in place across her mouth. He heard a slow, hissing sound from the respirator. It sounded like a giant heavily asleep.

"What we are most concerned about," the doctor said, clearing his throat, "is the trauma to her head. We won't know the extent of it until she regains consciousness."

What did he mean? Was she no longer herself? Would she wake up and have forgotten who he was? Forgotten how to talk, or laugh, or that two and two made four? Might she open her eyes and look at him not knowing who she even was herself? Gunder felt himself tumbling into a deep pit. But he clung to the thought of Poona. Her face appeared at the edge of this cavernous darkness, smiling.

He kept looking at his watch. Marie was tiny in the bed and her round face had lost all its contours. He had to let someone in on his secret about Poona. Someone he trusted, who would not laugh or make him doubt. Someone who was willing to do him a favour.

"Marie!" he whispered.

No response. Did she hear him?

"It's me. Gunder. I'm sitting by your bed."

He looked at the doctor despondently. His eyes brimming with tears.

"Everything is going to be fine," he said. "Poona and I are going to take care of you."

It helped to say her name out loud. He wasn't, after all, alone.

The clock was ticking. He could not leave Marie – what would she think? What would the doctors think if he popped his head round the ward sister's door and said "I'll be off now. I have to pick someone up at the airport." He tried to organise his thoughts, but they refused to let themselves be organised. Would he at last have found a wife, but at the same time lose a sister? He buried his face in his hands in despair. The doctor came over and stood close to him.

"I'm going now. Call . . . if there's anything."

Gunder rubbed his eyes hard. Who could he depend upon? He did not have close friends. Had never wanted any. Or had not managed to make any, he was no longer sure which. Time passed. The respirator tormented him with its hissing sound, he was almost tempted to switch it off to avoid having to listen to it. It interfered with his own breathing and made him breathless. Eventually he let go of Marie's hand and got up abruptly. Went into the corridor and found a payphone.

Gunder never took minicabs himself, but he knew the number by heart. It was on Kalle's Mercedes in black numbers. He answered at the second ring.

"Kalle. It's Gunder Jomann. I'm at the Central Hospital. My sister has been in a car crash!"

At first there was only silence at the other end. He could hear Kalle's breathing.

"That's dreadful," he said with feeling at last. "Is there anything I can do?"

"Yes!" Gunder said. "It so happens that I'm expecting a visitor from abroad. From India."

Not a word from Kalle, who knew about Gunder's journey to India and was beginning to realise the implication.

"She's arriving at Gardermoen from Frankfurt at 6 p.m. and is expecting me to meet her. But there is no way I can leave Marie. She's in a coma," he whispered.

"Oh? I see." Kalle's voice was barely audible.

"Would you collect her for me?"

"Me?" Kalle said.

"You have to drive to the airport and find her! With your taxi, you can surely park at the main entrance. Charge whatever you have to. But you need to leave right away if you're to make it. When she comes out of the arrival hall and doesn't see me, she'll probably go to the information desk. She's Indian," he repeated. "She has long dark hair, which is plaited. A bit younger than me. And if you don't see her you have to get them to page her. Her name is Poona Bai."

"Could you say her name again?" Kalle said uncertainly.

Gunder did as he was asked.

Kalle had finally collected himself. "Shall I take her back to your house?"

"No, bring her here, please. To the Central Hospital. My sister's married name is Dahl. She's in a neurology ward on the tenth floor."

"I need the flight number," said Kalle. "An awful lot of planes land there."

"I forgot it at home. But it lands at 6 o'clock. From Frankfurt."

Gunder sensed his despair was taking over. He thought of the fear that would grip Poona when she couldn't find him.

"Kalle," he whispered. "She's my wife. Do you understand?"

"No." Kalle sounded frightened.

"We were married in India on August 4th. She's coming to live in Elvestad."

Kalle stared wide-eyed through his front window. "I'm leaving right away!" he cried. "Stay with your sister, I'll take care of this."

"Thank you!" said Gunder. He wanted to cry with relief. "Tell Poona I'm so sorry."

Kalle started the car, but did not flick on the meter. A few minutes later the white Mercedes was roaring down the E6.

He went back to Marie's room. No change. To think that she could not breathe on her own. He imagined her lung as a flimsy balloon speared by the sharp bone splinters. Then it had collapsed. They had re-inflated it and reshaped it. The doctor had said that the cuts would heal on their own. This, too, was good. He looked at the clock. A nurse appeared at regular intervals. She looked at Gunder and smiled. Told him he needed a break, to go and get a bite to eat.

"I couldn't face food," said Gunder.

"I'll get you a drink."

Slowly he began dozing. The respirator was starting to make him sleepy; it was exactly like clockwork. Sucking the air out of Marie, forcing it back in, sucking it out. The time was 5.58 p.m. He thought, Poona's plane will be landing now. I hope to God that Kalle will have made it. That he will find her in the crowd. He stared down at his sister. Then it occurred to him that he had not asked a single question about the accident. What about the other car? What about the people in it? Why hadn't anyone said anything? He was smitten by the horrifying thought that perhaps someone had died. That Marie would wake up to a nightmare. He thought of Karsten who still knew nothing. Was he sitting somewhere with a foaming beer in front of him, perhaps listening to the raucous bellowing of German drinking songs? Soon Poona will be getting her luggage, he thought, and she too knows nothing of what has happened. Kalle is looking for her now. He could see clearly his greying head standing out among the crowd. The nurse reappeared. Gunder summoned up his courage.

"What actually happened?" he said. "The accident. What did she hit? Another car?"

"Yes," the nurse said.

"What happened to the other driver?"

"He's not doing so well," the nurse said.

"I do need to know what happened," he pleaded. "She may wake up and ask me. I need to know what to say!"

She looked at him gravely. "He's here. But we couldn't save him."

She bent over Marie and pulled up her eyelids. He saw the dead expression in them and gulped. A man had died and perhaps it was Marie's fault.

Then another nurse arrived. She held a cordless phone in her hand. His heart leapt in anticipation. It was Kalle.

"I couldn't find her," he said, out of breath. "She must have gotten another cab."

Gunder panicked. "You didn't see her at all?"

"I looked everywhere, and they paged her, but she must have got her luggage and cleared customs really quickly. I asked at the information desk if anyone of that name had been there looking for help and they paged her while I was waiting, but no-one came."

"What time did you get there?" Gunder stammered.

"I'm not quite sure. I drove as fast as I could," he said unhappily.

Gunder felt sorry for Kalle, who now had a bad conscience for no reason at all.

"She's probably gone to your house," Kalle suggested. "Perhaps she's sitting on your doorstep. I'll drive up there now."

"Thank you," Gunder said.

He handed the phone back. The nurses looked at him enquiringly, but he said nothing. He could not face talking any more. Marie could not hear him anyway. An eternity passed and a message was passed to him that Poona had not been waiting at the house. Perhaps she had not been on the plane at all, Gunder thought, bewildered. Perhaps it would be all right to contact Lufthansa? They could confirm whether she had been on the flight. Once more he went out to the pay phone and called the airport. Eventually they confirmed it. Poona Bai had travelled with Lufthansa from Frankfurt. The plane had landed on time at 6 p.m. Gunder went back up in the lift. Looked at his sister in the bed. His body felt heavy and infinitely tired. Reluctantly he got up again and left the room. Stopped in the doorway of the duty sister's office. Explained that he had to go because something had happened, but he promised to return. Please would they call if there were any developments?

They looked at him in surprise. But of course they would call. So he went home. Sat behind the steering wheel lost in his own thoughts and was nearly home when a car swept towards him at great speed. It was way over on his side of the road. He threw his wheel sharply to the right and gasped. His heart skipped a beat. Things could happen so quickly! Why don't you get started sooner if it's that important! he snapped at the mirror. The rear of a white Saab disappeared round a corner.

It was 9.30 p.m. when he let himself in. He sat at his desk and looked at the photograph of him and Poona. The evening came and then the night. Everything inside him was in turmoil. Had she misunderstood? Should he call the police? Surely they couldn't just start a manhunt? Where would they look? He sat up the whole night. Every time he heard the sound of a car he leapt out of his chair and pulled the curtain aside. There is an explanation for everything, he thought. Any minute now a taxi would draw up in front of the house. She would be with him at last. He glanced at the telephone. It did not ring. That meant that Marie was still unconscious and had no awareness of her own condition, or of the man in the other car who had died. Of Poona who had not arrived.

He sat all the time with the photograph in his hand. Looked at the odd yellow bag she always wore around her waist. He had never seen anything like it. He remembered how she kissed him on the nose and caressed his face with her warm hands. How she lifted up his shirt and hid her face in there. She would sit like that and listen to his heart. He lifted up the photograph close to his eyes. Her face was so tiny. It disappeared altogether behind his fingertip.

CHAPTER 5

The next day, August 21st, a police car drove slowly along the highway towards Elvestad. The white bonnet gleamed in the sunlight. Two men stared through the windscreen. They could make out a crowd of people in the distance.

"There," Skarre said.

They saw a clearing to the left. A meadow, surrounded by dense wood. Inspector Konrad Sejer looked towards the edge of the wood where a police team was working. The whole meadow was cordoned off. There had been created a passageway, through which they would apparently have to pass. People got out of their cars quickly and headed out into the tall grass. It was already flattened in places. This furrow, Sejer thought, will stand out like an open wound for a long, long time. A number of bystanders had also gathered on the road. Youngsters on bikes, a few cars. And the press, of course, denied any closer access for now. Their camera lenses glinted aggressively. Sejer was easy to recognise by the way he walked. The long body moved steadily across the meadow. There was never anything hasty or rash about him. Similarly he always thought before he spoke. Young people who did not know him made the mistake of thinking he was dim. Others saw the calm personality and sensed a man who rarely did things he regretted and even more rarely made a mistake. The greying hair was cut very short. He was wearing a black roll-neck sweater and a brown leather jacket which was unbuttoned. The group made way for him so he could reach the front unhindered. Jacob Skarre followed two metres behind, Sejer blocking his view. But suddenly there she lay at their feet. Skarre swallowed down a huge quantity of air. What was it Holthemann had said on the phone? *A truly horrific crime.*

Sejer thought he had prepared himself. He stood still, his legs slightly apart, and stared at the woman in the grass. The sight confused him. He saw a plait coiling like a black snake in the yellow grass. The rest of her face was smashed to the bone. Her mouth was a gaping red and black hole. Her nose had been struck flat against her cheek and he could not find her eyes in this pulp of red flesh. He had to avert his gaze and saw a clenched fist. A gold sandal. A lot of blood. It had been absorbed by her clothes and run off her down into the dry grass. He touched the pretty, silk fabric of the turquoise dress, where it still was clean. Glimpsed her glittering jewellery. As he raised his head he noticed blood smeared all over the grass further away from the woman as though someone had dragged her further afield. Automatically all his senses began working. He recognised the smell, heard the sound of voices, felt the soft ground give under his feet. He stared up at the blue sky for a moment and slowly lowered his head.

She was very slender. He saw a slim foot. Thin brown ankles. Her feet were naked in the sandals. Tiny feet, smooth and neat. Her age was impossible to determine. Anywhere between twenty and forty, he thought. Her clothing was undisturbed. There were no cuts on her hands.

"Snorrason?" he said eventually.

"Snorrason is on his way," Karlsen said.

Sejer looked at Skarre. He was standing in a strangely rigid position, only his curls moved in the wind.

"What have we got so far?"

Karlsen took a step forward. His moustache that always had an elegant turn was messy. He had clasped his hand over his mouth in shock.

"The body was discovered by a woman. She called us from that house over there." He pointed towards the woods where Sejer could make out a small house. He saw the windows shining brightly through the leaves.

"She's been hit by something very heavy and probably blunt, we don't know what. Nothing has been found. There are extensive traces of blood, in fact all the way to that corner over there," he pointed to the wood on the other side, "and almost all the way down

45

to the road. As though he's dragged her around. There's a lot of blood down there to your left as well. Perhaps he attacked her there. Then she got away for a moment before he caught up with her again and carried on. But we think that she finally died here, right where she's lying now."

Karlsen paused. "Snorrason is on his way," he repeated.

"Who lives in the house over there?" Sejer nodded towards the wood.

"Ole Gunwald. Shopkeeper in Elvestad, he owns the one-stop shop in the middle of the village. He's closed today on account of a migraine. We've already spoken to him. He was home yesterday evening and last night. Around 9 p.m. he heard muted cries and later a car revving its engine. By the time he got up it had driven off. A while later the same thing happened again. Faint cries and the slamming of a car door. He also remembers that the dog barked. It's tied up in the yard."

Sejer looked again at the woman in the grass. This time the shock was less and in the pulp of shattered bones and muscles he could discern a screaming face. The skin on her neck was almost intact and he saw that it was golden brown. The black plait, as thick as her wrists, was apparently untouched. Intact and beautiful. Held together with a red band.

"And the woman who phoned?" He looked at Karlsen.

"She's waiting in one of our cars."

"What state is she in?"

"She's OK," he said and once more swept his hand across his mouth, the moustache now in a very sorry state. There was a silence for a moment while they all waited.

"We need to set up a hotline," Sejer said decisively. "At once. Door-to-door enquiries must begin immediately. Also talk to all the onlookers down there, including the kids. Skarre: put on some shoe protectors and walk every metre of the meadow. Walk in a tight spiral. Start down by the road. Take Philip and Siw with you. They can follow you. Anything you miss they'll spot. If you're in doubt as to whether something should be bagged, then bag it. Don't forget to wear gloves. Afterwards you'll set markers wherever you see blood traces and flattened grass. We need two people on duty for the rest of today and the next twenty-four hours. To begin with. Karlsen! Call the station and ask them to get a map of the area. A large-scale one and as detailed as possible. If you can, get hold of someone local who knows about any paths that might not be on the map. Soot! There is a cart track going into the wood at the opposite side of the road. Find out where it leads to. Keep your eyes peeled."

Everyone in the group nodded. Sejer turned once more to the body. Squatted down and stared at her. Let his gaze wander slowly over the remains of her face. He tried to make everything stay fixed. He tried not to breathe. She was dressed in something foreign, turquoise. A flimsy, long-sleeved dress over flimsy, billowing trousers. The fabric looked to be silk. But the thing he was most preoccupied with was a beautiful piece of jewellery. A filigree brooch. It surprised him. A Norwegian national costume brooch. So familiar and yet so strange on this exotic clothing. It was difficult to speculate where she came from because the face was so damaged and he could not make out her features. She could be born and brought up in Norway, or it could be her first visit. One gold sandal had slipped off her foot. He found a stick in the grass and flipped it over. There was blood on the sole, but he could detect three letters. NDI. The clothing made him think of India or Pakistan. He took his mobile from his pocket and phoned the station. No women were reported missing. Yet. A few metres from the body lay a yellow bag. An odd, furry thing shaped like a banana. It had a zip and was to be worn around the waist. Astonishingly, it was perfectly clean. He speared the bag to the ground with the stick and using two fingers unzipped it. Lipstick. Mirror. Paper tissues. Coins. Nothing else. No purse or papers. Nothing about who she was. Her nails were painted blood red. She wore two silver rings, not very valuable ones. There were no pockets in the dress, but perhaps there were labels on her clothes. But for the time being he could touch nothing. She is the unidentified victim, he thought. Until someone calls and asks about her. On the air, on the radio and television and all the newspapers she will just be "the unidentified victim".

*

As he went back down the pathway between the plastic strips he glanced at the three officers walking up and down the meadow. They looked like children playing follow-my-leader. Each time Skarre stopped and knelt down so did the others. He could see Skarre's transparent plastic bag and that there was already something in it. Then he made for the police car. The woman who had found the body was waiting for him. He greeted her, got into the car and drove a hundred metres or so further down the road and then stopped. The people standing by the road stared at them. He opened the window so that fresh air could circulate in the car.

"Tell me how it was," he said calmly.

The firm voice helped her. She nodded and put a hand over her mouth. The fear of the words she had to find and say out loud shone from her eyes.

"Do you want me to start right from the beginning?" she said.

"Yes, please," he said steadily.

"I came here to pick mushrooms. There are many brittlegills around Gunwald's house. He doesn't mind me picking them, he can't be bothered himself. He's often ill," she explained. "I had a basket on my arm. I came just after 9.00 in the evening." She paused for a moment, then she said, "I came from that side." She pointed towards the road. "I turned off the road and walked along the edge of the wood. Everything was quiet. Then I noticed something dark in the grass some distance out in the meadow. It worried me a little. But I went on and began picking mushrooms. Gunwald's dog barked, as it always does when it hears someone. I thought of this dark thing, whatever it was. It made me feel uncomfortable and when I moved I kept my back to it. It's strange when you think about it. As if I knew everything all at once, but refused to believe it. I found many brittlegills – by the way, where's my basket?" She gave Sejer a perplexed look, before pulling herself together and carrying on. "Not that I care about the mushrooms. That wasn't what I meant. I was just thinking of the basket—"

"We'll find the basket," he said.

"I found quite a few chanterelles, too. Saw that there were plenty of blueberries. I thought that I would come and pick those another day. I was there for half an hour. When I was ready to leave, for some reason I didn't want to walk past the dark thing in the grass. So I kept to the edge . . ."

"Yes?" he said.

"But I couldn't help looking at it anyway. It looked like a big bag of rubbish, one of those black bin bags. I wanted to go on, but stopped again. It looked as if some of the rubbish was spilling out. Or, it crossed my mind, perhaps it was a large dead animal. I took a few steps back. I don't know how far away I was when I noticed her long plait. Then I saw her hair band. It was then that I knew what it was." She stopped talking and shook her head incredulously. Sejer did not want to interrupt her.

"A hair band. And then I ran," she said. "Straight to Gunwald's house. Banged on his door. Screamed that we had to phone. That there was a body in the meadow. Gunwald got so frightened. He's not young any more. So I waited on his sofa. He's sitting there still, all on his own. It isn't far from his house. Surely she must have screamed?"

"He only heard faint cries."

"I suppose his TV was on," she said, fearful herself.

"Perhaps. Where is your house?"

"Closer to the middle of Elvestad."

He nodded and handed her his mobile phone.

"Perhaps there's someone you'd like to call?"

"No."

"You need to come down to the station. It could take a while. But we'll give you a lift home."

"I've got plenty of time."

He looked at her and cleared his throat carefully.

"Have you looked under your shoes?"

She gave him a baffled look, unsure of what he meant. Bent down and slipped them off; they were light summer shoes with a white rubber sole. "There's blood on them," she said fearfully. "I don't understand. I was so far away."

"Are there any people of ethnic origin living in Elvestad?" he asked her.

49

"Two families. One from Vietnam and one from Korea. The Thuans and the Tees. They have lived here for years. Everybody knows them. But it couldn't be any one of them."

"It couldn't?" he said.

"No," she said firmly, and shook her head. "It couldn't be."

She stared again at the meadow. "Imagine that I thought it was a bag of rubbish."

Gunder was still in his chair long after the sun was up. He had fallen asleep in an impossibly awkward position. He jerked awake when the telephone rang, sprang up and snatched at the handset. It was Bjørnsson from work.

"So, are you working from home today as well?"

"No, no," he said, "it's not that." And he had to support himself against the desk. He had got up too quickly.

"Are you unwell?" Bjørnsson said.

Gunder looked at the clock, startled at how late it was. Something was throbbing in his head.

"No. It's my sister," he said. "She's in hospital. I have to go there now," he went on without actually meaning to because everything in his head was in chaos and he had no idea how to confront this day.

"I'll call and let you know more later."

Then he staggered into the bathroom. Peeled off his clothes. Showered with the door wide open so that he would hear the phone if it rang again. But it did not ring. After a while he called the hospital himself. There was no change. She was still in a coma, but her condition was stable, they said. Nothing is stable any more, thought Gunder miserably. He could not face eating, but brewed a pot of coffee. Sat in his chair again, waiting. Where had Poona spent the night? Why did she not call? Here he was, like an abandoned dog. He sat by the phone like this for a long time more asleep than awake. Marie could wake up at any moment and there would be no-one by her bedside. Poona might ring any second and say, "I think I'm lost. Please would you pick me up?" And then her laughter at the other end of the phone, a bit embarrassed perhaps. But time passed and no-one phoned. I have to call the police, he thought in despair. But that was as much as to acknowledge that something was wrong. He switched on the radio, but went to his desk and stayed there. He listened while all the misery in the world was quietly summed up on the radio. The volume was low, but he still caught every single word, without them making any sense to him. When suddenly he raised his head, it was because he heard the name Elvestad. Loud and clear. He got up and walked over to the radio. Turned up the volume. "Woman of ethnic origin. Beaten to death."

Here, in Elvestad? thought Gunder, exasperated. And then an inspector: We don't know the woman's identity. No-one has reported her missing. Gunder listened intently. What were they saying?

Woman of ethnic origin. Beaten to death.

He collapsed across the desk, trembling. Just then the shrill ring of the telephone cut savagely through the room, but he did not dare answer it. Everything was swimming before his eyes. Then finally it settled. He tried to straighten his body. Felt stiff and weird. He turned his head and looked at the telephone and it occurred to him that he should ring Marie. He always did when something was wrong. But now he couldn't. He went into the hallway to fetch his car keys. Poona was probably at some hotel in town. The other one, the woman they had referred to on the radio, had nothing to do with him. After all there was so much crime everywhere. He would write a note and stick it on the door, in case she arrived while he was out. My wife Poona. He saw his own face in the mirror and was shocked. His own eyes stared back at him, wide with naked fear. Just then the phone rang again. Of course, that would be her! No, he thought, it's the hospital. Marie's dead. Or perhaps it's Karsten from Hamburg who wants to know how she is; he is on his way to the airport to catch the first available flight. It was Kalle Moe. Gunder remained standing, holding the handset in his hand, sloping over his desk.

"Gunder," said Kalle. "I just wanted to know."

His voice was timid. Gunder said nothing. He had nothing to say. He thought of lying and saying: Yes, she's sitting here now. Had got lost, of course. A taxi driver from town who didn't know his way around out here in the countryside.

"How did it go?" Kalle said.

Gunder still did not answer. The news he had heard on the radio was still buzzing in his head. Perhaps Kalle had heard it too, and now the poor fool had put two and two together and made five. Some people were like that, of course: always imagining the worst. And Kalle was a worrier.

"Are you there, Gunder?"

"I'm on my way to the hospital."

Kalle cleared his throat. "How is your sister?"

"I haven't heard anything, so I suppose she hasn't woken up yet. I don't know."

There was silence once more. It was as if Kalle was holding something back. Gunder was definitely not coming to his rescue.

"No," said Kalle, "I just started to worry. I don't know if you've heard the news, but they've found a woman out at Hvitemoen."

Gunder held his breath, and then he said, "Yes?"

"They don't know who she is," Kalle said. "But they're saying she's foreign. And she is, well, I mean – they've found a woman's body, that's what I meant to say. That's why I started to worry, you know me. Not that I supposed there was any connection, but it's not very far from your place. I was scared that it could be the woman I was looking for yesterday. But she arrived all right, didn't she?"

"She'll be here later today," said Gunder with conviction.

"You got hold of her?"

Gunder cleared his throat. "I have to go now – should be at the hospital."

"Of course."

He heard Kalle's uneasiness at the other end.

"And I need to pay you for the trip," said Gunder hurriedly. "I'll catch you later!"

He put the telephone down. For a while he stood, hesitating. A note for Poona, that's what he was going to have done.

He could leave the key outside. Did they put the key under the mat in India? He found pen and paper, but then he realised that he didn't know how to write in English. Could only speak it a bit. It will be fine, he thought, as he left the house with the door unlocked and got into his car.

Hvitemoen was a kilometre out of Elvestad towards Randskog. It was not on his way to the hospital and he was relieved about that. It seemed to him that there were more people about than normal. He passed two white outside-broadcast vans and two police cars. Parked in front of Einar's café was a whole row of cars. And bikes and people. He looked at all of it as he accelerated past, frightened.

Once he was safely at the hospital he took the lift. He went straight to Marie's room. A nurse was leaning over her. She drew up when he entered the room.

"Who are you?" she said.

"Gunder Jomann," he said. "I'm her brother."

She bent over Marie once more. "All visitors must report to the duty office before they come on to the ward," she said. Gunder said nothing. He stood at the foot of the bed, bewildered and feeling guilty. Why was she like that? Were they not glad that he had finally arrived?

"I did sit here all of yesterday," he said, still ashamed. "So I thought it would be all right."

"Well, I wasn't to know that," she said, smiling half-heartedly. "I was off duty yesterday."

He did not answer her. The words were all tangled up in a hairball which stuck in his throat. He wanted to ask her if there was any change. But he could feel his lips trembling and he did not want her to see him cry. Carefully he sat down at the edge of the chair and folded his hands in his lap. My wife has disappeared, he thought frantically. He wanted to shout out to the woman standing by the bed regulating a drip feed just how difficult it all was. Marie, his only sister, in a coma, her husband in Hamburg. And Poona who had vanished into thin air. He did not have anyone else. He wanted the nurse to leave. And not return. He would prefer the blonde one who'd been there yesterday. The one with the friendly smile who had brought him a drink.

"Has anyone told you that as a relative you may stay at the hospital overnight?" she said.

Gunder was surprised. Yes, they had told him that, but he had had to find Poona. He did not want to tell her that. Eventually she left the room. He bent over Marie. There was a low gurgling noise coming from the tube. That meant that it was busy collecting saliva from her mouth – which was what the blonde nurse had explained to him. But if he pulled the cord to call a nurse then the sour one would probably be the one who came back. He could not face that. For a while he sat listening to the sound of the respirator, pushing air into Marie in long hissing drags. He thought that if the gurgling got any worse he would have to call them. And he would have to put up with whichever nurse it was who came.

They had urged him to talk to her, but now he was lost for words. The night before he had been so looking forward to seeing Poona again despite everything that had happened. "Marie?" he whispered. Then he gave up and let his head drop. He had to focus on the future. Karsten would suddenly appear in the doorway and take over the whole dreadful business. It occurred to him that there was a radio above the bed. Could he switch it on? Would it disturb Marie? He leaned forward and unhooked the radio. It was covered in white canvas. First he found the volume button and turned it right down. He held it close to his ear and heard a low hissing, tuned it until he found P4, which broadcast news every hour and it was coming up for 10 a.m. He waited tensely until a voice interrupted the music and read the news. Inspector Sejer has told P4 that the body of a woman found at Hvitemoen has not yet been identified. Police have also stated that the woman had been the victim of an attack with a blunt instrument, but will give no further details. Sources contacted by P4 claim that the body had been subjected to an assault of a violence very rare in Norwegian crime history. Police have now set up a hotline for the public and are asking everyone who was in the area of Hvitemoen near Elvestad yesterday afternoon, evening and night to contact them. All activity in the area is considered to be of interest. The body was discovered by a woman from Elvestad who was out picking mushrooms. They gave a telephone number. It was an easy number to remember and it burned itself into Gunder's brain against his will. The gurgling from Marie's tube interrupted his train of thought. It was getting worse. If he pulled the cord and the sour one came running she might think that he thought she was not doing her job properly. But there had to be more of them on duty. Perhaps it would not be the dark one who came. Then the door opened all by itself and to his delight he saw the blonde nurse enter. She came over to his chair and put her hand on his shoulder. "Your brother-in-law has been contacted. He's on his way home."

Gunder nearly wept from relief. Then she went to Marie's bed to remove the saliva from the tube. Gunder allowed himself to close his eyes. Finally his shoulders relaxed.

"Was everything all right yesterday?" she said, looking at Gunder from across the bed. He opened his eyes. He thought his voice would break.

"You mentioned some problems," she said.

She leaned forward again, but she was still listening. He had a feeling that she understood a great deal.

"Everything will be easier once your brother-in-law gets here," she said. "Then you won't have to manage on your own."

"Yes," he said. "It'll get better then." He summoned up his courage and looked at her. "Is she going to wake up?" he said feebly.

He looked down at Marie in the bed. That was when he noticed the nurse's name-badge for the first time.

"Yes, I think so," the girl called Ragnhild said. "She'll wake up."

CHAPTER 6

In the woman's gaping mouth Sejer counted three or four teeth which were still in the right place. What must the pathologist have thought when he saw this broken woman?

Bardy Snorrason had worked at his steel slab for many years. It was fitted with guttered edges and there was an outlet at the end where blood and fluids from the corpses could be hosed away and disappear down the drain. He could smell her, rank and raw. The chest and abdominal cavities were open.

"I want you to think out loud," Sejer said, studying the pathologist.

"I'm sure you do." He pushed his glasses down his nose and peered at Sejer over the frame. "This face speaks for itself." He turned his back and began leafing through a pile of papers. He muttered to himself, "This is so awful that it makes you want to shut up for once."

Sejer knew better than to push him. The woman's presence was deafening. That which must have escaped from her throat in her last moments echoed between the walls. He had to weigh his words. Respect her in some pathetic way, as she lay there naked on the slab with her chest opened up and the crushed head starkly lit by a work lamp. Because she had been hosed clean of blood, her injuries were there for him to see in a different way from when she was lying in the grass.

"She was wearing an outfit of silk," Snorrason said. "As far as I can see, the silk is very high quality. The clothing is produced in India. Her sandals are plastic. A wristwatch from Timex is also of modest quality. Her underwear was plain, cotton. In her bag were several coins, German, Norwegian, Indian. Oh yes, and on the bottom of her sandals it says 'Miss India'." Another pause. Papers rustled. "She suffered repeated blows to her head and face," he said.

"Is it possible to estimate how many?"

"No. I'm saying 'repeated blows' because it's impossible to number them. But we're talking very hard blows. Between ten and fifteen." Snorrason went over to the slab and stood behind the woman's wrecked head. "The skull has been smashed like a jar. You can no longer make out its original shape. A skull is fragile," he said, "though the top of your head is quite robust. The injuries are greater when you hit the back of the head or the temple. Here we're talking about a very destructive force. Whoever killed this woman attacked her in a violent rage."

"How old is she?"

"Around forty."

Sejer was surprised. Her body was so neat and slender.

"The weapon?" he said.

"The weapon was big and heavy, possibly blunt or smooth, and it was wielded with considerable force. I try to comfort myself and perhaps you too, since you look as though you need it" – he glanced across at Sejer – "that the majority of the blows were inflicted after her death. You can say what you like about death," he said, "but it sweeps away all this misery."

A long pause followed. Sejer felt a little outside himself, floating almost. He sensed a long period ahead with little sleep and much anxiety. That he could not escape from. He would not be able to forget this woman for a moment, she would be with him every hour of the day and night. In his head like a silent cry. He stared into the future to the moment when the culprit was identified and brought in. He would be sitting close enough to smell him and sense the vibrations when he moved in the same air space. Take his hand. Nod sympathetically. Approach this person with kindness. He felt a faint prickling at the back of his head. Snorrason was leafing through his papers once more.

"As I said. She's around forty years old, perhaps a bit younger. Height 1.60. Weight 45 kilos. As far as I can establish, she was healthy. She has a tiny scar from four stitches on her left shoulder. Incidentally, the filigree brooch is from Hardanger."

"That was quick," Sejer said, clearly pleased.

"I have a woman working for me on the case. She has one just like it." He thought for a while. "There were traces of fighting all over the meadow. Did he toy with her, do you think, like a cat?"

"I don't know," Sejer said, "I don't understand how he would dare to. It's still light at nine o'clock. Ole Gunwald lives just at the edge of the woods. The road goes right past. There is an audacity here which makes me think that the killer is chaotic. With no sense of judgment at all."

"Has anyone come forward yet?" Snorrason said.

"Car sightings. But the only thing I want to know right now is who she is."

"You should talk to all the jewellers in the area. They will likely remember if a foreign woman bought a filigree brooch from Hardanger. I don't suppose that happens so often."

"Presumably they keep a list of all sales," Sejer said. "On the other hand, I find it hard to believe that she bought it herself. I think it's a present from someone in Norway. A man, perhaps. And in that case a man who's fond of her."

"You get a lot out of a little," Snorrason said, smiling.

"I'm thinking aloud. When I saw her lying there in the grass, in those delicate clothes, the brooch was sparkling almost like a declaration of love."

"Well," Snorrason said, "perhaps love turned into something else. This doesn't look particularly loving."

Sejer went round the room once. "Yes," he said. "Bear in mind that it is possible to kill out of love."

Snorrason nodded reluctantly.

"You'll call when the post-mortem report is ready?"

"Of course. This is a priority."

Sejer pulled off his shoe protectors. Later he sat in his office with Skarre. The contents of a plastic bag tipped on to his desk. Sejer spread them all out with his index fingers. Looked through the array of bits and pieces and spotted an earring that he recognised at once.

"You certainly did a thorough job. The victim was missing one of these."

"It's flattened," Skarre said. He got up and went abruptly to the sink where he had a violent coughing fit.

"Take your time," Sejer said.

Skarre turned around and looked at him. "I'm OK," he said. "Let's get to work."

Kalle Moe, the minicab driver, was not a man given to gossip. However, it was becoming too much for him. He sat in his white Mercedes, thinking, a deep furrow in his brow. Minutes later he went up the steps to Einar's Café. There were more people there than usual. Einar flipped two hamburgers over and put cheese on them. He nodded to Kalle.

"Coffee, please," Kalle said.

The steam from the cup warmed his face. Linda's shrill laughter could be heard over in the corner.

"How lovely to be young," Kalle said. "Not even death affects them. They're like fat, smooth farmed salmon."

Einar pushed a bowl of sugar cubes across the counter to him. His narrow face was as closed as ever.

"Nasty business," Kalle persevered, with a furtive glance at Einar.

"Why should we be spared?" Einar said, shrugging.

Kalle didn't follow. "What do you mean?"

"I mean what happened here. After all, it happens everywhere."

"Not from what I've heard. Apparently this is truly horrific."

"They always say that," Einar said.

Kalle sipped his coffee. "At first I was scared. I thought of the Tee and the Thuan families."

"It's none of them," Einar said.

"I know. But I straight away thought of them."

Once more Linda's laughter echoed through the room.

"Goldilocks," Einar said with a resigned look in her direction. "That's what the boys call her. And it's not a compliment."

"No, it isn't, is it?" Kalle said.

Silence again. "So they don't know who she is?"

Einar laid the hamburgers carefully on the bottom half of each bun and put the other half on top. He whistled out into the room and a young boy came running.

"Haven't heard anything," he said. "But there are journalists all over the place. They claim the hotline is buzzing."

"That's all to the good," Kalle said.

He was thinking about this business with Gunder. However, something held him back. Nevertheless if he didn't say it, Einar would hear it from someone else. And perhaps a worse version. Kalle was a truthful person, he didn't want to exaggerate, but he longed to get it off his chest. So that Einar would say, really, are you mad! Jomann went and got himself married? In India? He was just about to speak when the door opened and two men entered. Both had green bags slung over their shoulders.

"Newspapermen," Einar said. "Don't talk to them!"

Kalle wondered at Einar's reaction. It sounded like an order, but he didn't protest. The two men came over to the counter, greeted first Kalle then Einar and then took in the surroundings. Einar nodded reservedly and took their order of Coke and rissoles. He worked swiftly with his back to them. Kalle was still standing there with his coffee. He suddenly felt exposed, no longer protected by Einar.

"A terrible thing," one of them said, looking at him. Kalle nodded, but he said nothing. He remembered that he had his travel log in his pocket, so he took it out and set about studying the record of his regular jobs with a look of concentration.

"Such a tragedy probably seems like an earthquake in a small place like this. How many people live here?"

It was a simple question. The girls in the corner had fallen quiet; they watched the journalists with interest. Kalle had no choice but to reply.

"A couple of thousand," he said coolly, and stared into his notebook.

"But she wasn't from around here, am I right?"

The other one stuck his head forward. Einar turned around and slammed two plates on the counter. "When the police don't know who she is, you surely don't expect us to?" he said.

"There's always someone who knows something," the journalist said knowingly, offering Einar a sour smile. "And it's our job to find out."

"You'll have to do that somewhere else," Einar said. "People come here to eat and relax."

"Food looks good," the other one said and bowed. They raised their eyebrows at each other and made their way to a table by the window, keeping an eye on the two girls.

"Let's hope they don't get their claws into Linda," Einar said, lowering his voice. "She doesn't know what's good for her."

Kalle did not understand Einar's ill humour. But perhaps he was brighter than most and knew best how to handle these hyenas from the city. He reached out for the pot to refill his cup.

"Have you heard about Gunder's sister?" Einar gave him a quizzical look. "She's in hospital, in a coma. On a respirator," Kalle said.

Einar frowned. "Why? Have you spoken to him?"

"He called me. It was a car crash."

"Really?" Einar said tentatively. "Did he call to tell you that? You two aren't usually so close."

"No." Kalle hesitated. "It so happens that Gunder was expecting a visitor from abroad, but instead of going to the airport he had to be with his sister in the hospital. That's why he called me. He asked if I would drive to Gardermoen and get this . . . visitor."

"I see," Einar said. Something was at work beneath the red hair. Kalle wasn't sure what.

The journalists were watching them. Kalle spoke as quietly as he could. "You know Gunder went to India?" he said.

Einar nodded. "His sister said so. She was here buying cigarettes."

"But do you know what he did down there?"

"On holiday, I suppose?"

"Yes and no. But the thing is that he went and got married down there. To an Indian woman."

Einar looked up then. His eyes were wide with genuine surprise.

"Jomann? To an Indian woman?"

"Yes. That's why he called me. Because his wife was arriving on

61

this plane. So he sent me to pick her up. Because he had to stay with his sister."

Einar was shocked. Kalle couldn't stop talking now.

"He explained everything, which flight and so on. Her name and what she looked like. He was very upset that he couldn't go himself. So I drove there." Kalle swallowed and looked at Einar. "But I couldn't find her."

"You couldn't find her?" Einar said, bewildered.

"I looked everywhere, but I couldn't find her."

Einar was now openly staring at him. An impulse made Kalle turn. The journalists were still watching them. He lowered his voice still further.

"So I called Gunder at the hospital and explained what had happened. We agreed that she'd probably taken another taxi and gone to his house. That she would be waiting there. After all, she had his address. But she wasn't there either."

A long pause followed. Einar could tell where Kalle was going with this. He looked haunted.

"Then I heard the news – about the dead woman at Hvitemoen. I got really scared. There aren't many foreign women around here. So I called him."

"What did he say?"

"He sounded strange. Didn't really answer my questions, said something about her probably being on her way. I've begun to think that it's her. That someone killed her on her way to Gunder's. Hvitemoen – that's not very far from Gunder's house. Just one kilometre."

"Just one kilometre," Einar said. "So, do you know her name?"

Kalle nodded earnestly.

"You have to call the police," Einar said firmly.

"I don't think I can," Kalle said. "Gunder needs to call himself. But I don't think he dares. He's pretending that nothing's happened."

"You have to talk to him," Einar said.

"He's at the hospital," Kalle said.

"But what about his brother-in-law?"

"He's in Hamburg," Kalle said. He suddenly felt exhausted.

"This hotline," said Einar. "You can call anonymously."

"No, if I call, then I'll give my name. After all, I'm not doing anything wrong by calling. But it will make them go straight to his house."

"Well, they won't find him if he's at the hospital."

"They'll find him sooner or later. And what if I'm wrong?"

"It's good if you're wrong, I suppose," Einar said.

"I don't know. I don't know him that well either. He is very private, is Gunder. Doesn't say much. Could you call?"

Einar rolled his eyes.

"Me? No, I couldn't." He dismissed the idea. "You're the one who was involved in this."

Kalle put his cup on the counter.

"It's only a phone call," Einar said. "It's not the end of the world."

Once again there was the sound of Linda's shrill laughter. One of the journalists was standing bent over the girls' table.

"I'll think about it," Kalle said.

Einar lit a cigarette. He watched the journalists in animated conversation with Linda and Karen. Then he opened the door to his office. A tiny room where he could take a break or could sit and do his bookkeeping. Behind the office was a cold-storage room where he kept the food. He opened this door, too. For a while he stood, at a loss, staring into the narrow room. His anguished eyes rested on a large brown suitcase.

CHAPTER 7

The press descended like flies, behaving as though they owned the whole village. They were on the prowl, their mouths their weapons. Every one of them had their own point of view and an original headline which no-one else had thought of. They took dramatic photographs, which showed nothing at all because they had not been allowed close to the scene of the crime. Nonetheless, they had crawled on their stomachs and focused in on it through the rushes and the grass with their camera lenses. So that man's incomprehensible inhumanity to man could be portrayed in the form of white tarpaulin with a few withered flowers in the foreground. They had a huge talent for empathetic facial expressions and they perfectly understood people's need for their fifteen minutes of fame.

The young certainly appreciated the excitement. At last we've got something to look at, said Karen. Linda preferred the ones in uniform, reporters are so scruffy, she complained. They had stopped giggling. Both had acquired an expression of mature horror. They discussed the awful murder in subdued voices and were emphatic in their conviction that it could not have been committed by anyone from the village. They had lived there all their lives, after all, and knew everyone.

"Where were you around nine o'clock last night?" one of the journalists asked them. He watched their young faces as they retraced the hours.

"I was with her," Linda said, pointing at Karen.

Karen nodded. "You left at a quarter to nine. Why nine o'clock?" she said.

"The murder is supposed to have happened around nine o'clock," the reporter told them. "A shopkeeper who lives near the crime scene has said that he heard faint cries and the revving of an engine. Halfway through the evening news."

Linda was saying nothing. You could tell that she was trawling through a myriad of thoughts. Then it came to her, what they had been giggling so foolishly about just now. When she had ridden home from Karen's, she had passed the meadow at Hvitemoen. She was back there now in her mind. Zooming along noiselessly on her bike. She had spotted a car parked on the roadside and had to swerve. Then she had glanced at the meadow and seen two people there. They were running after each other like in some giddy game, it was a man and a woman. He had caught her and pushed her over. She had seen arms and legs flail about violently and was suddenly really shaken because she had known at once what she was seeing. Two people who clearly wanted to have sex. Quite explicitly, in the open while she was going by on her bike and could see everything. She was both embarrassed and aroused at the sight, while feeling cross at the same time because she was still a virgin. A fear that she might die an old maid had nagged her for a long time. That was why she made sure she always behaved as if she was up for it. But those two people! Linda thought it through. The journalists were waiting. A disturbing idea came to her. What if they had not been playing at all? What if he was trying to catch her, if what she had seen was not a game, but the actual murder? It didn't look like a murder, though. The man ran after the woman. The woman fell. Arms and legs. Suddenly she felt nauseous and gulped down her soft drink.

"You passed Hvitemoen on your bike?" the journalist said. "About nine o'clock?"

"Yes," Linda said. Karen noticed the change in her and recognised the seriousness of it because she knew Linda well.

"It's an awful thought. Perhaps it happened just afterwards."

"But you didn't see anything? Along the road or in the vicinity?"

Linda thought about the red car. She shook her head decisively.

"Not a living soul," she said.

"If you did think of something, you should call the police," the journalist said.

She shrugged and became uncooperative. The two men got up

65

and eased the straps of the camera equipment over their shoulders. Glanced sideways towards Einar at the counter. Karen leaned forward across the table.

"Imagine if that was them!" Her voice was trembling.

"But the people I saw were doing something else!" Linda objected.

"Yes, but perhaps they had sex first and then he killed her afterwards. That's quite common, isn't it?"

Linda now had something momentous to think about.

"I think you should call," Karen said.

"I hardly saw anything!"

"But if you think about it? Perhaps you'll remember more after a while?"

"There was a car on the road."

"There you are!" Karen exclaimed. "They're interested in cars. Any type of car which was in the vicinity. They're mapping all movements in the area. What make of car was it?"

"A red one."

"You don't remember anything else?"

"I was busy swerving to avoid it," Linda said.

"But what did you see then? What did they look like?"

"I don't remember. A man and a woman."

"But pale or dark, fat or thin. Things like that?"

"Dunno," Linda said. They were silent for a moment. Einar was at work behind the bar.

"But how about the car? If you think about it. Old or new. Big or small?"

"Not very big. Paintwork was quite nice. Red anyway."

"Is that all you can remember?"

"Yes. But if I saw one like it, I'd recognise it. I think."

"I think you should call," Karen said again. "Talk to your mum, she'll help you."

Linda pulled a face at the idea. "Couldn't we ring together? What if I say something stupid? Do I have to give them my name?"

"Dunno. You won't say something stupid. They'll just note down what you say and compare it with other stuff they know. If more people have seen a red car, they'll start looking for a red car.

Something like that."

Linda was still stricken by doubt. Caught between the desire actually to have seen something and the fear of deluding herself. All the same, it was tempting. "The police have a key witness in the Hvitemoen case. The witness spotted a car and we now have a partial description of two people seen in the area."

What had they in fact looked like? She remembered something blue, dark blue perhaps, and something white. The man wore a white shirt. The woman was dressed in something dark. She wanted to go home and watch the news.

"I have to think about it," she said.

Karen nodded. "Before you call you need to write everything down so you know what you want to say. They'll probably ask you a lot of questions. Where you were coming from, where you were going, and what you saw. What time it was."

"OK," Linda said. "I'll write it all down."

They emptied their glasses and shouted "see ya" to Einar. His expression told them he was miles away.

Gunder had let go of Marie's hand. He was sleeping soundly now, his chin resting on his chest. He was dreaming of Poona. Of her smile and the large white teeth. He dreamt of Marie as a little girl, considerably chubbier then. While he was sleeping, the door opened and two nurses rolled in a bed. Gunder woke up and blinked in confusion.

"I think you should lie down," Ragnhild said, smiling. "Look. Some sandwiches for you. And there's coffee, if you'd like some."

He jerked upright in the chair. Looked at the bed and the food. The dark-haired, sullen nurse did not look at him. They checked the drip-counter and cleaned the tube. Lie down? He ran his hand over his forehead and felt the tiredness like a lead weight on his head. What if Karsten turned up while he was sleeping? He had a tendency to snore sometimes. He imagined his brother-in-law, pale with worry after the long journey from Hamburg. He imagined himself snoring on the bed or with his mouth full of sandwich. He looked away from the food. There was pâté and ham with cucumber and a glass of milk. But some coffee, perhaps?

"I think you should lie down," Ragnhild said again.

"No," said Gunder appalled. "I'll have to stay awake. In case anything happens."

"It'll be a while before your brother-in-law gets here. We can wake you in an hour if you want us to. But you need some food at least."

He stared at the newly made-up bed.

"You won't help your sister by wearing yourself out," she said gently. The dark-haired nurse said nothing. She opened a window and closed the catch with a bang. Her movements were hard and determined. He considered the option of sleeping in the bed and being woken by this dark-haired witch.

"You do what you like," Ragnhild said. "But we're here to help."

"Yes," Gunder said.

They left. He looked at the food. It was wholemeal bread. He fetched the tray and balanced it on his lap. Ate quietly. The food became him and it surprised him. Afterwards he felt sleepy. He drank two cups of coffee at high speed and felt it scald his throat. It was good coffee. The respirator was working. Marie's hands were yellowish against the white sheet. He put the tray on a table by the window. Sat on the edge of the bed for a moment. Perhaps Poona had arrived. Perhaps she was at home at Blindveien waiting for him. He remembered that the door was unlocked. To leave the house without locking the door was so unlike him. He rubbed his eyes hard. Pushed off his shoes. Turned and saw the white duvet with the sharp folds. Just a short nap, he thought. His body was stiff and aching after the long time spent in the chair. He leaned back and closed his eyes. He was asleep in seconds.

He awoke with a start. Karsten was standing watching him. Gunder leapt up from the bed so quickly that he felt dizzy and collapsed back on the bed.

"I didn't mean to alarm you." His brother-in-law looked tired. "I've been sitting here a while. They told me everything. You must

68

be worn out."

Gunder got up for the second time, this time gingerly.

"No. I was at home last night. But I slept in a chair. I must have dozed off," he said, taken aback.

"You've been asleep a long time." Karsten fumbled with his hands helplessly. "You can go home now, Gunder. I'll sit here. I'll stay tonight."

They looked at one another. Karsten seemed older than usual as he sat on the chair by the bed. "I can't imagine how this is going to end," he mumbled. "What if her brain's been damaged? What's going to become of us?"

"They don't know anything about that yet," Gunder said.

"But what if she stays like this forever?" He buried his face in his hands.

"They think she'll wake up," Gunder said.

"They said so?"

"Yes."

Karsten watched his wife's brother, but he did not say anything. His suitcase and a briefcase were against a wall.

"We were out sailing," he said. "I didn't take my mobile."

"I understand," Gunder said. "Don't give yourself a hard time." Gunder felt better because his brother-in-law had arrived and because he had had a rest. The thought of Poona also returned along with the alertness. And the dead woman at Hvitemoen.

"So you've been to India?" Karsten said. "Found yourself a wife and everything. She's here now, I suppose?" He sounded embarrassed.

"Haven't you heard the news?" Gunder said, tense.

His brother-in-law shook his head.

"There's been a murder at Hvitemoen. A foreign woman. They don't know who she is."

Karsten was bemused by Gunder's strange changing of the subject. And at that moment Gunder collapsed and buried his head in his hands.

"Karsten. There's something I have to tell you."

"Yes?" Karsten said.

Just then the door opened and the sullen, dark-haired nurse swept into the room.

"It can wait." Gunder got up abruptly and buttoned his jacket.

"Go home now and get some rest," Karsten said.

He pulled up outside his driveway. Sat at the wheel and stared through the window. Then, without being clear of his reasons for doing so, he drove on towards Hvitemoen. He wanted to drive slowly past, to have a look at this place everyone was talking about. He knew it well. Opposite the meadow a cart track led down to a lake. They called the lake Norevann. When he was a boy he used to go swimming there with Marie. Or rather she had swum. He had splashed about in the shallow water. He had never learned to swim. Poona doesn't know that, he thought, feeling embarrassed all of a sudden. As he approached, he started looking left, so that he would not miss it. Coming around the bend he noticed two police cars. He stopped the car and sat there watching them. Two policemen were at the edge of the wood. He saw red and white striped tape everywhere and was so flustered that he reversed rapidly so that the car was hidden by the trees. He did not know that the red Volvo had already been spotted. He sat very still and tried to get a sense of what he was feeling. If what had happened out on the meadow involved Poona in any way then he would have felt it, wouldn't he? He put his hand in his inside pocket and got out the marriage certificate, which he carried close to his heart. Read the few lines and the names on the paper over and over. Miss Poona Bai, born on June 1st, 1962, and Mr Gunder Jomann, born on October 10th, 1949. It was a pretty piece of paper. Champagne coloured with a border. The seal of the courthouse at the top. Actual proof. Now he didn't think anyone would believe him. He sighed deeply and crumpled a little. He was startled by a sudden loud noise and he jerked to one side. A policeman was tapping on his window. He folded the document.

"Police," the officer said.

Well, obviously, Gunder thought in a flash of irritation. The man was wearing a uniform, after all.

"Everything all right?"

Gunder gave him a mystified look. Nothing was all right. However, it occurred to him that it was no wonder he was being asked the question. His face felt grimy. His clothes were creased after the many hours spent in the bed at the hospital. He was worn out and needed a shave. He had pulled over on the roadside and was sitting there like some lost soul.

"I just needed a rest. I live close by," he said hurriedly.

"May I see your driving licence and vehicle registration documents?" the officer said.

Gunder looked at him tentatively. Why? Perhaps he thought he had been driving while intoxicated? That's probably how it appeared. He could safely breathe into the device, he had not had a drink since he was in Mumbai. He found the vehicle registration documents in the glove compartment and pulled out his wallet. The officer kept watching him. Suddenly he was interrupted by the crackling of his walkie-talkie. He sniffed and muttered something which Gunder did not hear. Then he made some notes, put the walkie-talkie back on his belt and studied Gunder's driving licence.

"Gunder Jomann, born 1949?"

"Yes," Gunder said.

"You live close by?"

"Towards the village. A kilometre from here."

"Where are you heading?"

"I'm on my way home."

"Then you're going the wrong way," the officer said, scrutinising him.

"I know," Gunder stuttered. "I was curious, that's all . . . about what has happened."

"What do you mean?" the officer said. Gunder felt like giving up. Why was he feigning ignorance?

"The foreign woman. I heard the news."

"The area has been cordoned off," the officer told him.

"So I see. I'm going home now."

He got his documents back and was about to drive off. The officer stuck his head inside the car as if he wanted to snoop around. Gunder froze.

"I know I look tired," he said quickly. "But the thing is that my sister's in hospital. She's in a coma. I've been watching over her. It was a car accident."

"I see," the policeman said. "You'd better get home and have a rest."

Gunder stayed for a while until the man had disappeared. Then he drove another ten metres, turned the Volvo on the dirt track and headed home. The officer was all the time watching him. Speaking into his walkie-talkie.

Behaved rather strangely. Seemed as if he was scared of something. I wrote down his details just in case.

No suitcase in the hall, no Poona in the living room. The house was empty. The rooms were dark, it had been daylight when he left and he had not left any lights on. He sat in his armchair for a long time, staring stiffly into space. The incident at Hvitemoen disturbed him. He had a feeling of having done something stupid. The policeman had behaved strangely. Surely it was no-one's business if he went driving and no-one's business where he stopped. Gunder felt dizzy. This business with Poona, everything that had happened in India, perhaps it was all a dream. Something he had made up sitting in Tandel's Tandoori. Who goes abroad and practically picks a wife, like others pick fruit in harvest time? It must be this book, *People of All Nations*, which had put ideas into my head. He could see the red spine on the shelf. Forced himself to switch on the light. Turn on the TV. There would be news in half an hour. At the same time he was petrified, he didn't want to know any more. But he had to know! They might come out with something which absolutely eliminated Poona. The victim might turn out to be from China. Or from North Africa. The victim, who is in her early twenties, the victim, who has yet to be identified, has a very unusual tattoo which covers her back. His imagination ran riot. Outside, all was quiet.

CHAPTER 8

As always, Konrad Sejer's lined face displayed the appropriate formal expression. Not many people had ever heard him laugh out loud, even fewer had seen him angry. But his expression betrayed tension; there was an alertness in the grey eyes which bore witness to solemnity, curiosity and passion. He kept his colleagues at a distance. Jacob Skarre was the exception. Sejer was twenty years his senior, nevertheless the pair was often spotted deep in conversation. Skarre was munching yet another jelly baby. Sejer was sucking a Fisherman's Friend. In addition Skarre was the only one in the department who had achieved the feat of persuading the inspector to go out for a beer after work. And on a weekday too. Some people thought Sejer was weird and arrogant. Skarre knew that he was shy. Sejer addressed him as Skarre when they were in company. He only ever called him Jacob when they were alone.

Sejer had paused at one of the drinking fountains. He bent down over the jet and slurped up the cool water. He felt a certain dread. The man he was looking for might be a pleasant man. With the same hopes and dreams in life as he himself had had. He had been a child once; someone had loved him very much. He had ties, obligations and responsibilities, and a place in society he was about to lose. Sejer walked on. He never wasted much time thinking about his own affairs. However, deep inside this formal character was a huge appetite for people. Who they were, why they behaved as they did. Whenever he caught a guilty person and obtained a genuine confession he could close the case and file it. This time he was not so sure. Not only had the woman been killed, she had been beaten to a pulp. To kill was in itself extreme. To destroy a body afterwards was bestial. He held many and frequently contradicting views about the concept of crime;

primarily he was concerned with all the things they had yet to discover.

There was a woman in his life. Sara Struel, a psychiatrist. She had her own key to his house and came and went as she pleased. There was always a slight excitement in his body when he climbed the thirteen floors to his flat and reached the top. He could see from the narrow, dark crack between the door and the doorstep whether she was there or not. He also had a dog, Kollberg. It was his one personal extravagance. Sometimes at night the heavy animal sneaked up on to his bed. Then he would pretend to be asleep and not notice. But Kollberg weighed 70 kilos and the mattress sagged mightily when he settled at the foot of the bed.

He came into the duty office and nodded briefly to Skarre and Soot, who were manning the hotline.

"Do we know who she is?"

"No."

He looked at his watch. "Who are the calls coming from?"

"Attention-seekers, mostly."

"That's inevitable. Anything interesting at all?"

"Car observations. Two callers have reported seeing a red car drive towards Hvitemoen. One has seen a black taxi going at a hell of a speed towards town. There's hardly any traffic along that stretch, apart from between 4 p.m. and 6 p.m. Plus a number of complaints about journalists. Any other news?"

"The reports from the door-to-door interviews are being typed up now. All forensic samples have been sent off," Sejer said. "They promised to make it top priority. We've got forty people working on this case. He won't get away."

He studied the list of incoming telephone numbers. The numbers were preceded by the same four digits, which identified them as mostly people from Elvestad or the vicinity who were calling. As he was standing there, the phone went again. Skarre pressed the speaker button. A voice could be heard in the room.

"Hello, I'm calling from Elvestad. My name is Kalle Moe. Is this the police?"

"It is."

74

"It's about the business at Hvitemoen."

"I'm listening."

"It's actually about a friend of mine. Or rather, an acquaintance. He's a really decent bloke, so I'm a bit worried that I might be causing problems for him."

"But you're calling all the same. Can you help us?"

Sejer took note of the man's voice: middle-aged and very nervous.

"Perhaps. You see, it so happens that this acquaintance of mine, he lives alone and has done for years. A little while back he went on holiday. To India."

The mention of India made Sejer pay attention.

"Yes?"

"And then he came back."

Skarre waited. A silence followed. Soot shook his head dismissively.

"Well, then, on the afternoon of August 20th, he called because he needed help."

"He needed help?" Skarre said to nudge the long-winded story to a useful point.

"His sister had fetched up in hospital following a car crash. Seriously injured."

Another silence. Skarre rolled his eyes. Sejer put a finger to his mouth.

"He had to go to the hospital immediately, of course, to be with her. It's a terrible business. But he called me because he was in fact supposed to have been at Gardermoen."

"Gardermoen airport?" Skarre said.

"He was expecting a visitor from abroad. And – would you believe it? – he told me that during his fortnight in India he had managed to get himself married!"

Skarre smiled. The man's reaction to something so bizarre was expressed in an excited crescendo.

"So this woman I was asked to collect, she was, in other words, his wife. His Indian wife."

Sejer and Skarre exchanged glances.

"Ah!" Skarre smiled, affected by the man's excitement.

"But as it turned out, I never found her."

The caller struggled with his complicated story. The three men listened intently. They recognised that this was important, the very first step on the way to a result.

"She was supposed to land at 6 o'clock," the narrative continued. "But she never turned up."

"Why hasn't he called himself?" Skarre said.

"That's what's worrying me. I did call him later to know if she had arrived. Perhaps taken another taxi. You see, I'm a taxi driver in Elvestad. In fact, the only one," he said. "Or she might have gone to a hotel, something like that. But his reply was so vague. I don't think he dares to think about it. He's not quite himself and it's all become too much for him, with his sister and everything. That's why I'm calling."

"What is his name?" Skarre said, fumbling for a pen.

"Gunder Jomann. He lives a little out of the middle of Elvestad, Blindveien 2. It's a dead end. I don't know if he's at home now; he may be at the hospital. Anyway, as I said, I'm really worried. Perhaps she tried to find her own way when Jomann wasn't there to meet her as she had expected. And then something happened to her on the way."

"I understand," Skarre said. "Do you have her name?"

"Yes," he said. "I put it somewhere on a piece of paper, but I'm wearing a different shirt today. I put it in my breast pocket."

"Can you find it for me?" Skarre said.

"That shirt could be in the washing machine. Damnation!" he said. "You're not going straight to his house now, are you?" he said. "I could be quite wrong."

"By no means," Skarre said firmly. "We're grateful for your help. We'll look into it."

He hung up. They looked at one another.

"We're going straight there," Sejer said.

The powerful headlights from a car swept across his yard. Gunder was startled. Could it be Karsten? He ran his hands over his balding head and hurried into the hall. Reluctantly he opened the door. When he saw the police car he took a step back. Sejer came up the steps with his hand held out.

"Jomann?"

"Yes."

His handshake was firm.

"I'm Inspector Sejer, this is my colleague Skarre. Could we come inside for a moment?"

Gunder led the way and stopped in the living room. He looked at the two men. One was around two metres tall and close to him in age. The other was a good deal younger and had big blond curls.

"Perhaps you know why we're here?" Sejer said.

Gunder stuttered. "I suppose it has something to do with the accident?"

"Your sister's, you mean?"

"Yes."

"I'm sorry to hear about your sister," Sejer said. "How is she doing?"

"Her husband has come back from Hamburg. He's with her now. He has promised to call. She's still in a coma."

Sejer nodded. "This is about something else."

Gunder's heart sank. "Then please sit down," he said softly. He gestured vaguely. He seemed tense. It looked as if he wanted to run from the house. Sejer and Skarre sat on the sofa and looked about the tidy, orderly room. Sejer watched Jomann fiddling with something on the wall, a little further away.

"I'm sorry," Gunder said as he joined them. "There was just something important I had to write down. There's a lot happening these days, a lot happening, normally I'm on top of things, but as you know, suddenly everything comes crashing down and knocks you completely off . . . off . . ."

He bit his lip and gave them a terrified look.

"We're here because of your wife. Has she arrived safely?"

Gunder swallowed. "My wife?"

"Yes," Sejer said. "Your Indian wife. We understand that you were

77

expecting her to arrive at Gardermoen on the 20th and that you sent a friend to collect her. Has she arrived?"

Sejer already knew the answer. Gunder hesitated. They were moved by his evident despair.

"Kalle called you?" he said feebly.

"Yes," Skarre said. "Perhaps we can help?"

"Help?" Gunder said. "In what way? Everything's gone wrong lately. I haven't been to work either, not for several days. No-one knows if Marie will regain consciousness. Or how her head will be if she wakes up at all. She's all I have."

"Yes," Sejer said. "And your wife. You were married recently, isn't that so?"

Gunder was silent once more. Sejer let him sit on in silence.

"I was," came the almost inaudible reply.

"You were married on a holiday in India?"

"Yes."

"What's her name?" said Sejer kindly.

"Poona," Gunder said. "Poona Bai Jomann." His voice was tinged with pride.

"Have you any idea why she has not arrived as planned?"

Gunder looked out of the window for a moment. "Not really."

"What steps have you taken so far to find her?"

"I don't really know what to do. Should I go looking for her on the roads? And then there's my sister, there has been so much going on with her."

"Perhaps your wife has relatives?"

"Only an older brother. In New Delhi. But I don't remember his name." He felt ashamed. Imagine forgetting the name of his own brother-in-law.

Sejer recognised that feeling of unease in his stomach.

"What do you think has happened to her?"

"I don't know!" he shouted with sudden intensity. "But this much I do know, you think that she's the one they found at Hvitemoen!"

Gunder began to shake uncontrollably. Skarre closed his eyes. Simultaneously he thought: we don't know this man. He's at the end of his wits, but we don't know why.

78

"We don't believe anything of the kind," Sejer said. "What we're trying to do at this stage is to eliminate her from our enquiries. Sometimes we work in this way. We don't know who the victim is and that troubles us. So we thought we would ask you a few questions. We can probably decide here and now if we need to undertake further enquiries."

"Yes," Gunder said. He was doing his best to be calm.

"Let's begin. Do you have a photograph of your wife?"

Gunder looked away. "No," he lied.

"Indeed?"

"We didn't have a proper wedding photograph taken. There's only so much you can do in a fortnight," he said curtly.

"Yes, of course. I was thinking more of an ordinary photograph. One that you perhaps took of her on another occasion?"

"No, I have no such thing."

He's not telling us the truth. He doesn't want us to see it.

"But naturally you can describe her. Perhaps that's all we need."

Gunder closed his eyes. "She's pretty," he said and a broad smile creased his face. "Very slim and light, not a large or a heavy woman. Indian women aren't as big. I mean, as big as Norwegian ones."

"No, they're not." Sejer smiled. He allowed himself to be charmed by this shy man and the simple way he expressed himself.

"She has brown eyes and black hair. It comes down to her waist, it's that long. It is always plaited in one long plait."

The two men nodded. Sejer looked anxious.

"How would she normally be dressed?"

"Ordinary clothes. Like Norwegian women. Unless it was a special occasion. Then she wore sandals. That's all they wear there. Low-heeled brown sandals. She worked at a tandoori restaurant and needed sensible footwear. But for going out she wore different clothes and shoes. When we were married she wore a sari and gold sandals."

There was a profound silence in Gunder's living room.

"On the other hand," he said, quickly because the silence alarmed him, "lots of Indian women have long plaits and gold sandals."

"I quite understand," Sejer said. "Is there anything else?" he said. "Do you want to tell us about your stay there?"

Gunder gave him a puzzled look. All the same it was good to talk about Poona to someone who was willing to listen to him.

"How did you celebrate your wedding?" Sejer said.

"It was a simple wedding. Just the two of us. We had dinner at a very smart restaurant, which Poona knew about. We had a main course, dessert and coffee. Then we walked round a park and made plans for all the things that needed doing to the house and the garden. Poona wanted to get a job. Her English is good and she is a hard worker. Not many Norwegian girls could keep up with her, believe you me." Gunder felt hot and his face was flushed. "She'd bought me a present. An Indian wedding cake, and I had to eat all of it. It was pretty awful, sweet and sticky, but I managed to get it down. Well, when it comes to Poona, I'd have eaten an Indian elephant if she'd asked me."

This confession made him blush. Sejer felt a terrible sadness.

"What did you give her?" Sejer smiled.

"I have to admit that I had made arrangements in advance," Gunder said. "I thought I might meet someone. I knew what I would find, I know how beautiful Indian women are. After all, I've read books. I brought a piece of jewellery. A Norwegian filigree brooch."

Not a sound in the small room.

"Jomann," Sejer said gently, "in order not to overlook any possibilities in this serious matter, I am going to ask you to come with us."

Gunder went pale. "But it's late in the evening," he muttered. "Surely we can do this in the morning?"

They asked him to bring a jacket. They waited outside the front door and called the station. Gunder Jomann was coming to look at the victim's jewellery. The earrings, the rings. And the brooch. The two men were standing outside when they saw a car drive slowly by. It stopped at Gunder's letterbox and they noticed the driver reading the name on it.

"Press," Sejer said, his eyes narrowing. "They don't miss much."

"They sleep in their cars," Skarre said grimly. Then he turned to Sejer. "He was very proud of his Indian wife."

Sejer nodded.

"Why didn't he call?"

"Because he refuses to believe it."

Gunder came out of the house. He had put on a brown tweed jacket. For a moment as he stood there fumbling with the buttons he looked like an oversized, petulant child who did not want to leave home. So they wanted him to go look at some jewellery. He supposed he could not refuse. All the same, he was annoyed. Besides, he was tired and had so much on his mind. But of course it was awful that no-one knew who she was.

No-one said much during the half-hour it took them to drive from Elvestad to the police headquarters. When Gunder thought about it he could not remember a single previous occasion on which he had spoken to a police officer. Until that grumpy fellow out at Hvitemoen. But these two were pleasant. The young one was open and gentle, the older one courteous and reserved. He had never been to the police station either. They took the lift. Gunder thought of Karsten and hoped that he had managed to get some sleep. I have to get back to work, he thought. This mess cannot go on.

They were in Sejer's office. He switched on a lamp and pressed a number on his telephone.

"We're here. You can come up."

He showed Gunder to a chair. Gunder felt the enormous gravity in the room; he looked at the door, to that which was approaching. It is only some jewellery. He forgot to breathe. Did not quite understand this tension simply because he was being asked to look at a few pieces of jewellery and say that he had never seen them before. Never. The younger one offered to take his jacket, but Gunder wanted to keep it on. A woman police officer came in. Gunder noticed her shoulders, which seemed broad because of the epaulettes. She wore thick-soled black shoes with laces. In her hand she held a brown paper bag and a long yellow envelope. The paper bag was large enough to hold a loaf of bread, Gunder thought. What was this? She put these items on the desk and went out again. What was in the long envelope? In the brown bag? What were they thinking of him? What was the real reason they had come for him? He felt dizzy. Only the desk lamp was on; it threw a harsh light on to the surface of the desk, lit up the inspector's blotting pad, with its map of the world. Sejer pushed the blotter to one side; it stuck to the surface and there was a painful tearing noise as he tugged it loose. Then he picked up the envelope, which was fastened with a paper clip. Gunder's heart was pounding. All sound in the room ebbed away, only his heartbeat remained. Sejer tipped up the yellow envelope and there was a faint jingling sound as the jewellery spilled on to his desk. It settled and sparkled in the lamplight. An earring with a small ball. It did in fact resemble a pair which Poona had worn one day when they were out together. Two tiny rings, quite anonymous, and a large red band, a hair band probably. But then something else . . . partly hidden by the rings and other things. A beautiful filigree brooch. Gunder gasped. Sejer raised his head and looked at him.

"Do you recognise this?"

Gunder closed his eyes, but he could still see the brooch. He saw every detail of it because he had looked at it so many times. But then he told himself that many more exactly like it must have been made. So why should this one just happen to belong to Poona?

"It's impossible to say for certain," said Gunder hoarsely. "Brooches can be so alike."

Sejer nodded. "I understand, but can you eliminate it for us? Can you say that this one is definitely not the one you gave to your wife?"

"No." He coughed into his palms. "I suppose it does look like it. Perhaps."

Skarre nodded silently and caught his boss's eye.

"The woman in question," Sejer said, "is, as far as we can ascertain, from India."

"I understand that you think it's her," Gunder said in a firmer voice. "There's no other way. I guess I'll have to see her. The victim. So we can finish this once and for all." His voice was now so distorted by his irregular breathing that it came out in a rasping staccato.

"I'm sorry. That won't be possible."

"Why not?" Gunder said, surprised.

"It's not possible to identify her."

"Oh, you don't understand what I mean," Gunder said nervously.

"If she's my wife, then I'll know at once. And if she's not then I'll know that too."

"It's not that," Sejer said. He looked towards Skarre as if he was asking for help.

"She's very hard to recognise after what's happened to her," Skarre said carefully.

"What do you mean, hard to recognise?"

Gunder remained sitting, staring at his lap. Finally he grasped what they were telling him.

"But how else will we know?" His eyes were wide with fear.

"The brooch," Sejer said. "Is this the brooch you gave to your wife?"

Gunder began to sway in his chair.

"If you think it is, then we have to contact her brother in New Delhi and ask for his help. We haven't found her papers. But perhaps you know the name of her dentist?"

"I don't think she went to the dentist that often," Gunder said miserably.

"How about other distinctive features?" Sejer said. "Beauty spots or birthmarks. Did she have any of those?"

Gunder swallowed. She had a scar. She had once had a glass splinter removed from her shoulder and she had a fine, narrow scar paler than the rest of her skin. On her left shoulder. She had had four stitches. Gunder sat thinking of this, but he said nothing.

"Scars, for example?" the inspector said. Again he looked intently at Gunder. "The victim had a scar on her left shoulder."

It was at this point that Gunder snapped. "But the suitcase?" he cried out. "You don't travel from India to Norway without a suitcase!"

"We haven't found a suitcase yet," Sejer said. "The assailant must have got rid of it. But she did have a bag. It is quite distinctive."

He began opening the paper bag. Slowly the yellow bag appeared. Sejer gave thanks to an otherwise cruel fate. The bag was clean, not bloodstained.

"Jomann," Sejer said. "Is this your wife's bag?"

Gunder had been holding on, hoping against hope for so long. It felt strange, almost good, to let himself fall.

83

CHAPTER 9

The image of the broken man haunted Sejer. The instant when he finally gave up. His voice as he begged and pleaded to see his dead wife. I must have rights, Jomann had said. Can you really deny me those?

He could not. Only ask him to spare himself. She would not have wanted you to see her like this, he said. Gunder was a shadow of his former self as he walked down the corridor. A woman police officer would drive him home. To an empty house. How he had waited for her! Bursting with excitement like a little kid. Sejer thought of the marriage certificate which he had proudly shown them. This vital document, proof of his new state.

"Her name is Poona Bai," Sejer said later on, standing in the open doorway to the duty office. "From India. Here in Norway for the first time."

Soot, who was manning the telephone, looked up at him, wide-eyed.

"Are we going public with this?"

"No. We don't have any documentation. But there's a man in Elvestad waiting for her. They were married in India on August 4th. She was on her way to join him." He leaned forward to read the screen. "What have you got there?"

"A young woman," said Soot excitedly. "Just called. You've got to get over there. Linda Carling. Aged sixteen. Cycled past Hvitemoen on the 20th, just after 9 p.m. A red car was parked at the side of the road and a man and a woman were up to something in the meadow."

"Up to . . . ?" Sejer said. He was instantly alert.

"She had a hard time finding the right words," Soot said. "Her impression was that they were about to have sex. They were running

84

after each other, as though they were playing. Then they fell over in the grass. Later on she realised that she might have seen the victim and the killer, that they might have had sex first and he'd killed her afterwards. Neither of them saw her go by."

"There was no sexual intercourse," Sejer said brusquely. "Mind you, he might have tried it. What about the car?"

He was unaware that he had clenched his fists.

"A red car. And the red is interesting," Soot said. "Karlsen came in. A man in a red Volvo parked by the scene of the crime yesterday evening. Just sat there. They took his details, in case. He was acting strangely."

"What was his name?" Sejer said.

"Gunder Jomann."

The duty office fell silent. "That's the husband," Sejer explained. "And it's not likely to be him."

"How can we be so sure?"

"My guess is that he was at the Central Hospital. His sister's a patient there. I'll check that. Skarre, you go to Linda Carling. Worm all the information you can out of her. She saw the car!"

"Understood," Skarre said. "But isn't it a bit late?"

"We spare no-one in this case. Anything else?" He looked at Soot.

"Nothing of importance."

"Something's bothering me," Skarre said as he put on his leather jacket. "The murder weapon. What did he hit her with? There were no big stones in the grass there. Assuming he drove there and kept tools in the car then I can think of nothing that matches her injuries. What do people ordinarily keep in their cars?"

"A jack, perhaps?" Sejer said. "A tyre lever. Screwdrivers, stuff like that. Snorrason says something heavy. We have to search the area again. There's a lake on the other side of the road. Norevann. He could have ditched the murder weapon there. And the suitcase. Plus we have to find her brother."

"Brother?" Soot said.

"Her only relative, and Jomann's brother-in-law. We have to locate him as soon as possible."

"We're off," Skarre said eagerly.

Linda's need for attention knew no bounds. Being with people, being noticed all the time, was vital to her. When she was alone she was in the shade. But right now she was in the sunlight. A police officer was on his way! She sashayed around, looking for her hairbrush. Sprayed on her mother's Lagerfeld perfume. Then she ran outside and looked down the road. Still no car in sight. She opened a window to hear it the sooner and tidied the coffee table. The teenage magazine *Girls* was open at the centrefold with a portrait of Leonardo DiCaprio. She binned it. Kicked off her slippers and walked around in bare feet while thinking about what she was going to say. It was crucial that she kept a cool head and told it exactly as she had in fact seen it, not what she thought she had seen. But she did not remember a great deal and that annoyed her. She relived the bicycle ride in her mind and tried out some sentences to herself. What little she had to give him. They would send a man, of course, it never crossed her mind that it might be a woman police officer though she knew they existed. When finally she heard engine noise and tyres crunching the gravel, her heart leapt fiercely. She heard the doorbell, but lingered a while; she did not want to dash out like a kid. Then she worried that she might have made too much of an effort and ran into the bathroom to muss it a bit. When the door was at last opened, Skarre looked straight at a girl who was warm and breathless, with flushed cheeks and a cloud of hair framing her face. She smelt strongly of perfume.

"Linda Carling?" he said, smiling.

Something happened in Linda's head at that very second. Mesmerised, she gazed at the young officer. The porch light lit up Skarre's blond curls. His black leather jacket gleamed. His blue eyes struck her like lightning. She felt giddy. Suddenly she was important. She lost the power to speak and her body stiffened like a tightened bow in the open doorway.

Skarre looked at her with curiosity. This girl might have passed Hvitemoen at the moment the crime was committed. And yet, was she a reliable witness? He knew that women made better witnesses than

86

men. She was young, her eyesight was probably good. Besides, it was still light at 9 p.m. She had gone by on her bike, not in a car. In a car you would be past in four or five seconds. He also knew that what she was about to tell him would in all likelihood be all that she remembered. If she remembered more details later there was every reason to be doubtful. People had this compulsive need to complete a picture. An internal harmony. What was now a series of fragments of an incident could turn into more, given time. And he detected her eagerness to be helpful. Skarre knew his witness psychology, he knew all the factors that affected someone's experience of what they actually saw. The relativity of impression. Age, gender, culture, mood. The way he would ask the questions. Besides, she seemed unfocused, fidgety and nervous. Her body was in constant motion, she gestured excessively and tossed her head. The heavy perfume wafted towards him.

"Are you on your own?"

"Yes," Linda said. "My mum is a long-distance lorry driver. She's hardly ever at home."

"Long distance? I'm impressed. Would you like a similar career?"

"You call that a career?" she laughed. "No, never ever."

She shook her head. Her white hair reminded Skarre of glass wool. They sat down in the living room.

"Where had you been?"

"With a friend. Karen Krantz. She lives out Randskog way."

"Is she a close friend?"

"We've known each other for ten years."

"You're in the same class?"

"I'm about to go to technical college to train as a hairdresser. Karen is going to sixth-form college. But apart from that we've always been in the same class."

"So what were you doing at Karen's?"

"We watched a video," said Linda, "'Titanic'."

"Ah," Skarre said. "With DiCaprio. That's a love story, isn't it?"

"Yes, it's a love story," said Linda, smiling. He noticed how her eyes sparkled.

"So, in other words, you were affected by the mood of that film when you left Karen?"

She shrugged flirtatiously. "You could say that. I was in a romantic mood."

That's why you believed they were playing, Skarre said to himself. You saw what you wanted to see, what your brain was expecting. A man running after a woman to make love.

"What were you thinking as you cycled along the road? Can you tell me that?"

"No." She hesitated. "My mind was very much on the film."

"Were any cars going in the opposite direction to you on your way home?"

"None," she said positively.

"As you approached Hvitemoen, what was the first thing you saw?"

"The car," she said. "First I saw the car. It was red and it wasn't parked straight. As if it had stopped suddenly . . ."

"Go on," Skarre said. "Talk freely, if you can. Forget that I'm sitting here listening."

Linda looked at him in amazement. That would be quite impossible.

"I looked around for the driver. It had to belong to someone. Then I saw two people in the meadow, in the wood practically. They were running. Away from me. I saw the man more clearly because he was closer to me and he blocked my view of her. He was wearing a white top. A white shirt. He was waving his arms about a lot. I thought he was trying to frighten her."

She fell silent; in her thoughts she had now turned again as she approached the car.

"What could you see of the other person?"

"She was smaller than him. Dark."

"Dark? In what way?"

"Everything was dark. Her hair and clothes."

"You're sure it was a woman?"

"She ran like a woman," Linda said simply.

"Did you see the man's hands? Was he holding anything?"

"I don't think so."

"Go on."

Skarre made no notes. Everything she said burned into his brain.

"Then the car was in my way. I had to swerve. Then I had another look. The man had caught up with her again and they both fell over. Fell over in the grass."

"So they must have been partially obscured when you were watching from the road. Or could you still see something?"

"The man was, er, on top," she said, colouring a little. "I saw arms and legs. But then my bike wobbled and I had to watch the road."

"Did you hear anything?"

"A dog barking."

"Nothing else? Shouting or screaming? Or laughter, maybe."

"Nothing else."

"The car," Skarre said. "What do you recall of it?"

"That it was red."

"There are lots of shades of red. What kind?"

"Bright red. Fire engine red."

"Good," Skarre said. "Did you notice any details about the car as you passed it? Was there anyone in it?"

"No, it was empty. I did look inside."

"Registration plates?"

"Norwegian plates. But I don't remember the number."

"But it was facing you, as though it had come from Elvestad?"

"Yes," she said. "But it wasn't parked straight."

"Were the doors open?"

"On the passenger side."

"Did you see the interior of the car? Was it light or dark?"

"Dark, I think. I'm not sure. The paintwork was nice."

"You've no idea of the make or model?"

"No."

"And you're sure that no-one saw you?"

"Quite sure," she said. "They were only interested in each other. And anyway, a bike doesn't make any noise."

Skarre thought for a moment. Then he smiled at her.

"If there's anything you need, call me at the station. On this number."

He handed her his card. She clasped it hungrily. Jacob, it said.

Skarre. She didn't want him to go, the whole thing had taken not even ten minutes. He thanked her and shook her hand. His hand was warm and firm.

"Tomorrow we'll have to ask you to show us the place where you saw the two of them. And where the car was too. As accurately as you can. Can you manage?"

"Absolutely," she burst out.

"Then we'll send an officer or two round tomorrow morning."

"OK," she said, disappointed.

She clutched the card. Knew that there was nothing else. The memory flickered, blurred, without detail. She said a quick prayer that more things, that something decisive would come to her in her dreams. She had to see this man again! He was hers. She had been waiting for him. Everything was right. His face, his hair, his blond curls. The uniform. She tilted her head and lowered her eyes bashfully, as she had a habit of doing.

If there's anything you need!

What did he mean by that? He could have meant anything. She locked the door behind him and tiptoed into the living room. Hid behind the curtain and watched him drive away. We'll send round an officer or two. Pooh! She went to the bathroom and cleaned her teeth. Ran up the stairs to the first floor. Stood in front of the mirror in her room and started brushing her hair in long strokes. It became static and started giving off sparks.

"Well, his name is Jacob," she said to the mirror. "How old is he? Twenty something. Definitely not yet thirty. Of course he's handsome. We're going out on Saturday, probably down the 'Stock Exchange'. They won't allow me in? I'm with a police officer, I'll get in anywhere! Am I in love? I'm head over heels." She watched her glowing cheeks. "I'm telling you, Karen, this time it's for real! This time I'm willing to go very far to get what I want. *Very far indeed!*"

Once more she heard engine noises from the drive. A heavy, throbbing diesel engine, familiar and at once unwelcome. Her mum was home. She switched off the light and slipped under the duvet. She did not want to talk now. When her mum found out, she would take everything away from her. Control it. She was the witness. What did they call it? Key witness. I'm Jacob's key witness, she thought, and closed her eyes. Her mum let herself in downstairs; she heard the faint click of the lock. Linda breathed as regularly as she could when her mum peeped in. Then it went quiet again. In her thoughts she was at Karen's house. I'm off now. Call you tomorrow. Then she got on her bike. The first part of the journey was a gentle downward slope towards the main road. The weather was mild and pleasant. Her bike made no sound as she rolled downhill. I'm cycling along in this beautiful weather. Stay focused, remember everything, trees to my left and right, not a soul on the road. I'm all alone and the birds are quiet because it's evening now, but not yet dark, and now I come out of the bend and I'm coming towards the meadow at Hvitemoen. In the distance I can see a red car. What does the registration plate say? Can't see it! Damn! I'm getting closer and have to swerve. There's movement to my right, some way away, there are people in the meadow. What are they doing? Running around like kids, even though they're grown-ups. She's trying to get away, but he's holding her arm. He's faster, it looks as if they're playing, it's almost like a dance, that's where I swerve to avoid the car; there's no-one in it, but I notice something white on the side window. A sticker. And I'm in the middle of the road before the bend and have to move quickly to the side, but I look across at the meadow one more time, where the two of them have just fallen over in the long grass. The man lies on top of the woman. I see an arm reach out and the man bending over and I'm thinking, God! They're going to have sex in the middle of the meadow, they're mad! He's wearing a white shirt; she has dark hair. He's bigger than she is, broader. His hair, is it blond? I've passed them now and I take a last look. They've disappeared in the grass. But the man was blond and there was a sticker in the car window. I absolutely have to ring Jacob.

Gunder had no wish to go home to the empty house. He would rather have stayed at the police station, in Inspector Sejer's office, the whole night. Close to the jewellery. Accessible in case someone should turn up with definitive information about the woman who had died. It couldn't be Poona! After all, he had not been allowed to identify her. I'm a coward, Gunder thought, I should have downright insisted. He thanked the policewoman and shuffled up the steps. He did not bother to lock the door behind him. He went into the living room, took out the photograph of Poona and himself from the drawer where he had hidden it. He looked at the yellow bag. What if they were wrong? They must have made hundreds or thousands of those banana-shaped bags. Marie, he thought, my job. Everything's falling apart. What did the man on the plane say? The soul remains at Gardermoen airport. Gunder understood now what he meant. He sat at his desk, a crumpled shell. He got up, sat down again and then wandered restlessly about the house. A flittering moth searching for the light.

CHAPTER 10

The police station was buzzing. Thirty men working at full stretch. They were all outraged at what had happened. A foreign woman wearing a Norwegian filigree brooch had arrived here, newly wed perhaps. Someone had attacked her as she neared her new home. They wanted to solve this crime, get the man. Their unspoken unanimity straightened their backs and steadied their gaze. First, the press conference. It robbed them of precious time, but they wanted to look the Norwegian people in the eye and say: "We will take care of this."

Sejer would have preferred not to be there, facing the reporters and their cameramen. A little metallic forest of microphones on the table. He recognised the ominous itching. He suffered from eczema and it was always worse when he felt ill at ease. Holthemann, his head of department, was sitting on his left and Karlsen was on his right. There was no escape. The demands of the media and the nation had to be satisfied: photographic material, investigation strategy, updates, information about the composition of the team, their experience, previous cases they had investigated.

Then the bombardment began. Did they have a suspect? Were there any clues which might suggest a motive? Had the woman been sexually assaulted? Had she been identified? Was there any significant forensic evidence from the crime scene? Had it been established where the woman was from, or her age? How many leads did they have? Had they yet carried out door-to-door interviews? And how great was the risk that the killer would strike again?

How the hell would I know? flashed through Sejer's mind. What could he say, if anything, about the murder weapon? Was it possible that the killer had left no trace at all? This witness on a bicycle, was that someone from the village? Furiously they scribbled. Sejer put a Fisherman's Friend in his mouth. His eyes watered.

"When will the post-mortem report be ready?"

"Not yet. When it is, it will be comprehensive."

"Would it be possible to take pictures of her?"

"Absolutely not."

Silence, as everyone's imagination worked overtime.

"Are we to understand, then, that you consider this a particularly brutal crime? In the context of the history of Norwegian crime in general?"

Sejer looked over the crowded room. "I do not think it would be constructive to compare unrelated cases, in terms simply of brutality. Not least for the sake of the deceased. Nevertheless, I am willing to say that, yes, there is in this killing evidence of a degree of savagery which I have not had to witness at any time hitherto in my career as a policeman."

He could already see the headlines. Simultaneously, he thought of all the things he could have achieved during the hour the press conference lasted.

"As to the killer," someone piped up, "are you working on the assumption that the man or men are local?"

"We're keeping an open mind."

"How much do you know that you're not telling us?" a woman said.

Sejer could not help smiling. "A few minor details."

At this point he spotted Skarre at the back of the room. His hair was standing straight up. He was trying to keep calm while the last questions were being answered. Holthemann too, sitting beside him, had noticed Skarre. He leaned towards Sejer and whispered, "Skarre's got something. He's gone bright red."

Finally it was over. Sejer whisked Skarre with him down a corridor.

"Tell me," he said, out of breath.

"I think I got something. From a minicab office. On August 20th at 6.40 p.m. one of their cabs drove from Gardermoen airport to Elvestad. The manager gave me the name of the driver. His wife answered and says he'll be home soon. She'll get him to call straightaway."

"If that driver had half a brain he'd have got in touch with us long ago. What's his name?"

"Anders Kolding."

"A taxi from Gardermoen to Elvestad? That would cost a fortune, wouldn't it?"

"Between 1,000 and 1,500 kroner," Skarre said. "But don't forget that Jomann had given her money: Norwegian as well as German."

They waited, but no-one telephoned. Sejer gave him thirty minutes, before dialling the number. A man answered.

"Kolding."

"This is the police. We gave your wife a number and we have been waiting for you to call."

"I know, I know."

A young voice. Turmoil in the background. The cries of a squalling child could be heard.

"We want you to come down to the station."

"Now? Right now?"

"Right this minute, if possible. Tell me about this ride from Gardermoen."

"I drove a foreign lady to Elvestad. Now, where was it? Blindveien. But there was no-one at home. So she got back into the cab and asked me to drop her in the middle of Elvestad. By the café."

"Yes?"

"That's where she got out."

"She got out by the café?"

"She went *into* the café, to be precise. It's called Einar's Café," he said.

"Did you see her after that?"

"Hell, no. I drove back."

"Did she have any luggage?"

"One heavy brown suitcase. She only just managed to drag it up the steps."

Sejer pondered this. "You didn't help her?"

The angry cries rose and fell in the background.

"What's that?"

"So you didn't help her with her suitcase up the steps?"

"No, I didn't. I was in a hurry to get back to town. That's a long way without a fare."

"And that was the last time you saw her?"

"That was the last time."

"I'll be expecting you, Kolding. There's a chair waiting here for you."

"But I've got nothing more to tell you. The wife needs to go out and my kid's hysterical. It's a really bad time."

"You've just become a father?"

"Three months ago. A boy."

He didn't sound overjoyed at this development.

"Bring him with you," Sejer said. "Simple as that."

"Bring the kid?"

"I expect you'll have a baby carrier."

He hung up and turned to Skarre.

"I'll deal with Anders Kolding," he said. "You go to Einar's Café."

Gunder dragged himself to the telephone. He dialled the office's number and Bjørnsson answered.

"It turns out," he stammered, "that I need a few days at home. I'm not a hundred per cent. And my sister is still in a coma. I'll have to get a sick note."

Bjørnsson was surprised. "Perhaps you caught something in India."

"It was very hot there. Perhaps I did."

Bjørnsson told him to get well soon, spotting an opportunity to poach some of his customers.

Gunder called the hospital and the friendly nurse answered.

"There's no change, I'm afraid," she said. "Her husband's just left. He had things to do at home."

"I'm coming over right away."

"Only if you can manage it," she said. "We'll call if there's any change."

"I know," he said forlornly. "But I'm coming anyway."

He needed to be close to his sister, even though she could not now be a help to him. He had no-one else. Karsten and he had never been close. Marie would have told him about his marriage to Poona, but Gunder did not want to talk about his fears, it seemed inappropriate. What could he say? It was best to keep it under wraps until they knew for certain. After all, nothing *was* certain. Gunder was worried that Kalle Moe would phone back. Perhaps he felt badly for having telephoned the police? He forced himself to go into the bathroom. Did not have the strength to shower, just shaved and brushed his teeth. He had not eaten for ages, his head felt fuzzy. Then he reversed the car out of the garage, and drove into town.

Marie was as before. It was as if time had stopped. He clasped her hand on the sheet. He realised at once how good it felt to sit like this, completely still, holding his sister's hand. They had asked him to talk to her, but he had nothing to say. If Poona had been at home in their house, pottering about in the kitchen, or outside in the garden, he could have told Marie about that. Poona is tending to the roses. They're at their most beautiful now. Or, Poona is cooking chicken for me today. Spicy red chicken. But there was nothing to say. Gunder sat by the bed very still. At regular intervals a nurse came in and it was a new one this time, a small, chubby one with a plait.

"You mustn't give up hope," she said. "It can take time."

The extra bed was still there. Possibly Karsten had slept there during the night. Gunder felt that everything was different now; he too would lie down and rest whenever he felt tired. A couple of hours later he went into the corridor to call a doctor. He never went to the doctor's so this presented him with something of a problem. Who to call? Not the doctor in Elvestad, he had to find someone in town. Then it dawned on him that he was in a hospital. They'd told him to ask if there was anything he needed. He hesitated, went back again and stopped outside the duty nurse's office. The blonde one got up straightaway.

"I was just wondering," he said, lowering his voice so that the others would not hear him. "I need a sick note. I have to take a few days off to get through this. Is there someone here who can help or should I go somewhere else?"

"I'll have a word with the doctor. You can go back to your sister, I won't be long."

He thanked her and went back again. The respirator was working steadily and it soothed him that all she had to do was rest while the machine kept her alive. The machine never tired. It did its job with a perseverance human beings simply did not have. Later the doctor came to see him and filled in the forms for him. He had brought a plastic bag with him. It contained Marie's belongings. Her handbag and a bouquet of flowers. He unwrapped it. Red roses. With a card. "Dear Poona. Welcome to Elvestad."

If Poona had gone into Einar's Café, someone must have seen her. And subsequently worked out who she was. The owner of the café, at the least. But he had not called. Why not? Skarre noticed two cars parked outside the café, a green estate car and a red Toyota. Burgundy, Skarre thought automatically, not red like a fire engine. As he pushed open the door he spotted a jukebox. He stopped for a moment to admire it, wondering what sort of music it played. To his surprise he saw that practically everything was old. Nearly twice as old as he was. Then he tore himself away and went to the counter. Two women sat at separate tables by the window, drinking coffee. A red-haired, lanky man sat behind the counter with a newspaper on his lap.

"Are you doing the door-to-door interviews?" Einar said quickly.

"I am," Skarre said, smiling. Because he always smiled, he seemed perfectly harmless and quite free of suspicion.

"Is there somewhere private we can talk?"

"That bad, eh?"

Einar opened the flap so that Skarre could come through. They went into Einar's office. It was messy and there was hardly any floor space, but Einar pulled out a chair for Skarre. He himself sat on a beer crate.

"I had a call from a minicab firm," Skarre said. "And it led to me coming here."

Einar was at once on his guard.

"A cabbie drove a woman here on August 20th from Gardermoen. He dropped her at this café. The last thing he saw was the woman lugging a suitcase up your steps."

Einar sat still, listening.

"The woman was from India. She was dressed in a blue top with matching trousers. She had a long plait all the way down her back."

Einar nodded once more. It looked as though he was thinking hard.

"So now I want to ask you," Skarre said, "if such a woman came in here on the evening of the 20th?"

"Yes, she did," Einar said, reluctantly. "I remember her."

"Then perhaps you can tell me what happened?" Skarre said, still smiling.

"There's not much to tell. She dumped the suitcase by the jukebox and ordered a cup of tea," he said. "Took a seat in the far corner. I only had Lipton tea. But it seemed to be OK."

"Did you talk to her?"

"No," he said firmly.

"Did you see the suitcase?" Skarre said.

"The suitcase? Well, I guess I saw a brown suitcase. She put it down by the jukebox. Then she came over to the counter and asked for tea. She looked stressed, as a matter of fact. As though she was waiting for someone."

Skarre tried to build an idea of the sort of person Einar was. Introverted. A stickler. And guarded.

"How long was she here?"

"A quarter of an hour maybe."

"I see. And then?"

"The door slammed and she was gone."

Silence followed, while they both thought.

"Did she pay with Norwegian money?"

"Yes."

"And now, afterwards, what thoughts do you have about this woman?"

Einar shrugged, unconcernedly. "That it was probably her. The woman they found at Hvitemoen."

"Precisely," Skarre said. "It's that simple. And you never thought of calling us?"

"I didn't *know* it was her. A good many people come here."

"Not a great number of Indian women, I imagine."

"We've some immigrants here, or refugees or whatever they call themselves. It's not easy for me to tell the difference. But, yes, I should have considered the possibility. So all I can do is apologise," he said sullenly. "However, now it appears you've worked it out all by yourselves."

"We usually do," Skarre said. "So. Which way did she go?"

"No idea," he said. "I wasn't looking out of the window and I wasn't interested anyway."

"Anyone else at the café at that time?"

"No-one," he said. "Too late for the coffee crowd and too early for the beer drinkers."

"Did she speak English?"

"Yes."

"But she didn't ask you any questions? Nothing at all?"

"No."

"She didn't ask to borrow the telephone, or something like that?"

"No."

"What was your opinion about who she was or where she was going? A foreign woman, alone, with a huge suitcase, out in the countryside, in the evening."

"Nothing. I'm not very interested in people. I serve them, that's all."

"Was she pretty?" Skarre said. He looked directly at Einar Sunde. Einar gave him a baffled look. "That's a strange question."

"I'm just curious," Skarre said. "I've never seen her."

"You've never seen her?"

"Not until it was too late."

Einar blinked.

"Pretty and pretty," he looked down at his hands. "I'm not sure. Yes, in a way. Very exotic. Slender, neat. And they dress like women, if you know what I mean. No jeans or track suits, those awful clothes we wear. Her teeth stuck out a great deal."

"But apart from that. How did she act? Confidently? Anxious?"

"I've told you. She looked stressed," he said. "Lost."

"And the time? What time was it when she left?"

He frowned. "Might have been 8.30 or thereabouts."

"Thank you," Skarre said.

He got up and left the office. Opened the flap and went out into the café. Stayed there for a moment looking around. Einar followed him. Grabbed a cloth and started wiping tabletops here and there.

"You can't see the table by the jukebox when you're standing behind the counter," Skarre said slowly.

"No, I told you. I didn't see her leave. I heard the door slam."

"But the suitcase. You said it was brown. How did you see that?"

Einar bit his lip. "Well, perhaps I did go out into the room after all. I really don't remember."

"No," Skarre said. "Thank you very much."

"Don't mention it."

Skarre took four steps and stopped once more.

"Just one small thing." He raised his index finger to his mouth. "I mean, frankly . . . Countless requests for help in the papers and on TV, requests for absolutely anything that might be relevant to a foreign woman being in Elvestad on the 20th. Why on earth didn't you call?"

Einar dropped the cloth. Fear showed momentarily in his face.

"I don't know," he said. His eyes flickered.

Linda was duly described in the paper as a key witness. Unnamed, of course. But all the same. She cycled around at random, just to be seen. No-one knew, only Karen. And her mother. She kept on asking.

"But for God's sake, what did you see?"

"Hardly anything," Linda said. "But maybe I'll begin to remember more in time." She had called Jacob with the latest news. The blond hair. The sticker in the car window. Sensed this particular value she had finally acquired. She cycled towards the centre of the village and Gunwald's shop was on her right. An old moped was on its stand outside. Even though she never shopped at Gunwald's she could wander inside and let on a little bit. A single word would flutter like a butterfly from ear to ear that she was the one, Linda Carling, the witness on the bike. People would look at her, come over to her, and talk about her.

Linda saw the killer.

The shop had a special smell. Of bread and coffee and sweet chocolate. She nodded to the shopkeeper and went over to the icebox. Took her time. Gunwald lived right next to the meadow. If he'd been standing by his window he would have seen what she had, but closer. Unless he was short-sighted. He wore spectacles with thick lenses. Gunwald didn't have any of the new, cool ice creams, just the old fashioned Pinup and Krone ones. She chose a Pinup, tore off the paper and placed the ice cream between her sharp front teeth. Then she rummaged round her pocket for money.

"So you're out and about today?" Gunwald said. "Every time I see you you've grown half a metre, but I still recognise you. You walk like your mother."

Linda couldn't stand this type of comment, but she smiled anyway and put the money on the counter. A newspaper was open next to his till; he was reading about the murder. A truly horrific crime, a headline called it.

"I can't even begin to understand this," Gunwald said, pointing at the newspaper. "Here. In Elvestad. Something like this. I'd never have believed it."

Linda placed her lips over the chocolate coating and it started to melt.

"Think about the killer! He goes around reading about himself in the paper," he went on.

Linda's teeth bit through the soft chocolate coating.

"Well, he got a surprise today," she said.

"Really?"

The shopkeeper pushed his glasses down his nose.

"Today he'll read that he was actually seen. Practically while committing the murder."

Gunwald's eyes widened.

"What's that? It doesn't say so here." He had another look at the page.

"Yes it does. Down there." She leaned over the till and pointed. "A key witness has come forward. The witness passed the crime scene on a bike at the crucial time and noticed a man and a woman in the meadow, where the victim was later found. The witness also noticed a red car parked on the roadside."

"Good God!" Gunwald said. "That witness, could that be someone from around here?"

"It must be," said Linda, nodding.

"But then they might have a description and all that. They'll probably catch him now. Like I always say, not many of them get away with it in the end."

He carried on reading. Linda ate her ice cream.

"She must have seen something," she said. "Anyway, the police don't give away everything. Perhaps she saw much more than it says there. I suppose they have to protect witnesses like that."

She imagined Jacob in her living room, being responsible for her life. She felt a delightful chill down her spine.

Gunwald looked up at her. "She? It's a woman?"

"Doesn't it say so?" said Linda innocently.

"No. Just 'witness'."

"Hm," Linda said. "It might have been in another paper."

"It'll be clear soon enough," Gunwald said. He took another look at Linda and the half-eaten ice cream.

"I didn't think young women ate ice cream," he said, laughing. "They're always watching their weight."

"Not me," Linda said. "I don't have any problems with that."

Then she left the shop, licked the stick quite clean and got on her bike. Perhaps there would be someone she knew at the café. Two cars were outside. Einar's estate car and Gøran's red one. She parked her bike and stood for a while staring at Gøran's car. It wasn't big, but not small either. Newly washed, the paintwork in good nick. And red like a fire engine. She went over to the car and took a closer look. On the left side window was a round sticker. ADONIS it said. Then she made up her mind to have a look from further away, to view it from the same angle as she had seen the other car out at Hvitemoen. She crossed the road to Mode's Shell petrol station and stood there looking. In some ways it could have been a car like that. Whatever that was. But a lot of cars looked the same. Her mum used to say that cars had no distinguishing features any more. But that was not altogether true. She went back across the road and walked up close to the car. Gøran drove a Golf. So now she knew that. And there were lots of cars sporting stickers. For example her mum had the yellow sticker for the air ambulance in the rear window of her car. She went into the café where a crowd was gathered: Gøran, Mode, Nudel and Frank. The man called Frank was known by another name which people used when they wanted to say something derogatory or make a friendly joke: Margit's Achievement. This was because his mother, Margit, had moaned and groaned during the entire pregnancy, paralysed by fear of the birth. The doctor said that it would be a big baby, he had weighed more than six kilos. He was still big. They nodded to her and she nodded back. Einar was sullen as always. She bought a Coke, then went over to the jukebox and put in a one-krone coin. It only took the old-fashioned sort, they were in a bowl next to it and were used over and over. When they were all gone Einar would empty the jukebox and put the coins back in the bowl again. There was never one missing. A miracle, Linda thought. She looked through the titles and picked out "Eloïse". While she was standing there Gøran came over. He stopped and gave her a hard look. She noticed that his face was badly scratched. She looked away.

"Why were you studying my car?"

Linda jumped. She had not realised that anyone would have been able to see her.

"Studying your car?" she said, frightened. "I wasn't studying anything."

Gøran watched her intently. She noticed more scarlet stripes on his face and on one of his hands. He went back to his table. She stayed standing, listening to the music, confused. Had Gøran been in a fight? He wasn't normally aggressive. He was a cheerful, chatty guy with lots of confidence. Perhaps he'd had a row with Ulla. They said that she was worse than a Tasmanian Devil, when she got mad. Linda didn't know what a Tasmanian Devil was, but it would appear to be something with claws. Gøran and Ulla had been going out for a year now and Karen used to say that that was when the rows began. She shrugged and sat by the window. The others looked the other way and she felt unwelcome. Baffled, she sipped her Coke and stared out of the window. Should she call Jacob and tell him about this incident? If she remembered something she only had to call. Now she'd seen Gøran's car, seen the resemblance.

"Good afternoon. It's Linda."

"Hello, Linda. Is that you again? Does this mean you've got something else to tell me?"

"It may not be important, but it's about the car. I wonder if it mightn't have been a Golf."

"You've seen one like it?"

"Yes. Precisely."

"In Elvestad?"

"Yes, but it's not the one because I know the guy who owns it, but it looks like it. If you know what I mean."

She was lost in her dreams. Wondering and wondering. How many red cars were there in Elvestad? She thought about that. Gunder Jomann had a red Volvo. But apart from that? She thought hard. The doctor. He had a red estate car, similar to Einar's. She sipped her Coke and stared out of the window. Listened to the voices from the other table. "Eloïse" was ended. Einar was making a clatter with ashtrays and glasses. She was convinced that Einar went around with a cloth like that at home. He wiped the seats and tables and window frames and probably his wife too and kids and everything. But Gøran and the red scratches. He terrified her.

CHAPTER 11

Anders Kolding was twenty-five years old. Slim build with brown eyes and a small mouth. He wore his cabbie uniform which was far too big for him and white sports socks in black loafers. His eyes were bloodshot.

"The baby?" Sejer said.

"He's asleep in the car. Couldn't risk waking him now. He's got colic," he said. "And I'm working shifts. I sleep in the car between trips."

He placed a well-worn money changer on the desk. The leather cover was fraying.

"This murder in Elvestad – have you heard about it?"

"Yes." He looked at Sejer guiltily.

"Did you ever wonder that it could be the woman you drove from Gardermoen?"

"Not really," Kolding said. "I mean, not straightaway. I drive all kinds of people. Lots of foreigners."

"Tell me everything you remember about this woman and the drive," Sejer said. "Don't leave anything out." He made himself comfortable in the chair. "If you saw a hedgehog cross the road as you drove into Elvestad, you'll tell me."

Kolding chuckled. He relaxed a little and took hold of the money changer again. He stayed in his seat, fiddling with it while he was thinking. This business with the Indian woman had haunted him all the way into his dreams. He didn't tell Sejer that.

"She came walking towards the car with a heavy brown suitcase. Almost unwillingly. She kept looking back as though she didn't want to leave. I took the suitcase and wanted to put it in the boot, but she said no. She was very confused. Kept looking at the clock. Looking over her shoulder towards the airport entrance. So I waited patiently. Besides, I was tired, as far as I was concerned I could've had a little snooze. I opened the door, but she didn't want to get in. I asked her in English if she was expecting someone and she nodded. For a while she stood there holding the car door. Then she wanted the boot opened. I opened it and she fiddled with the suitcase. There was a brown folder buttoned on to the outside, a kind of document case. She unbuttoned it and got in at last. She sat on the edge of the seat gazing out of the window. Stared towards the entrance to the arrivals hall, stared down along the taxi rank and kept looking at the clock. I was pretty confused myself. Did she want a cab or not?"

Kolding needed a break. Sejer poured him a glass of Farris mineral water and handed it to him. Kolding drank it and put the glass down on Sejer's blotting pad, next to the Panama Canal.

"Then I turned to her and asked her where she was going. She unzipped the brown folder and took out a scrap of paper with an address. An address in Elvestad. That's a long way, I said. Expensive, too. Takes about an hour and a half. She nodded and pulled out some bank notes to show that she had the money. I don't know my way round out there, I said, so we'll have to ask around. She looked lost. I studied her in the wing mirror, her eyes were full of despair. She was still rummaging around in her bag as though she was looking for something. For a while she sat there studying the remains of her plane ticket as though there might be something wrong with it. She didn't want to talk. I tried a few times, but her answers were brief, in reasonable English. I remember her long plait. It fell down over her shoulder and reached to her lap. She had a red band in it and I remember that it had tiny gold threads in it."

You're quite a find, Sejer thought. If only it had been you riding past Hvitemoen on your bike!

Kolding coughed into his hands, breathed in through his nose and continued. "There are houses dotted all over the area and not all of them are numbered. A few kilometres outside the centre of Elvestad I finally found Blindveien. She looked so relieved. I went up the gravel drive and felt just as relieved as she did. She smiled for the first time and I remember thinking that it was a shame about her teeth. You see, they really stuck out. But apart from that she was pretty. I mean, when she closed her mouth. I got out of the car and so did she. I wanted to lift the suitcase out, but she gestured that I should wait. Then she rang the door bell. No-one there. She rang and she rang. I shuffled around the drive, waiting. She got more and more upset. She looked as if she was going to cry. Are they expecting you? I asked her. Yes, she said. Something must have happened. Something is wrong.

"She got back into the car. Didn't say a word. I didn't know what she wanted to do, so I waited too. And the meter was running, we were into big numbers now. Isn't there someone you can call? I asked her, but she shook her head. Then she asked me to drive her back. When we got to the village centre she asked me to stop. By the café. She said she'd wait in there. I lifted the suitcase out of the car and she gave me the money. The fare came to more than 1,400 kroner. She looked totally worn out. The last thing I saw was her dragging her heavy suitcase up the steps. I drove over the road to fill up with petrol. There's a Shell station there. And then I drove back into town. I couldn't get her out of my mind. I thought about how far she'd come and then she'd ended up in front of a locked door. Someone must have played a nasty trick on her. It was really cruel," Kolding said. He put the money changer down and looked at Sejer.

"No, she wasn't tricked. The man who was supposed to meet her at the airport was prevented from doing so. She never knew why. But if she'd known, she would have forgiven him."

Kolding looked at him, wondering what that could mean.

"On the way between Elvestad and the house, did you notice anything? People along the road? Parked cars?"

Kolding had not seen anything. Traffic had been light. To further questions he said that he had been a cab driver for two years, was married and was the father of a three-month-old screaming child. In addition he confirmed the approximate timings.

"When you filled up the car," Sejer said, "who was behind the till at the petrol station?"

"A young woman. Blonde."

"Did you buy anything else?"

Kolding looked at him, surprised. "Bought anything? You mean from the kiosk?"

"Anything."

"Well, as a matter of fact, I did buy a battery for my car," he said after a while.

Sejer considered this for a moment. "You bought a battery for your car at Elvestad petrol station?"

"Yes. It was a special offer. You won't get a car battery that cheap in town," Kolding said.

"And this battery, where is it now?"

"In the car, of course. My own car, I mean."

Sejer imagined a car battery, how heavy it might be. With hard, clean surfaces. If you smashed it against a human head it would do considerable damage. The thought made him look carefully at Kolding's face. He imagined Poona sitting in his car.

"What else did you do at the petrol station?"

"Nothing much. I had a Coke while I was there. Looked at the CD stand. Leafed through a newspaper."

"So you spent quite a time in there?"

"Only a few minutes really."

"You didn't see the Indian woman leave the café?"

"No, no."

"And afterwards. Where did you go?"

"Back to town. No return fare to be had in Elvestad. Had no choice but to drive back on my own."

"Your cab. What make is it?"

"Mercedes. A black one."

"How many people live in New Delhi?"

They were in the canteen. Sejer prodded his food.

"Millions, I guess," Skarre said. "And we don't know his first name."

Sejer did not like the idea that Poona Bai had a brother who was unaware of what had happened. He removed the garnish from his sandwich. They ate in silence.

"Time's passing," he said eventually.

"Indeed," Skarre said. "It tends to."

"A guilty person spends his time wisely. He creates an alibi. Gets rid of the evidence."

"Such as the suitcase," Skarre said, between mouthfuls.

"And the clothes he wore. His shoes. If he has sustained any injuries as result of the struggle then they heal. Tell me about Einar Sunde."

Skarre pondered. "Sullen. Uncooperative. Doesn't see any need to be in the limelight."

"Or scared," Sejer said.

"Could be. But he was alone in his café when the murder took place. He'd hardly have locked the door, gone out and killed Poona and then come back in to flip hamburgers."

"We've only got his word for it that he was alone." Sejer wiped his mouth with the napkin. "This is turning into the kind of case where people are terrified to talk," he said. "Everything will be used against them later on. But I've been thinking about this young woman, Linda. That she did in fact cycle past them. Without seeing anything other than a white shirt."

"It happens."

"There must be a way of making her remember."

"You can't remember what you didn't actually see," Skarre objected. "The visual impressions might have been plentiful, but if the brain didn't interpret them then she'll never be able to recall them."

"Is there anything you don't know!"

"Basic witness psychology," Skarre said.

"Really! We didn't have that in my day."

"Surely you were taught psychology?"

"One lecture. Two hours. That was all."

"During your entire training?"

"I've had to work things out for myself."

Skarre looked at his boss in disbelief.

"I'm sorry to have to say it," he said, "but I'm not sure just how serious she is. She's too keen."

"If psychologists can get people to recall past lives, all the way back to the Stone Age, they should be able to revive Linda's memory of two people in a meadow four days ago."

"You're just not taking this seriously," Skarre said.

"I know."

He focused on the case again. "I've got an hour to spare now. I'll go to Hvitemoen. I'll take Kollberg, he needs some fresh air."

They put their trays back. Sejer went to the car park. As he approached his car he noticed it was bouncing violently. The heavy Leonberger sprang out. Not as agile as he used to be, Sejer thought, but then he wasn't a young dog any more.

He brushed copper-red dog hair from his trousers. Allowed the dog to relieve itself in the bushes. Then he drove to Elvestad. At Hvitemoen he parked in the place where Linda had seen the red car parked. It was marked with two orange cones. He let the dog loose again and started walking towards the bend from where Linda had come cycling. He turned his head and looked back. He could now observe his own car from a considerable distance. The sun gleamed on the paintwork and made it shine like silver although it was in fact blue. He walked briskly down the road with the dog beside him. A few paces on and he turned and looked over to the meadow where they had found the woman. A man or a woman would probably be visible from the waist up given the distance and the long grass. He looked at his car again. What was he actually seeing? That the car was big and wide and had metallic paintwork. At a glance it could pass for silver or grey. A car reckoned to be red might turn out to be brown. Or orange. He felt depressed, stopped by the roadside and looked down at the grass to make sure it was dry before he sat down. The dog sat next to him. It looked at him expectantly. Started sniffing his pockets. Sejer fished out a dog biscuit and told Kollberg to shake hands. His paw was large and heavy. The dog wolfed down the biscuit.

"Don't be greedy," he said gently.

Kollberg barked.

"No. I haven't got any more. You don't look all that well," he said pensively. He raised the dog's head and gazed into its black eyes.

"I'm not on especially good form myself. Because of what has happened." He looked out over the meadow again. At the black wall of spruces which partly hid Gunwald's house. There was a flash of light from the window. How had he dared? It struck him that none of this was planned. A man had happened to come across a woman. She had been hitchhiking, perhaps, or been walking along the road when he had driven past. Then, being an exotic-looking woman, she had aroused something in him. And he had stopped thinking rationally, had not taken into account that it was still more or less broad daylight and that anyone could come by. Like the Linda girl on her bike. How could a man develop such rage against someone he probably didn't even know? Though they couldn't be sure of that. Unless it was the case that she was a substitute for some other woman. Or all women. An aggrieved man who had not got his way, a big rejected kid. A man with great strength, or having an extreme weapon, he still didn't know what it could be. What did he keep in the red car? Sejer sensed that this was part of the answer. The weapon would tell them something about who he was. Had Linda really seen the two of them? It had to be them, the timings were right. The plane had landed at 6 p.m. She had got into Kolding's cab by 6.40. They'd reached Jomann's house at 8.00 and Einar's Café by 8.15. Sunde had said that she left the café around 8.30. Alone, out on the road. She'd met someone there. Had she walked along the road with the heavy suitcase? Anders Kolding had said it was big and that she had practically had to drag it up the steps into the café. A man had driven by. He imagined a red car and the driver spotting the dark woman. How utterly helpless and irresistible she must have seemed. A delicate woman in pretty clothes. Where was she heading? Back to Jomann's house presumably, it lay in that direction. Was she proposing to wait on the doorstep? If she had not been stopped on the road she'd actually have met Jomann. He was back at his house by 9.30. But she never arrived. After the immense journey from India, she had died 1,000 metres from his house. He imagined the man stopping and talking to her. Perhaps he pointed at the suitcase and asked where she was going.

I can give you a lift, I'm going that way anyway. So he took the suitcase and put it in his boot. Opened the door for her. She felt safe, she was in Gunder's home country, safe little Norway. They drove away. He asked what she was doing at Gunder's. Perhaps she said that he was her husband. Sejer stopped and zoomed in on that image, but then it slipped out of reach because he could not imagine what had triggered the rage and the attack. The car drove away from him. Disappeared behind the bend. The dog nudged him with its snout.

"In a place like this," Sejer said aloud and studied the wood and the meadow and Gunwald's house. "In a place like this people will protect one another. That's how it always is. If they've seen something they don't understand they wouldn't dare to say so. They think I must be mistaken, I grew up with him, we've worked together and anyway, he's my cousin. Or neighbour. Or brother. We went to school together. So I won't say anything, it must be a mistake. Human beings are like that. And that's a good thing, isn't it, Kollberg?" He looked at the dog. "We're not talking about evil here, but the good in people which stops them from saying what they know."

He sat there for a long time staring out at the meadow, listening for sounds. Linda had said she had not heard anything at all. His bleeper went off and he recognised Snorrason's number. He dug out his mobile phone and called.

"I've found something," Snorrason said. "It could be important."

"Yes?" he said.

"Tiny traces of white powder."

"Go on."

"On her bag and in her hair. Tiny amounts, but we've isolated it and sent it to the lab."

Sejer thanked him. Kollberg had got up. A white powder. Something that could be traced. Drugs? He threw a final look at the wood. Had the woman herself decided to run out in the meadow because she had seen Gunwald's house and believed that would be her safe haven? There was nowhere else to run to. Why hadn't she screamed? Gunwald had only heard faint cries. But perhaps his hearing was defective. Why had the man stopped his car at precisely this place, where he could so easily be seen? Perhaps she had opened the door, trying to get out while they were driving? Linda had explained that the door was open on the passenger side. Had she seen the cart road on the opposite side and tried to run down there? Down to Norevann.

He let the dog into his car and got behind the steering wheel. Closed his eyes. As he often did. Then the real landscape would vanish and different images form in his consciousness. They ran like a film, sharp and lucid. *Statistically, it's a man between twenty and fifty. Probably in employment, but not well educated. A man who lacks the words to express who he is and what he feels. He may have friends, but is not close to anyone. An unresolved relationship with women. A wounded personality.*

Sejer swung across the road and rolled slowly towards the water. After about 500 metres he reached a small bay with a pebble beach. No houses, no huts. He went down to the water. Stood there for a while, looking across to the other side. Not a soul to be seen. He stuck his hand in the water; it was very cold. Ran his wet hand across his forehead. On his right were dense, impenetrable woods. A narrow headland stretched out to the left. He walked out to the point. Found the remains of a fire, prodded it with his foot. The water here was black, possibly deep. He could have hidden her. Many did, throwing the body in the water, burying it. But nothing had been done to hide this murder. Nothing had been done to mislead them. The killer was disorganised, characterised by confusion and lack of control.

He drove back to the station.

CHAPTER 12

Skarre came bursting in. Munching a jelly baby as always.

"What about Anders Kolding?" he said expectantly. "Not our man?"

"Don't think so. Unless he killed her with a car battery which he claims to have bought at Elvestad petrol station. I'm going to talk to them. By the way, we also have the unpleasant task of checking on anyone with a previous conviction for sexual assaults."

"But he didn't rape her, did he?"

"It might have been his original intention. It sounds awful, but I wish he'd succeeded. There would've been more evidence."

"What are the chances that he's done it before?"

"Good. But he could be young and not have gone this far before now."

"Is he young?"

"This enormous rage – there's something young about it. I'm fifty," he said. "I don't think he's fifty. Thirty maximum."

"Thirty and strong."

"And deeply wounded. Possibly by a woman, or all women. He becomes very strong when he's angry. And he had a powerful weapon. What do you keep in your car, Jacob?"

Skarre scratched his curls. "A metal toolbox, small tools. A jack. A warning triangle. Stuff like that. Sometimes a hanger for my jacket."

"God help me!"

"A thermos, if I'm going to be driving for long. A torch."

"Too small."

"Mine is heavy. The biggest Maglite there is, forty centimetres long."

"It's too angular and would've caused a different type of injury."

"Then I've got 40 or so audio tapes in the glove compartment and

115

sometimes a bag of bottles for recycling in the boot which I don't always remember to get rid of. What's in your car?"

"Kollberg," Sejer said.

He went to the window. Skarre sidled up to him. For some time they stood there, thinking in the silence.

"He's counting the hours," Sejer said.

"He's collecting them," Skarre said.

"He's obsessed by time. The paper every morning. And the news. Whatever information is made public. He follows it, notices everything. Tries to work out what we know."

"That's not a lot," Skarre said. "How about Jomann?"

"He left the hospital around 9.00 that evening. They've confirmed it. It takes him half an hour to get home."

"And he met no-one?"

"A white Saab. They nearly collided."

"Well, I have been known to speed a bit when I'm on the highway," Skarre smiled.

A man entered the room. Gunder let go of Marie's hand. He recognised Sejer and it suddenly occurred to him that it was all a terrible misunderstanding. There must be thousands of banana-shaped bags. Sejer remained standing and watched the stooping man.

"How are you?"

Gunder looked at him forlornly. "I don't know what's going to happen. They're saying they'll have to move the tube to her neck because her throat's becoming sore. They'll simply cut a hole in her neck and stick the tube in there. I don't know what's going to happen," he said again.

There followed a silence between the two men.

"Have you found her brother?" Gunder said.

"No," Sejer said, "but we're looking. There are a great many people in New Delhi, we have to be sure we find the right one."

"He didn't want her to go," Gunder said sadly. "By the way, I'll pay for the ticket. Tell him that. It's my responsibility."

Sejer promised to let him know. Gunder ran a cold hand across his neck. "You'll tell me when I can bury her, won't you?" he said.

Sejer hesitated. "It'll be a while. Lots of things have to be cleared up first. We have to talk to her brother about where she's to be buried. Perhaps you should prepare yourself that he might want to take her home. To India."

Gunder turned white. "Oh, no! No, she must be buried here, at Elvestad church. She's my wife after all," he said anxiously. "I've got the marriage certificate." He patted his breast pocket.

"Yes," Sejer said. "I'm telling you this so you can prepare yourself. We'll find a way. However, it can take time."

"She's my wife. It's my decision."

Gunder was getting angry. This was something which hardly ever happened. All of his heavy body was trembling.

"In India it's their practice to cremate their dead, am I right?" said Sejer carefully. "What was her religion?"

"She was a Hindu," he said quietly. "But not practising. She would have wanted to be next to me. I'm certain of that."

They were silent once more.

"But what am I going to do if her brother wants to bring her back to India?" he asked in despair.

"I'm sure there are rules covering situations such as this one. You do, of course, have rights. A lawyer will be able to advise you, don't worry about it now. Think of yourself and your sister," he said. "There's nothing more, alas, that you can do for your wife."

"Yes! I can make sure that she gets a beautiful funeral. I'll organise it all. I'm on sick leave now. I don't mind where I sit. I've a bed here, too." He pointed at the bed by the window. "Karsten can't handle sitting here. Karsten is her husband," he said. "I feel sorry for Karsten. He's so frightened."

"I used to sit like this with my mother," Sejer said. "She died two years ago. Towards the end, she'd lie, staring into space, saying nothing. Didn't recognise me. I used to think that in some way she could sense that I was there. Even if she didn't know it was me, she'd sensed that someone was by her bedside. Knew that she was not alone."

"How did you pass the time?" Gunder said.

"I sat chatting to myself," Sejer smiled. "About all sorts of things. Sometimes I'd talk directly to her, other times just to myself. I'd be thinking aloud. When I left I really felt that I'd been to visit her. That I'd done something. If you just sit here and don't say a word it makes you depressed."

He looked at Gunder. "Just start talking. No-one can hear you in here. Tell her about Poona," he said. "Tell her everything that has happened."

Gunder let his head drop. "I don't know if I can."

"There's another way of looking at it. You might not believe in victim support. But you do have a sister. Tell her everything."

"But she can't hear anything!"

"Are you sure of that?"

Sejer patted Jomann on the back. "I know you've a lot on your mind. If you have any questions, just call. My numbers, home and work, are on this card."

"Thank you," Gunder said.

Sejer walked to the door.

"I do have something to tell you," Gunder said shyly, clearing his throat.

"Yes?"

"I have a photo of Poona. I hid it from you."

"Will you lend it to me?"

"If I get it back."

The hotline had gone quiet. Newspaper coverage had shrunk to smaller notices. Poona was no longer front-page news. Gunder had requested that his name be left out, but it became common knowledge anyway. He had never expected anything else.

Sejer finally found a peaceful moment to think. The white powder, what was it? He turned it over in his mind again and again as he stood staring at the wall map of Elvestad and its surroundings. The junction with the Shell petrol station, Einar's Café, Gunwald's shop. The road to Hvitemoen. The meadow and Norevann. Poona represented by a red cross, exactly where they had found her. The red car parked on the roadside. Linda Carling on her bike. Everything was in its place. He came from the centre of the village, Sejer thought, the car was facing Randskog. No, not necessarily. Perhaps he came from the other direction. He spotted her, went past her and turned round. The man was alone in the car and had acted on impulse. He'd had something heavy in his car. Poona weighed 45 kilos, the man could have been twice as heavy. Linda, he asked himself, what did you see? You know most of the people who live in Elvestad. Did you recognise him? Do you know something you're afraid to say?

He started scribbling on a notepad. She leaves the plane. Goes through to the arrivals hall. Out to Kolding. Then to Einar's Café. Alone on the road.

I didn't see her leave, I heard the door slam.

Was Einar telling the truth? Why did she leave? Walk down the road with that heavy suitcase. Because she was upset? When you walk, you're walking towards a solution. The Norwegian landscape with its yellow fields must have instilled trust in her; she came from a big city with twelve million inhabitants. Streets so packed with people that you could hardly walk. Out here, she walked alone. The dark woman like a foreign flower among the rosebays and dandelions.

He left the meeting room and went into the office. Pulled the folder out of his drawer. Leafed through it, reading. His own reports. Skarre's reports, witness statements. The telephone rang. It was Snorrason.

"Tell me you've got good news," Sejer said.

"The white powder. Magnesium."

"I'm bad at chemistry. What's it used for?"

"We can't say for certain the exact purpose this powder was used for. It can probably be used for a number of things. However, I have a few ideas. Otherwise we'll have to start asking around to find out. By the way, magnesium is also used in medicine, but in a different compound."

"Get in touch with me when you know something. And keep it out of the newspapers."

"Will do," Snorrason said.

Sejer replaced the handset and closed the folder. Magnesium, he thought. Magnesium powder. Who came into contact with magnesium? Someone who worked with chemicals? Did that tell us anything about his job? Kolding had bought a car battery, across the road from Einar's Café, while Poona was there, only a few metres away from where he was. He left the office and drove to Elvestad petrol station. Mode Bråthen was behind the till. He watched Sejer with quiet curiosity and appeared to relish the situation. The grey beanpole of a man towering by his counter with all his questions. Most people retreated instinctively. Mode leaned forward over the counter and examined him like a rare guest.

"I didn't do it," he said, smiling amicably. "Like I told to the guy who came out here the other day, it was my evening off. I was out bowling. Torill was working. She lives across the road. I could call her and ask her to come over."

"Well," Sejer said, his grey eyes observing him, "that's what I call service."

"Exactly," Mode smiled. "This is a Shell petrol station."

Two minutes later a young woman came in.

"It's quiet out here. Especially in the evenings. So I remember him well," she said eagerly. "He filled up with diesel and bought a Coke," she recalled.

"Nothing else?" Sejer said.

"Yes. A car battery. Plus he sneaked a peek at a newspaper, but he didn't buy it."

"So he spent a few minutes in here?"

"Yes," she said. "But he didn't say anything. Just wandered around."

"When did he leave? Do you remember?"

"No," she said, hesitating. "Perhaps around 8.30 p.m."

"Did you see his car as he left?"

"Yes. He must've picked up a fare. His light was turned off when he drove away."

"A fare? Out here? Was he heading into town?"

"No," she said. "He turned left towards Randskog."

Sejer frowned. "In other words, towards Hvitemoen?"

"Yes."

He gave young Torill a serious look.

"You're quite sure that he turned left? And not right, towards town?"

"Yes, for God's sake! I saw him indicate." She looked directly at him. "I'm one hundred per cent sure."

Well, I'll be damned, he thought. He remained standing outside, staring right across the road to Einar's Café. Imagine if Kolding had wandered round inside the petrol station killing time to see if Poona would reappear? Perhaps the thought of the Indian woman was troubling him, knowing that she was alone and helpless. Perhaps she'd come down the steps dragging the suitcase behind her. Kolding could have followed her and picked her up. With the car battery in the boot. Or did Torill remember wrongly? Claim against claim. There were always so many of them. However, Torill could scarcely have anything to hide. Kolding had sat in the hot car with Poona in the back. Watched her in the mirror. He was young. Trapped in a marriage with a screaming baby who clearly got on his nerves. Utterly exhausted, perhaps unstable. And, despite all the requests, he had never contacted the police.

Sejer drove steadily home. The images in his head came and went. Kolding's bloodshot eyes. His nervous hands fidgeting with the money changer. A runt of a man. On the other hand, if he had a car battery, he didn't need muscles.

Linda fetched a pile of old newspapers from the basement staircase. Then she sat down at the kitchen table and began slowly leafing through them. There was a great deal of coverage of the Hvitemoen murder. She found a pair of scissors and started cutting. There were several photographs of police officers, but none of Jacob. His face was beginning to fade. However, she could recall his voice and his eyes.

This business with the car. Every time she thought about the red car, she felt slightly scared. She hadn't called Jacob. Though it might

121

be a coincidence, it could be important all the same. What if she simply called and said "it could've been a Golf". Nothing else, nothing more exact than that. Then they could eliminate the others. It couldn't have been a Volvo, for example, or a Mercedes. The scissors tore through the paper, she had a good pile of articles and photographs now. Afterwards she put them in date order and put them in a plastic folder. For a moment she was tempted to underline certain sentences. A witness on a bicycle claims to have seen two people at the crime scene, they could have been the victim and her killer. Or: New vital witness in the Elvestad case. However, she wasn't that childish. She went into the living room and sat by the telephone with Jacob's card in her hand. Then she caressed her cheek with it, smelled it and pursed her lips. Tenderly she kissed his name, three times. It didn't matter what you did so long as you did it in the privacy of your own home. A rather alluring thought, come to think of it. Then she dialled the number. When he answered, she started shaking and had to force herself to sound calm and reflective, something she never was. She tried to be succinct, had decided to just say this one thing: it could've been a Golf. However, that wasn't enough for Jacob. She wasn't prepared for how the conversation would develop and lost control. Couldn't get away, couldn't hang up, because then Jacob would be gone.

"Do you know anyone who drives a red Golf?" he said.

Initially she was defensive and rather brisk. "No."

"Have you seen a car like that in Elvestad?"

"Possibly," she said then, "but no-one I know well."

"So you do know someone in Elvestad who drives a red Golf?"

Linda bit her lip. "He doesn't have anything to do with the murder," she said. "It's just that his car looks the same."

"We understand," said Skarre calmly. "I'm just interested in how you worked this out. That it might've been a Golf. That's why I'm asking. If you know his name, then I'd like you to tell me."

Linda stared out of the window at the garden and the trees. They stood like guardsmen with their pointed tops. Her heart pounded. Was he not coming over? Would she never see him again? Fear enveloped her. The sense of having set something in motion. The mere thought made her quiver. But give his name? And what about his injuries? He looked as though he'd been scratched.

"Are you there, Linda?" said Jacob. She melted instantly. He was begging her now.

"Gøran," she said. "Gøran Seter. Someone's scratched his face, too."

Just then white, violent lightning flashed across the sky again and again. No thunder could be heard, only a slight rustling. Summer lightning, she thought. It's just summer lightning. It's harvest time.

When Skarre saw this trembling young woman, he immediately thought of a slice of roast beef. Gossamer thin and raw, ready to be wolfed down. He asked God to forgive this greedy thought and smiled as amiably as he could.

Linda was not at all happy that everything she told him had to be written down and that she had to read it through and sign it.

"We can leave Gøran's name out, can't we?" she said anxiously.

"Of course," he said. "And a little bit of advice: keep this to yourself. That way you'll avoid problems later on. Gossip is not a trifling matter, neither is the press. By the way, have they been here?"

"No," she said. She didn't know how she would resist them if they turned up with cameras and everything. She hadn't told a soul about the Golf, and the reason her gaze was steady was because it was actually true. She struggled to think of other ways she could impress Jacob. He folded the statement and got up. She made a final, desperate attempt.

"When you find the man who did this, should I expect to appear in court as a witness?"

He looked at her and smiled. "I wouldn't have thought so, Linda. Your observations aren't accurate enough."

She felt indescribably disappointed. Then he was gone and she remained standing on the floor with her hand over her mouth. Her lips felt huge. She found the telephone directory. Looked under S and found Skarre, Jacob, 45 Nedre Storgate, and his telephone number, which she memorised twice. After that it was burned into her brain. She found the folder with the newspaper cuttings and went upstairs to her room. Stood for a while in front of the mirror. Then she read them all again. She had to keep this case alive. Had to blow on it the way you blew on embers. It had become something that sustained her, almost like a mission. She remembered reading about a detective from the national crime squad who had been taken off a case because he had started a relationship with a witness whom he later married. She wasn't even a key witness, not as important as she was. The thought of all the things she could set in motion made her feel flushed and excited. Then she remembered that Jacob had told her not to talk to anyone about this and she wasn't going to. Except to Karen.

CHAPTER 13

Rumours were flying. They crept in wherever there was the slightest crack. The murdered woman was Gunder Jomann's wife, come from India! If Poona had arrived safely they would hardly have let her off so easily! They would have scrutinised her mercilessly. Nevertheless, she didn't deserve to die and Gunder was treated with sympathy for his amorous excess. However, they were more interested in the fact that someone had seen Gøran Seter's car parked right at the crime scene. They were prepared for rumours to fly and didn't think for a moment that Gøran had killed someone; he was a fine young man and they all knew him. They were more interested in whoever it was who had not only seen a similar car, but also called the police. And given them Gøran's name. They sat drinking in Einar's Café. There was Frank, Margit's Achievement, a pale skinny guy they called Nudel, and Mode from the petrol station. Frank placed his huge forearms on the table. "Why don't they suspect me, eh? I've a red Toyota and I look like a savage."

"But your Toyota is brown," Einar argued from behind the counter.

"Rust-coloured," Frank stated. "It looks red at a distance."

"But come to think of it, Einar, I think you did it. It says in the paper that she was here, drinking tea."

Einar lifted a wire basket with chips out of the boiling fat. "Yeah. She trundled in here with her suitcase and everything and I threw her in the car and drove to Hvitemoen where I did her in and rushed back to flip burgers. Piece of cake." He sniffed.

"I think it was old Gunwald," Nudel said. "After all, he lives right by the crime scene and has been a widower for God knows how long. Then he sees a woman in a sari mincing down the road and races after her with his dick hanging out of his trousers."

This suggestion caused general merriment. Einar shook his head. "She didn't wear a sari. It was more like a trouser suit. Dark blue or turquoise. No, it's got to be someone from outside."

"Why, of course, since we're better than anybody else," Frank said. "As far as I'm concerned, I think he's from around here. There are now something like two thousand of us here. You can bet your life that this is where they're looking."

"No, it's Mode," Einar said. "He was sitting over at the petrol station doing his books and saw her leave my café. Then he jumped into his Saab and sped after her."

"My car is white," Mode said. "Besides, it was Torill who was manning the shop. I was bowling in Randskog."

Einar looked at him. "Is it true that you've bought yourself a bowling ball?"

"Yes!" Nudel exclaimed. "And not just any old ball. It is clear like glass. Weighs 21 pounds. And in the centre of the ball there's a tiny black scorpion. He calls himself Scorpio on the scoreboard."

"Christ, what a show-off," Frank shouted.

Mode was well and truly bullied. It bounced off. He was good at bowling and had a personal record score of 230.

Einar sneered. "We don't know if it was a red car. It's only some nitwit who's seen one like it. And got it into their head that it might be a Golf."

"A nitwit from around here. Since there are rumours about Gøran," said Frank.

"Probably that girl who always rides a bike," Nudel said. "Goldilocks. By the way, she was standing outside the other day gawping at Gøran's car. Afterwards she came into the café. He went over to her and asked her what she was staring at."

"Linda Carling?" Einar said.

"Precisely. The one who's always up for it. She called the cops. I bet you it's her."

For a while it was quiet while they all drank their beer. Frank made himself a wonky-looking roll-up. Einar sprinkled BBQ spices on the fried potatoes and carried the plate over to him.

"What does Gøran have to say about it?"

Frank snapped the Zippo lighter shut and smelled the food.

"Gøran is cool. He says they're talking to everyone."

"I've just remembered something," Mode said. "Gøran came into the café, it must have been on the day she died. No, the day afterwards. His face was scratched."

"Probably Ulla," Frank tittered. "She's worse than a cat."

"True, but all the same. I wonder if the cops have noticed."

"It'll have healed by now," Einar said. "Well, almost."

"So it's healed. But people have seen it," Nudel said.

Frank gave him a hard stare. "So if they come to you and start cross-examining you, you'll be sure to include that, is that what you're saying? That his face was scratched?"

"Of course not. I'm not stupid."

"Why shouldn't he say it?" Mode said calmly. "Are you afraid it might be him, perhaps?"

"Of course it's not him."

"Then why can't we mention the scratches?"

"To save him a lot of crap. It's a dead end, obviously."

At that very moment the door crashed open. Gøran entered followed by his dog. The table fell silent. Their faces were guilty. Gøran gave them a measured look.

"The dog," Einar said. "Outside."

"He can lie under the table," Gøran said and pulled out a chair. It made a screeching noise.

"The dog has to be outside," Einar said again.

Reluctantly Gøran got up and went out with the dog. He tied it to a fence and came back in. Einar pulled him a pint.

"Enjoy it while you can," Nudel laughed.

"Hell, yeah," Gøran said, "seeing that I'll be in the nick soon. Oh, I don't think it's that bad. They wanted to know where I'd been that day. Made a few notes and then they left. Lots of people in Elvestad have red cars. They'll be busy."

"Well, at least I've got an alibi," Frank chuckled. "Went to the pictures that night. Even saved my ticket. I'm bloody well not binning it now. You can't trust those people. Innocent people are convicted all the time."

"On the whole they get the right ones," Nudel said.

"Have you found out who gave your name yet?" Frank said, looking at Gøran.

"No, and I don't give a shit."

"It could be Linda. The one with the albino hair."

Gøran stared into his beer. "I thought it might be her."

"For Christ's sake, she also saw them out in the meadow."

"Saw the outlines of them," Frank corrected him.

"Says who?" Gøran said quickly.

"Karen."

"God only knows what she actually saw."

Gøran lifted his glass to drink. "She should watch her mouth. Damn it. If there's a madman about and she's babbling to the cops all the time, anything could happen. If I was her, I'd keep a low profile."

"That girl's never kept a low profile," Einar said.

"If she'd really seen something that was any use then the police would've got further. They're not even sure if they were the ones she saw."

"Well, that's what they're saying!"

Nudel waved his arms about in excitement. "Imagine everything that the cops know, but aren't saying. Perhaps they're saying she only caught sight of two people to protect her. But in fact she saw a lot more."

"I doubt it," Einar said, stacking the empty tankards in the dishwasher.

"That's how they do it," Nudel said. "They leak titbits to the press to keep them at bay while they actually know much more."

"Well, in that case you're innocent, Gøran," Einar said. "Otherwise they'd have nicked you ages ago. Linda knows very well who you are. If she'd seen you, she'd have told them long ago."

"Albinos are short-sighted," Gøran said flippantly.

"She's not an albino. She's just very blonde. But she's clueless. Why aren't you with Ulla?"

"Ulla is in bed, has a bug or something," Gøran said coldly. "Women really do my head in."

He drank slowly for a long time. His eyes became distant. The others watched him covertly. Narrow red stripes were still plain to see on his face and on the hand with which he held his glass.

"We were wondering if you'd been in a fight," Frank said. "As your face is a bit, how shall we say, decorated."

Gøran smiled. "That'll be my dog. Sometimes we try each other's strength. That animal constantly needs reminding who's boss."

"But what did the cops say?"

"They want to talk to everyone. Your turn will come." Gøran clenched the tankard in his fists.

"D'you hear that, Einar?"

"They've been here already." He shrugged as if he could not care less. "They sent a curly-haired schoolboy. He really made me wet my pants."

"Same one I saw," Gøran said. "Didn't seem very bright."

"The bright ones join the national crime squad," Frank said.

Mode was deep in thought. "I wonder if they've profiled the killer," he said. "That's the trend these days. The worst thing is it's usually accurate."

"Listen," Nudel said. "We're not exactly Chicago."

"No, but all the same."

Mode had a dreamy way of talking, as if he was thinking aloud. "I wonder if it's the case that killers prefer certain makes of car. I mean, tell me what you drive and I'll show you who you are."

The others laughed; they knew Mode's fondness for gross generalisations when it came to people's choice of cars.

"Take a Volvo, for example," Mode said. "A Volvo is an old man's car. A Mercedes likewise. Look at Jomann and Kalle Moe and you'll see it's true. He who drives a French car has a certain style and a sense of comfort and sophistication. But he is totally impractical. French cars are delightful, but impossible to repair yourself. Those who drive Jap cars are practical, but lack style and sophistication."

This gave rise to laughter all round, Frank's car being Japanese.

"Then there's the BMW," Mode mused. "That's for guys who want to get ahead. BMW drivers are complete show-offs. Whereas English cars are often driven by slightly feminine men. Then there's the Opel," he said. "An Opel is evidence of style, practicality and confidence. Not to mention a Saab!"

More raucous laughter at the table. Mode drove a Saab.

He took a sip of his beer and stared at Gøran. "When it comes to Skoda and Lada, I'd rather not say anything at all."

"That just leaves the Golf," Nudel said, looking around at the others.

Gøran listened, his arms folded across his chest.

"A Golf," Mode said, "is very interesting. A Golf is driven by someone with a temper. They want things to happen quickly and they are always on the move. They have their foot on the pedal all the time. Somewhat hot-headed, perhaps."

"I think you should offer your services to the police," Einar said over the counter. "With your knowledge of people and cars, you'd be invaluable."

"It's true." Mode laughed.

Einar switched off the dishwasher and flicked the light three times. The young men grunted reluctantly, but emptied their glasses and carried them to the counter. No-one crossed Einar. Sometimes they wondered why.

CHAPTER 14

It was late in the evening. The light was fading and the trees were already black silhouettes. Gunwald attached the lead to his dog and plodded along the edge of the wood. He couldn't bring himself to cross the meadow. He kept to the edges. The beagle was panting, its tongue hanging out of its mouth.

"Come on, fatso," Gunwald said. "You need the exercise and so do I."

They walked towards Norevann. After a hundred metres he stopped and turned. Looked back at the meadow. The silence troubled him and he was not sure why. He was deeply upset by what had happened. He knew everyone in the community. Now a stranger from outside had wrought death and destruction. If it *was* a stranger. Gunwald had never before been afraid of the dark. He shook his head and walked on. It was a walk he made every evening. It made him feel that he had done his duty for the fat dog. Not a great or forceful personality, you could say. Not a show dog. Just its silent companionship. The padding of paws. The familiar warning when someone came near the house. He had got to the end of the road and stepped on to a grassy mound leading down to the water. His steps became noiseless now. The clouds whispered above him, he felt the hair on his head move. Suddenly he heard a familiar sound. A car engine, still faint, but approaching fast. He looked at his watch. A car out at Norevann this late in the evening, he couldn't understand it. He disappeared in between the trees and waited while the dog did its business. Gunwald couldn't work out why he was gripped by this sudden fear. It was ridiculous, he had been taking walks here for years, and so had many others with or without their dogs. He listened for the car. It slipped quietly, almost reluctantly down the cart road. Came to a halt. The headlights beamed across the water giving off a cold, blue-white halogen light. Then they were turned off and it was dark again. A figure appeared. Went to the back of the car to get something. Walked out towards the point. Gunwald moved further back among the trees. Thought that the dog would start to bark now. But it didn't, it stood there listening attentively as well. In the dwindling light from the western sky Gunwald could see the silhouette of a man. He stood at the edge of the point carrying something, something big and heavy. It struck him that it looked like a suitcase. Then the man turned and looked around. Suddenly he swung his arm with great force and a huge splash was heard. Gunwald felt his heart pound. The dog stood next to him, spellbound. The man hurried back to his car. People throwing stuff into the lake probably meant nothing at all, Gunwald thought. Nevertheless he was shaking. The car which had come out of nowhere, the man who had looked furtively over his shoulder had frightened him. The man had reached his car. For a moment he stared into the twilight while Gunwald crouched down between the trees. The dog was smitten by its master's fear and froze. The man got into the car. Started up and reversed. Made a sharp turn and straightened up. Disappeared back to the road. Gunwald was very sure. That man was Einar Sunde.

He sat in his armchair for a long time, thinking. Should he report this? He remembered that it had said in the papers something about a missing suitcase. But this was Einar, a man he knew. Had known all these years. A hardworking family man with a spotless reputation. True, there were rumours that his marriage was in trouble and that the wife had secrets of her own. But Gunwald wasn't small-minded, he didn't judge people for such things. Einar had probably dumped some rubbish and that was, strictly speaking, illegal, but you didn't call the police just for that. If he were to call they would ask him who he was. And of course Einar had not killed a defenceless woman. He was certain of that. But perhaps it was important. Why had he thrown the suitcase into the water? Assuming it *was* a suitcase. He could call anonymously, he thought that was allowed. He closed his eyes and saw the silhouette once more. Suddenly he felt cold. Got up and went over to the cabinet, where he found a bottle of Eau de Vie. Poured himself a large glass. He didn't want to get mixed up in something like that. Young Linda Carling, however, she had cycled past and told them what she'd seen without hesitation. But then she was young and full of energy. He was old, well past sixty. But if he were to call and say: someone stood out at the tip of the point and threw something into Norevann. I was out with my dog. I didn't see who he was. And I didn't see what he dumped. But it could've been a suitcase. Then they would send out divers and find something. And if it turned out to be a sack of rubbish then there was no harm done. Call them now and tell them that. Don't mention Einar's name. He drank more Eau de Vie. Besides, though it was Einar's car, he might not have been the one driving. He had a son who sometimes borrowed the car. Ellemann. It could have been Ellemann Sunde. But he was short and this had been a tall man. It was definitely Einar's car. He had not seen the plates, of course, but he recognised the rear of it, it was always parked outside the café with its rear towards the road. A Sierra estate. He saw it every day from his own shop. Was the hotline open now, this late in the evening? He swallowed more Eau de Vie. It was hard to go to bed without telling anyone. Anyway, it struck him that Einar would never dump rubbish in the lake. He had a huge skip, which Vestengen Transport emptied once a month. Gunwald had never seen it full. It contained paper cups, styrofoam and coffee filters. He looked down at the dog. Caressed its head. "We'll call in the morning. It's time for bed now. You didn't bark," he whispered in disbelief. "And I'm damned if I know why you didn't. You always yap at the slightest thing."

The water was five metres deep and very muddy. Two divers were working away. Sejer stood at the tip of the point and saw the blurred figures arch like huge fish. Skarre sidled up to him.

"Tell me about Gøran Seter," Sejer said.

Skarre nodded. "Nice young man. Nineteen years old. Only child of Torstein and Helga Seter. Still lives at home in his old bedroom.

Works for a carpenter. Went to the gym in town on the evening of the 20th, the Adonis Health Studio. Passed Hvitemoen around 8.30 p.m."

"And afterwards?"

"Spent the evening with his girlfriend, Ulla. They babysat her sister's child."

"How did he react to your questioning?"

"He answered willingly. However, I noticed some red stripes on his face. Partially healed cuts."

Sejer looked up. "I see. Did you ask about them?"

"He'd been playing with his dog. He has a Rottweiler."

"This weight training – is he very committed to that?"

"Absolutely. We're talking about a bundle of muscles. Around 100 kilos, I'd say."

"Did you like him?"

Skarre smiled. At times Sejer asked some strange questions. "Yes, I did actually."

"We need to speak to his girlfriend."

"We do."

"I've been thinking of something," Sejer said. "Who goes out in the evening? Late in the evening, down to the lake. People with dogs?"

"Probably," Skarre said.

"If I'd lived where Gunwald lived, then this is just where I'd walk my dog."

"I don't think he takes it for walks. That dog's a real porker."

"Nonetheless we should talk to him. If it was him who called, he'll crack at the slightest pressure. He's not very tough."

"Crack under pressure?"

"We'll see what we find."

"He sounded strange on the telephone," Skarre said. "Reeled his words off as if he'd learned them by heart before slamming the phone down. Scared stiff."

"Why, do you think?"

"I think he was lying. Said he'd only seen the outline of a man. Perhaps he actually saw who it was. And that terrified him. Possibly it was someone he knew."

"Exactly."

Sejer stared into the deep. Bubbles surfaced and burst. One of the divers broke the surface and swam towards the shore. "There's something down there. Looks like a box."

"Could it be a suitcase?" Sejer said.

"It might be. It's heavy. We need a rope."

He fetched a coil of nylon rope and disappeared under the surface once more. The men on the shore held their breath. Sejer forced his eyes until he felt dizzy as he stood there leaning forward, peering.

"They're coming up. They're ready."

Two technicians pulled the rope in small tugs. Soon they saw something break the surface. They saw the handle to which the green rope was tied. Sejer closed his eyes with joy. He grabbed the handle and helped drag the heavy suitcase up on to the shore. For a while it lay there, soaking wet, glistening in the grass. It was an old suitcase of brown imitation leather with solid handles. Fastened to the suitcase was a brown folder of the same material. A nametag was attached to the handle, but water had erased the writing. He knelt on the grass and looked at the suitcase. He could not help but think of Jomann.

"How much water has got in?" Skarre said.

"Quite a lot. It's old and worn."

Sejer lifted the suitcase. "God, it's heavy. I don't see how she could've walked along the road with it."

"If that was what she did. She sat in the café drinking tea. Einar Sunde is the only one who saw her leave."

"But she was killed where she was found," Sejer reminded him.

"But what if there were two? If there was a customer at the café when Poona arrived?"

"And they both tried it on and one of them drove after her to finish it off?"

"Yes. Something like that."

Carefully Sejer lifted the suitcase into the car.

"Skarre. We'll check the contents of this. You go and talk to Gøran Seter's girlfriend."

135

"Yes, boss." Sejer rolled his eyes. "She works in the mall, sells perfume. It all fits, doesn't it? A beefcake and a painted doll, textbook stuff," Skarre said.

"Just get out of here," Sejer ordered him.

"Why the sudden hurry?"

"You said his face was scratched. Check his alibi."

The suitcase was unlocked. It was secured with two broad straps pulled tight. Sejer slid the locks open. Two sharp clicks were heard. Then he opened the lid. Wet clothes and shoes. For a while he stood staring at the exotic colours. Turquoise, lemon, orange. And underwear. It looked brand new and was folded into clear plastic bags. Two pairs of shoes. A sponge bag with a floral pattern. A bag with different-coloured hair bands. A hairbrush. A dressing gown, rose-coloured and silky. The clothes were folded neat and tight. Her few possessions looked lost and strangely misplaced in the meeting room. The objects overwhelmed them. She would have placed her belongings in the drawers in Jomann's bedroom. The brush on the chest of drawers, the sponge bag in the bathroom. The shoes in the wardrobe. In her mind she had imagined unpacking with her husband helping her. She had 1,000 metres to go when she died.

They found Poona's papers in the brown folder. Travel insurance and passport. On the photograph she was very young and looked like a ten-year-old. She didn't smile in the photograph.

"These things belong to Jomann," Sejer said. "Take care of them. They're all he's got left."

The men nodded. Sejer thought of Elise, his wife. Her hairbrush still lay on the shelf under the mirror; it had been there for thirteen years and would never be removed. Everything else had gone. Clothes and shoes. Jewellery and bags. But not the hairbrush. Perhaps Jomann, too, would put this hairbrush on the shelf under his mirror. How significant things could become.

He left the room and called the hospital. They told him that Jomann was at his sister's bedside.

*

The shopping centre was crowded. Surprising really that Gunwald was still in business, Skarre thought. He looked around for the perfumery and saw a counter between a wool shop and a key cutter. A girl was sitting behind the counter, reading. Skarre ran his eyes across bottles, jars, tubes and boxes. What did they use it all for, he wondered. A single shelf was set aside for men. He studied the bottles and looked at the young woman.

"What would you recommend for me," he said, "if I wanted to smell good?"

She turned towards him and gave him a professional once-over.

"Hugo Boss is good. And Henley. Depends if you want to be really noticed or not."

"I'd like to be noticed," Skarre said enthusiastically.

She picked a bottle from the shelf. Opened it and dabbed some on his wrist. He sniffed it obediently and smiled at her.

"Well, well," he said, laughing. "That's a bit frisky. How much is it?"

"390 kroner," she said.

Skarre nearly choked.

"You must remember that there are years of scientific research behind a fragrance," she said, businesslike. "They experiment for ages before they finally get it right."

"Mm," Skarre said. "You're Ulla, aren't you?"

She looked at him in surprise. "Yes. That's me."

"Police," he said. "You probably know why I'm here." Ulla had broad shoulders and huge breasts. They looked real. Otherwise she was slim with long legs and was very skilfully made up.

"Then I'll have to disappoint you," she said. "I don't know anything about that business at Hvitemoen."

"No, we didn't think so either," Skarre smiled. "But that's how we work. We turn every stone."

"Nothing will crawl out from under my stone," she said, pretending to be insulted. This caused Skarre to laugh with embarrassment.

"Of course not. I'm just trying to make an impression, but it doesn't work every time. Is there somewhere quiet we could talk?"

"I can't leave this place," she said quickly.

"Isn't there anyone you can ask, just for a minute?"

She looked around the large hall. There were two girls at the bakery counter and they didn't seem to have much to do. She waved to one of them and she came running over.

"There's a bench over there. We can go and sit there."

The cast-iron bench was terrible. Skarre solved the problem by sitting at the very edge and leaning forward.

"Just to make you aware. We're at the stage where we're eliminating people. Do you understand? We're trying to find out where people actually were on the evening of the 20th. And what they might've seen."

"Precisely. But I didn't see anything at all." She looked at him apprehensively.

"But I'll ask you anyway. Where were you on the evening of the 20th?"

Ulla thought back. "First I went to Adonis to work out. With a guy I know."

Skarre thought her choice of words for her boyfriend was strange, but he made no comment.

"We finished around 8 p.m. I took the bus from town out to my sister who lives a mile out of Elvestad. She is married and has a two-year-old boy. I babysat for her," she said.

"I see. How long were you there?"

"Till about midnight."

"And – this Gøran. He was with you?"

"No," she said abruptly. "I don't need company to look after a two-year-old. I watched TV and caught the last bus home."

"So your boyfriend didn't keep you company?"

She gave him a cutting look.

"Gøran," Skarre said.

"I don't have a boyfriend," she said.

Skarre rested his chin in his hands and looked at her. On one hand she wore a pretty ring with a black stone.

"You're not with Gøran Seter?" he said calmly.

"Used to be," she said, and he heard the despondency in her voice.

"It's over?"

"Yes."

"When was it over?"

"That very day," she said. "The 20th after the work-out. I'd had enough."

Time passed while Skarre digested the news and slowly took on board the significance of it.

"Ulla," he said quietly, "forgive me for asking you what might seem to be personal questions. However, I need to know some of the details surrounding your break-up with Gøran."

"Why?" she said, fearful.

"I can't explain. Please tell me what you can. Exactly when and how did it happen?"

"But why do I have to talk about it?"

"I understand that you think it's none of my business. But, actually, it is."

"Neither of us is mixed up with this case. I don't want to."

She clammed up again.

Skarre encouraged her. "You don't need to give details. Just give me a brief description of how it happened."

He focused his blue eyes on Ulla's green ones. That usually worked, and this time was no exception.

"We'd been together for nearly a year. We used to work out together at Adonis two or three times a week. I don't always work out three times, but Gøran does. So he picks me up and we go together. Work out for a couple of hours and then we leave. We were at Adonis on the evening of the 20th and I was determined to end it. I waited till we'd finished our work-out. Then we went to our separate changing rooms. I dreaded it," she admitted. "Decided to postpone it. Find a better occasion. But then it just came flying out of my mouth. We met at the exit like we always did. He bought a Coke, I bought a Sprite, which we drank outside. Then I told him. That I'd had enough. That I was going to catch the bus instead."

Skarre's thoughts took off in all directions.

"Ulla," he said, "what was he wearing? After the work-out. Do you remember?"

139

She gave him an uncertain look. "Now, what was it? Tennis shirt with a collar. White. And Levi jeans. Black. That's what he wears."

"How did he take it?"

"His face turned white. But there was nothing he could do. If it's over, it's over. So he said nothing. Just stormed off and threw himself into his car."

"Did he tell you where he was going?"

"No. But I stood there for a while watching him. He made a call, I remember. On his mobile. Then he drove off. The tyres squealed."

"Ulla," Skarre said calmly, "we'll be back to talk to you. But you've got nothing to worry about. Do you understand?"

"Yes," she said gravely.

"You can go back to work now," he said. Then he left the shopping centre and got into his car. Drummed his fingers continuously on the steering wheel. Gøran Seter had not been babysitting with Ulla. It was over. He'd been rejected. On his way home he passed Hvitemoen. He was alone in the red Golf and he was wearing a white shirt.

CHAPTER 15

Linda had called Karen repeatedly, but her mum kept saying that she was out. It was several days since they had last spoken. People stared at her when she went to the café or cycled down the road. They seemed hostile. She stood by the window staring into the dark garden. Rumours flew around, mercilessly, about whom the police had been to see and especially where they had been more than once. Her mum didn't seem particularly excited one way or the other that Linda had called the police. As far as she knew, there was no prospect of meeting Jacob again. She didn't know what she could do to make him come to the house. She had searched her memory over and over through confused snapshots, as they seemed, for further details. The two people in the meadow, the strange game. When she thought of it, it still seemed like a game. But Jacob had said that you saw what you wanted to see. No-one wanted to see a murder. A man running after a woman, like they do all the time. That's why she'd drawn that conclusion. Gøran had given her such an evil stare that day in the café when she had been looking at his car. Now he had probably made the connection. Not that she was scared of Gøran, but she didn't want to get him into trouble. She had just wanted to tell them about the car. Lots of people owned Golfs. They could be from any-where. But it was too late. They had talked to both Gøran and Ulla. Then she thought about Gøran's face, about the scratches on his face. Other people must have noticed them. They would have mentioned them in any case. She wasn't going to say anything else, not a single word. But she had to see Jacob again! She lingered by the window, thinking hard. Her mum had gone to Holland to bring back a load of tulips. The house was quiet, it was past 11 p.m. Suddenly she rushed out into the hall and locked the door. The sharp click of the lock frightened her. She sat at the kitchen table.

When the telephone rang she leapt up and gasped. Perhaps it was Karen ringing back at last. She lifted the handset and called out her name. But no-one answered. She could hear someone breathe. Confused, she remained where she was, holding the handset.

"Hello?"

No reply. Just the dialling tone. She put down the handset, her hands trembling. Now they had started to scare her, too. She sat on the sofa, biting her nails. Outside the wind rustled in the trees. No-one would hear her if she screamed. Fear threatened to overpower her. She switched the TV on, then switched it off again. If someone came to the door she wouldn't be able to hear them with all that noise. She decided to go to bed. Quickly she brushed her teeth and ran up the stairs. Closed the curtain. Pulled off her clothes, crept under the duvet. Lay there listening. She had a strong feeling that someone was outside. It was silly. There had never been anyone outside the house apart from the deer that came to eat the fallen apples no-one could be bothered to pick up. She turned off the lamp and hid under the duvet. The man who had done that terrible thing would never come to her house. He was probably in hiding. Three hundred people had called the hotline. Imagine, she was just one of three hundred.

Suddenly she heard a sound. It was quite distinct and not something she had imagined. A thump against the outside wall. She jerked upright in her bed. Sat listening breathlessly. Then a kind of dragging sound. Linda felt sick. She bent over in the bed, hugging herself. Someone was outside! Someone was in the garden. She put her feet on the floor, ready to jump. Any minute now someone would start fiddling with the lock downstairs. There was a rushing noise in her ears, she couldn't think. Then everything went silent. The room was in total darkness. She went to the window and stuck two fingers behind the curtain. Stared out through the narrow gap. At first all she could see was the darkness. But then her night vision took over and she glimpsed the trees outside and the faint light from the kitchen which fell softly on the lawn. Then she saw a man. He was staring right up at her window. She backed into a corner and stayed there gasping. This is the punishment, she thought. He would take his revenge now because she had phoned. In a blind panic she dashed out and ran down the stairs. Grabbed the telephone and dialled Jacob's number, the private number in Nedre Storgate, which she knew by heart. She panted down the receiver when he answered.

"Someone's here," she whispered desperately. "He's standing outside in the garden staring up at my window."

"Sorry," she heard, "who's this, please?"

"Linda," she shouted. "I'm home alone. There's a man in the garden!"

"Linda?" Skarre said. "What are you talking about?"

His voice was a great relief. She started to cry.

"A man. He tried to hide behind some trees, but I saw him."

Skarre finally understood what this was about and adopted a professional and reassuring tone of voice. "You're home alone and you thought you saw someone?"

"I did see someone! Quite clearly. I heard him too. He was pressing up against the wall."

Jacob Skarre had never in all his life experienced anything like this. He sat for a while, thinking. Decided to talk to her and calm her down, she was probably overwrought.

"How did you get my home number?" he asked.

"From the directory."

"Yes, of course. Of course you did. But I'm not on duty now, you know."

"No. But what if he tries to get in?"

"Have you locked the door?"

"Yes."

"Linda," he said. "Go to the window. See if he's still out there."

"No!"

"Do as I say."

"I daren't!"

"I'll wait. I won't hang up."

Linda sneaked over to the window and peeked out into the garden. It was deserted. For a time she stood there, staring in confusion, then she came back to the kitchen.

"Was he there?"

"No."

"Perhaps it's something you've imagined? Because you're scared?"

"You think I've lost it. But I haven't!"

"I don't think that. But what you're scared of won't happen, Linda."

"Everyone knows what I've said," she sniffled. "Everyone in the area."

"Are they unkind to you?"

"Yes!"

She gripped the handset as tightly as she could. He mustn't hang up. She wanted to talk to Jacob till dawn.

"Listen to me, Linda," Skarre said urgently. "Many people are too cowardly to call. They see all sorts of things, but don't want to get involved at any cost. You've been brave, you've told us what you knew. And provided us with the possible make of the car, nothing else. No-one can accuse you of anything."

"No, but I'm thinking of Gøran," she said. "I bet he's mad."

"He has no reason to be," Skarre said. "D'you know what? I suggest you go to sleep now as quickly as possible. Tomorrow you'll see things in a more positive light."

"Aren't you coming over to investigate?"

"There's probably no need. However, I can call the station and ask them to send over an officer if you really want me to."

"I'd rather you came," she said, meekly.

Skarre sighed. "I'm off duty," he said. "Try to relax, Linda. People do go out for walks, you know. Perhaps it was a night wanderer taking a short cut through your garden."

"Yes. I'm sorry." She pressed the handset so hard against her ear that it felt like Jacob was inside her head. "Well, I'm not going to say anything any more," she said obstinately.

"But surely you've told us everything you know by now?"

"Yes," she said.

"Then that's that. Go to bed. I understand that you're afraid. It was a terrible thing that happened," Skarre said.

Don't hang up! a voice was screaming in her head. Jacob! Don't!

"Goodnight then, Linda."

"Goodnight."

Gunder's cheeks were sunken. He was unshaven and his shirt had a dark rim round the collar. Just as well Marie can't see me, he thought. He stared down at Poona's belongings, which were spread out on the table. The clothes were dry, but stained from the dirty water. You could still see how beautiful they were. These are my wife's clothes, he thought. The nightgown and the hairbrush. When he closed his eyes he could recall how she used to lift her hair forward across her shoulder to brush it.

"We'll bring them home to you as soon as possible," Sejer said.

Gunder nodded. "It'll be good to have something," he said bravely.

"There's one more thing," Sejer said. "We've received a letter from the police in New Delhi. You can see it if you wish."

He nodded and took the sheet of paper. Struggled a bit with the English wording.

"Mr Shiraz Bai, living in New Delhi, confirms one sister, Poona, born on June 1st, 1962. Left for Norway on August 19th. Mr Bai will come to Oslo on September 10th to take his sister home."

Gunder gasped. "Back? To India? But she's my wife! I've got the marriage certificate here. Surely I'm her closest relative? Can he do this?" Gunder was so upset that he stood on the floor shaking. The blue eyes shone with fear and the letter trembled in his hands.

Sejer tried to calm him down. "We'll help you with this. I'm sure we'll find a solution."

"I must have some rights. A marriage is a marriage."

"It is," Sejer said. He opened a drawer in his desk. "However, at least I can let you take this home." He handed Gunder a slim envelope. "Her brooch."

Gunder had to wipe away a tear when he saw the beautiful piece of jewellery.

"She'll be buried with this," he said firmly.

Carefully he put the brooch in his inside pocket and hugged his jacket tightly around himself.

"We're chipping away at this case," Sejer said. "It will be solved."

Gunder looked down at the floor.

"I know that you've other things on your mind," Sejer said. "You're a widower now."

This made Gunder raise his head. Sejer had called him a widower. It felt like restitution. He drove home and called his brother-in-law to tell him about Marie. He always did that when he returned from the hospital. Though there wasn't much to tell.

"It's odd that someone can lie as still as that," he said to Karsten. "And not even blink. Imagine if she loses her voice."

"It'll just be a bit hoarse," Karsten said. "They can probably rehabilitate it."

"Everything will need rehabilitating," Gunder said sadly. "Her muscles are wasting away. They say that her body is turning soft. They say . . ."

"All right, all right. We'll just have to be patient. I don't want to hear any more. I don't understand a word of it anyway."

Fear crept into his voice. Karsten had not mentioned Poona at all, though by now it had leaked out who she actually was. Gunder was deeply hurt. He stood there fiddling with the curly telephone cable. Karsten didn't come to the hospital. Gunder personally was happy to sit by his sister's bedside. He spoke quietly and sombrely to her about everything that had happened. They've found her suitcase now, Marie. With her clothes. And her brother's coming. I'm so worried. I took his sister from him. True, Poona said they weren't especially close, but all the same. He advised her against going. And he was right.

He sat there, talking in this way. Thus he coped with his thoughts, one by one.

He was still on sick leave and did not want to return to work. The days came and went, sometimes Bjørnsson called to chat. He seemed perky. He had finally got the chance to show them what he was made of, now that their senior sales person was away. But Svarstad had asked for Jomann. And according to Bjørnsson had stood there gawping in the doorway when he heard the lengthy story. He had never believed that Jomann had the courage to go abroad and find himself a wife.

"In an earlier interview with one of our officers, Jacob Skarre, you stated that you were with your girlfriend Ulla on the evening of August 20th."

Sejer looked at Gøran Seter, who smiled back at him. The scratches on his face were now reduced to faint lines.

"That's correct."

"However, the interview with the young lady revealed the following: she's no longer your girlfriend and she didn't spend the evening with you. You worked out together at Adonis Studio from 6 p.m. to around 8 p.m. Thereafter she ended the relationship. At which point you drove off in anger, alone in the car. And subsequently passed Hvitemoen sometime between 8.30 p.m. and 9 p.m."

Gøran Seter's eyes widened. He was a heavily built man with blond hair with bright red stripes. His hair stood up. His eyes shone intensely. Sejer was reminded of pearls of mercury.

"So Ulla's ended it again?" He let out a bemused laugh. "She tends to do that. It happens all the time, I've stopped taking it seriously."

"I'm less interested in whether you're still in a relationship or not. You have previously stated that you were with her later that evening, at her sister's, and that's not correct."

"It is. But excuse me, why do I have to answer this?"

"We're investigating a murder. A great many people have to answer a great many questions. You are, in other words, just one of many. If that makes you feel better."

"I don't need to feel better."

Gøran was strong and convincing. The smile never left his face.

"Ulla likes to stir," he explained.

"Not according to my officer."

"Well, he spoke to her for a few minutes. I've known her for over a year."

"So you still maintain that you spent the evening with her?"

"Yes. We were babysitting."

"Why would Ulla lie about this? To a police officer?"

"If he was attractive that would probably be reason enough. She goes for everyone. Wanted to appear available, I guess."

"That's a bit cheap, in my opinion."

"You can't have any idea what lengths girls will go to to make themselves look interesting. They'll stop at nothing. Ulla is no exception."

"Have you been to her sister's house before?"

"Yes." His smile broadened. "So I can describe to you the living room and the kitchen and the bathroom. What a shame, eh?"

"How were you dressed when you left Adonis?"

"Tennis shirt. White probably. Black Levis. That's what I wear."

"You showered after the work-out?"

"Of course."

"Nevertheless you took another shower later on?"

Brief pause.

"How do you know that?"

"I've been speaking to your mother. You were home by 11 p.m. Went straight to the shower."

"If you say so."

Still he smiled. No fear or anxiety. The heavy body rested in the chair, carefully sculpted.

"Why?"

"Felt like it."

"Your mother also said that when you came home that night you were wearing a blue T-shirt and grey jogging pants. Did you change again after your work-out?"

"My mum's memory is not all that great, in my opinion."

"So you're the only one in the village who can think straight, is that it, Gøran?"

"No. But honestly, she doesn't notice stuff like that. However, I do work out in a blue T-shirt and grey jogging pants."

"So after you left Adonis wearing a clean white shirt and before you came home, did you change back into your sweaty work-out clothes?"

"No, I'm telling you. It's Mum who's getting it mixed up."

"What did you wear on your feet?"

"Trainers. These ones."

He stretched out his legs and showed him.

"They look new."

"Not at all. They've been worn."

"Can I see the soles?"

He lifted his feet. The soles of the trainers were white as chalk.

"Who did you call?"

"Call? When?"

"You made a call in your car. Ulla saw you."

For the first time Gøran looked serious.

"I called someone I know. Simple as that."

Sejer considered this. "This is your situation as of today. You passed the crime scene in your car at the crucial time. You drive a red Golf. A similar car was seen at the scene, parked on the roadside. A witness saw a man wearing a white shirt out in the meadow. He was with a woman. You're lying about where you spent the evening. Several witnesses have remarked that your face was scratched when you turned up at Einar's Café on the 21st, the day after the murder. Your face is still scratched. I'm sure you can appreciate that I need an explanation for this."

"I had a fight with my dog. And I don't go around assaulting women. I don't need to. I have Ulla."

"That's not what she says, Gøran."

"Ulla says a lot of things." He was no longer smiling.

"I don't think so. I'll be back."

"No. I won't have you bothering me. Sod you."

"My only concern is for the dead woman, no-one else," Sejer said.

"Your lot are never concerned about anyone."

Sejer went out into the yard. He had a strong feeling that Gøran Seter was hiding something. But everyone is, he thought, and it doesn't have to be a murder. That's what made this job so difficult, there was a touch of guilt in everyone, which put them in a bad light, sometimes quite undeservedly. The ruthlessness of it, digging into other people's lives, was the part of the job he most disliked. So he closed his eyes and summoned up the image of Poona's battered head.

CHAPTER 16

Sara was waiting for him, sitting on the sofa, with a pot of coffee ready. Kollberg his dog was lying at her feet. He was dreaming he was chasing something, his paws were twitching as though he was racing at great speed. Sejer wondered if dogs experienced the same nightmarish feelings when they dreamed, the sensation of running on the spot.

"He'll never grow up," Sejer mused. "He's just an overgrown puppy."

"Maybe something happened in his childhood," Sara laughed and poured him some coffee. "What do you know about Kollberg's first weeks?"

Sejer thought back. "He wasn't quick enough. Always the last one to get to the food. Pushed around by the other puppies. It was a big litter, thirteen in all."

"Then he's been starved of attention. And you picked the puppy you ought never to take."

He chose to ignore this. "But since then he's had far too much. This starvation – it'll pass, surely?"

"Something like that never passes," Sara said.

They turned off the lamps and sat in the twilight. A candle burned on the table. Sejer thought of Poona.

"Why did he destroy her face?" he said. "What does that mean?"

"I don't know," she said.

"There must have been a reason for it."

"Perhaps he thought she was ugly."

Sejer was astonished. "What makes you say so?"

"Sometimes it's that simple. You're bloody ugly too, he thinks, his fury is provoked and he crosses a line." She sipped her coffee. "What do you think? Is he desperately unhappy now?"

"Not necessarily. But I'd like to think he was."

"You're so upright," she smiled. "You'd like remorse."

"In this case it would be entirely appropriate. But when we catch him he'll above all be concerned with his own survival. Make excuses for himself. Defend himself. He has rights too, he'll say."

Sara got up and squatted on the floor next to Kollberg, scratching its back. He saw the heavy animal rock backwards and forwards contentedly beneath her hands.

"He has a lump under his coat," she said. "Here. On his back."

Sejer gave her an uneasy look.

"In fact, several," she said. "Three or four. Have you noticed, Konrad?"

"No," he said.

"You need to get him to a vet."

There was a trace of fear in his normally calm face.

"You know," she said, "at his age these things happen. And a dog his size – how old is he now?"

"Ten."

He remained on the sofa. Didn't want to touch the lumps. Fear filled him like freezing water. He got up reluctantly and searched with his fingers through the thick fur.

"I'll call first thing in the morning."

He sat down again and reached for his tobacco pouch to make a roll-up. His daily ration was one whisky and one roll-up. Sara looked at him lovingly.

"You're a man with enormous self-control."

Sejer had shut her out. Escaped from this business with the dog and gone to some other place. She could tell it in his eyes.

"There's not much through traffic in the area," he said in a far-away voice.

"Where are you now?" Sara said, confused.

"In Elvestad. Chances are that he's local."

"Good for you. I don't suppose many people live there?"

"More than 2,000."

"I could call the vet. and make an appointment. Or I could take him. You've got a lot on."

He lit the roll-up. It was unusually thick.

"You might as well roll two slim ones," she teased him.

"They might just be cysts. Filled with fluid."

She heard the anxiety in his voice and how he suppressed his fear. The lumps did not contain fluid, she was sure of that.

"We've got to get them looked at. He's finding the stairs difficult."

"For all I know we've already spoken to the killer," he said.

Sara shook her head. She kept on stroking Kollberg's back. The dog was aging. He didn't want to see it. His brow was deeply furrowed. The business with the lumps reminded him of something. He was in a place which was shut off to her.

"He's thinner, too. When did you last weigh him?"

"He weighs 70 kilos," Sejer said stubbornly.

"I'll get the bathroom scales."

"Are you mad?" He frowned. Once she was out of sight he sprang up from the sofa and knelt down. Raised the dog's heavy head and looked into the black eyes.

"You're not sick, are you, old chum? You're just getting on a bit. So am I."

He placed the head softly on the dog's front paws. Sara came back with the scales.

"Hang on," he said. "He's not a circus elephant."

"We'll try," she said. "I'll get a cold potato."

The dog sensed that something was about to happen and got up eagerly. They wound the scales to zero and nudged him on to them. They pushed his paws together and Sara supported his sides. He recognised the familiar smell of food and wanted to co-operate. After much encouragement Kollberg finally shook hands while he stood wobbling on his three remaining legs. Sejer looked down at the digital display: 54.9 kilos.

"He's lost 15 kilos," said Sara.

"It's his age," he said.

Kollberg swallowed the potato and lay down.

She snuggled up to Sejer's chest. "Tell me a pretty fairy tale," she pleaded.

"I don't know any fairy tales. Just true stories."

"Then we'll have a true one."

He put the cigarette on the edge of the ashtray. "Many years ago we had some trouble with a petty criminal called Martin. That wasn't his real name, but like you I have a duty of confidentiality."

"Martin is fine," she said.

"Martin was a familiar face. Did all sorts of things: car theft, fraud, stole from people's garages. He had a rather weak character and served an endless series of sentences, usually three to four months. He also drank. Apart from all that, he was a rather charming fellow, except that he had awful teeth. He had only a few rotten stumps left. He would put his hand in front of his mouth whenever he laughed. But we liked him and were concerned about him. We were afraid that one day he'd be caught up in serious crime. We discussed what might be done to rehabilitate him, and we thought about his teeth, whether it was worth fixing them. We contacted social services and asked for funding to replace his teeth; he had no resources of his own. They asked us to submit an application, which we did. We wrote that it was an important part of his rehabilitation. Teeth *are* important, you know. And believe it or not, we got the funding. Martin had to go through with it. During his sentence he went to the dentist three times a week and when eventually he finished he had a mouthful of flawless, bright white teeth. Like yours, Sara."

He inhaled her hair. "Martin was a new man," he recollected. "Held his head high. Cleaned himself up, got a haircut. Then there happened to be a woman working in the prison library. She lived on her own with her daughter and had taken this job to earn some extra money. She fell in love with Martin. He completed his sentence and moved in with her. He still lives with her and is a good father to her child. He has never offended from that day to this."

Sara smiled. "That was almost better than a fairy tale," she said.

"It happens to be true," he said. "But the man we're dealing with here has bigger problems than Martin."

"Yes," said Sara sadly. "He needs more than a dentist."

*

154

September 10th. Shiraz Bai had arrived in Norway. He was installed at the Park Hotel at Gunder's expense. Sejer rang Gunder.

"If you wish, we can arrange a meeting at the police station, that way you don't have to be alone with him. He'll probably have questions which might be difficult to answer. He speaks English, but not too well."

Gunder stood by the telephone, mulling it over. Looked at the photograph of Poona. Wondered if he resembled his sister. He's my brother-in-law, he thought. Of course I need to go. But he didn't want to. He imagined an endless list of stinging accusations. How would he find the courage to face that?

It seemed important to look his best. He showered and put on a clean shirt. Tidied all the rooms. Perhaps Bai would like to see the house which was to have been Poona's home. The fine kitchen and the bathroom with the white swans. He drove slowly into town. Skarre was waiting for him in reception. That was really very considerate, Gunder thought. They understood so much. He hadn't expected it. He entered the inspector's office and saw him straightaway. A lean man, not particularly tall, and so like his sister that it startled him. Right down to the protruding teeth. His face was pock-marked and his skin was darker than Poona's. He was wearing a nice blue shirt and pale trousers. His hair was greasy and needed cutting. His gaze was evasive. Gunder approached cautiously when Sejer introduced them. He looked into his brother-in-law's solemn face. He saw no accusation, his expression was completely closed. Just a brief nod. The handshake was an unwilling touch. They were each offered a chair, but Bai declined. He remained standing by the desk as though he wanted this to be over and done with quickly. Gunder had already sat down. He was filled with melancholy. He was close to giving up on it all. Marie was still in a coma. His world was coming to an end.

Skarre, whose English was better than Sejer's, led the conversation.

"Mr Bai," he said, "is there anything you'd like to say to Jomann?"

Bai looked askance at Gunder. "I want to take my sister home. She never arrived. Home is India," he said in a low voice.

155

Gunder stared at the floor. At his feet. He'd forgotten to polish his shoes, they were grey with dust. He was screaming inside, pleas he could not put into words. Bribes. Money, perhaps. Poona had said he was very poor. Then he felt ashamed.

"Perhaps we can talk about it," he said hesitantly.

"No discussion," Bai said abruptly, pressing his lips together.

He looked angry. Not sad about his sister, not weighed down by grief. Not horrified by what had happened, which the police had explained to him down to the last detail. He was angry. Silence followed while the four men in the room waited for each other. Gunder did not have the strength to talk about his rights as a husband or raise the subject of Norwegian and Indian law, or of his own broken heart. He felt powerless.

"I have a single request," he said eventually. His voice was close to cracking. "Just one request. That you come to my house and see Poona's home. What I wanted to give her!"

Bai made no reply. His face was hard. Gunder bowed his head. Skarre looked insistently at Shiraz Bai.

"Would you like to see Mr Jomann's house? It's important to him to show it to you." The question was an appeal, bordering on being an order.

Bai shrugged. Gunder wished the floor would open up and let him fall down into an endless darkness, perhaps all the way down to Poona. Then he would find peace at last. Peace from this stubborn man with the bitter face. From everything that was difficult. Marie, who might wake up and dribble like an idiot. His head was full of noise. I'm going to faint, he thought. I have never fainted in my life. But he did not. He felt how his face, too, became hard and closed.

"Would you like to see Mr Jomann's house?" Skarre repeated. He spoke in an exaggeratedly slow manner as if he were speaking to a child.

At last Bai nodded, an uninterested nod.

"Let's go then," Gunder said nervously and jumped up from the chair. He had an important task ahead of him and had to act while he still felt capable of it. Bai hesitated.

"We go in my car," Gunder said. "I will take you back to the hotel."

"Is that all right with you?" Skarre said, looking at Bai, who nodded in return. The two men walked side by side down the corridor. Gunder heavy and broad with his bald crown and Bai dark and lean with his thick blue-black mane.

Skarre said a silent prayer that Bai would soften. Sometimes it happened that his prayers were answered.

He went back to Sejer's office and took a bag of jelly babies from his pocket. The plastic rustled as he opened the bag.

"Do you still believe in God?" Sejer said, studying him with a friendly gaze.

Skarre picked a jelly baby from the bag. "The green ones are my favourites," he said, avoiding the question.

"Perhaps your faith has started to fray?"

"When I was a boy," Skarre said, "I used to put a jelly baby in my mouth and keep it there till the sugar had dissolved. Then I'd take it out again and it would be clear as glass. They look better without the sugar," he said thoughtfully.

He sucked his green one for a long time, then took it out. "Look!"

It dangled from his fingers and was quite transparent.

"Coward," Sejer smiled.

"What about you?" Skarre said, confronting his boss. "How do you feel about the power?"

Sejer raised his eyebrows. "How do you mean?"

"You once said you believe in a power. Godless as you claim to be, you must have found something else. Strange, isn't it? We do need something."

"Yes. I believe in a power, but we exist as independent entities," Sejer said. "We don't talk to one another."

"Lonely, in other words. You can't ask for anything, you can't find fault with it and rage at it."

"So that's what you do when you say your prayers at night?"

"That too." He took a red jelly baby.

"Say a prayer for Gunder," Sejer said. He stuck his arms into the

157

sleeves of his jacket and walked to the door. Switched off the ceiling light.

"May the force be with you," Skarre said.

Gunder opened the car door for Shiraz. He was now overcome with humility. Poona would have wanted him to receive her brother well. If she could see them now, see this childish defiance between them, she would have frowned. He with his clenched jaw. Shiraz with his eyes narrowed. It'll be over soon, Gunder thought; he didn't believe that fate would ever smile on him again. But he promised to try hard. They drove out of town. It was a beautiful autumn day and the landscape appeared very exotic to Shiraz. Gunder started to talk. Short sentences in English which Shiraz understood. I grew up here. Lived here all my life. It's a quiet place. We all know one another. House built in 1920. Not big, but in good condition. Garden. Nice view. Very nice kitchen, he said. Shiraz kept looking out of his window.

"We have shops and a bank and a post office and a café. A school and a kindergarten. A pretty church. I want to show you the church."

Shiraz said nothing. Deep inside he must have known what Gunder was trying to do. They drove to Elvestad Church. A pretty wooden church with a gently sloping graveyard, still green and lush. There were even a few flowers here and there. The church was rather small, but it brightened up the landscape, blinding white against the dark green. Gunder stopped the car and got out. Shiraz stayed sitting inside. But Gunder didn't give in. He was in action now, this was his last move, the last of his strength was mobilised for this one project. To keep his dead wife. He opened the door on the passenger side, stood there waiting, expectantly. Shiraz got out reluctantly. Peered out on the church and the graves.

"If Poona is allowed to stay, this is where she will lie. I will visit her grave every day. Plant and decorate with flowers. I have plenty of time. All the time I have left I will give to Poona."

Shiraz said nothing, but he was listening. He did not know if he thought the place was pretty. He looked rather surprised. Gunder started walking among the graves. Shiraz followed him at a fair distance. He saw Gunder stop by a grave and approached him cautiously.

"My mother," Gunder said. "Poona would not be alone."

Shiraz stared at the gravestone.

"Do you like it?" Gunder said, watching him. Shiraz shrugged. Gunder hated that he only shrugged. Poona never did that; she always answered clearly and precisely.

"Now we go to the house," Gunder said, and walked back to the car. He was still focused, but it sapped his strength. They pulled up in the yard. Bai looked at the garden and the view.

"Apples," Gunder said, pointing at the trees. "Very good apples."

Shiraz nodded. They went into the hall. He showed him the living room, wandered around, pointing, took him to the kitchen, the bathroom and upstairs. There were two bedrooms. A large one, which was to have been his and Poona's, and a smaller one which was a spare bedroom. Marie slept there when she came to visit. Used to sleep there.

"Your room. If you came to stay," Gunder said. "We wanted to invite you." Shiraz looked into the simple room. A bed was made up with a crocheted bedspread. Blue curtains and a lamp on the bedside table. If Shiraz was impressed he did not show it. They moved on to the rest of the house. Gunder wanted Shiraz to say something, but he said nothing at all. They had finished, they had been everywhere. Gunder made coffee and took some griddle cake out of the freezer. Marie had made it, using butter and sugar and cinnamon. Gunder knew they used a lot of cinnamon in India, perhaps Shiraz would like it. But he would not touch the cake. He did put a lot of sugar in his coffee and did not like that either. Gunder felt despondent once more.

"I must take my sister home," Shiraz said. His voice was no longer hard, but it was still firm. Then Gunder gave up. He collapsed in his chair, sobbing. He did not care what this man might think. His eyes were filled with tears. He had no more words left, they were all used up. Shiraz was silent while Gunder sobbed. The wall clock ticked relentlessly on.

159

Gunder did not know how long he had been sitting like this. He was vaguely aware of movement on the sofa. Shiraz had got up. Perhaps he was going to leave the house in protest and walk the long way back into town. But that was not what he did. He walked around the house. Gunder did not mind. He could snoop all he wanted. Out of the corner of his eye he saw that Shiraz had found the photograph of Poona and him above the desk. Then he went out into the kitchen. Gunder remained in his armchair, tears still flowing. Shiraz was now out in the hall, then he disappeared upstairs. Gunder heard his footsteps, light, cautious steps. He came back downstairs and went out into the yard. Gunder could see him in the garden. He stood under the apple trees, taking in the view. Finally he returned. Both cups of coffee were now cold. Shiraz sat down on the edge of the sofa.

"My sister can stay," was all he said. Gunder could not believe his ears and stared at him in amazement.

"She can stay," Shiraz repeated. "And you must pay. For everything."

"Of course," Gunder stammered. "I will pay for everything. Only the best for Poona!"

He glowed with relief and leapt out of his chair. Clumsily Shiraz started to retrieve something from his shirt pocket and finally extracted an envelope. He handed it to Gunder.

"Letter from my sister. All about you," he said.

Gunder took the letter from the envelope and unfolded the sheet of paper. Poona's writing, neat like embroidery with a black pen. However, he didn't understand a word of it.

"It's in Indian," he said, bewildered. "Do not understand."

"Is written in Marathi," Shiraz said. "Get someone to translate."

Then he got up and nodded to Gunder. "Back to Park Hotel," he said.

Gunder wanted to shake his hand. Shiraz hesitated, but he held out his hand too; it was lean and bony. He squeezed slightly harder than the first time. "Very nice house," he said, bowing.

Gunder was suddenly buzzing with plans. He would arrange Poona's funeral and had a thousand things to do. He did not have a date yet, but there were many things that needed organising. Which undertaker should he employ? What should she wear in the coffin? The brooch. He stood, holding his brother-in-law's hand, overwhelmed with gratitude.

"I have a sister, too," he said quietly. "In hospital."

Shiraz gave him a questioning look.

"Car accident," Gunder said. "She is not awake."

"Very sorry," Shiraz said softly.

"If you ever need anything," Gunder said, cheered by this snippet of sympathy, "you call me."

"I have a better picture," Shiraz said. "Beautiful picture of Poona. I send it to you."

Gunder nodded. They left the house.

He dropped Shiraz at the hotel. Then he went straight to Marie at the hospital. Sat by her bed and took her hand. For the first time in a very long time, he felt at peace.

CHAPTER 17

Gunwald was stacking the shelves with jars of baby food. There were strong rumours going about that the police had been to see Gøran Seter several times. He did not understand that. What about the suitcase? Not that it was Einar from the café who had killed the poor Indian woman, but all the same. I did my duty, he told himself, and lined the jars up in perfect, straight rows.

He read the newspaper assiduously every day. After the murder he sometimes bought several papers. He made a strange discovery. It was new to him, as he had always had just one newspaper. What they wrote did not add up. One said that police did not have a single important clue. Another that they had a crucial sighting and were following a lead. It was hard to know what to think. And he was troubled by the business of the suitcase. It was full of Indian women's clothing. Should he call again and say that it was Einar? He crushed the packaging flat and carried it out into the back yard. Threw it into the container. He didn't want to be a part of this story in any way. When he came back in he saw Mode from the petrol station leafing through his newspaper.

"Do you have any currant buns?" he wanted to know. Gunwald fetched the buns.

"They're never going to get to the bottom of this," Mode said. "No doubt about it."

"What makes you think so?" Gunwald said.

"If they don't catch him right away, they'll never get him. Quite soon they'll have to cut back on the manpower and the case will be shelved. Meanwhile some other poor sod is murdered and that takes priority. Such is life."

Gunwald shook his head. "They sometimes solve cases like this several years later."

"Rarely," Mode said, opening the bag. He bit into a bun.

Gunwald was troubled by the idea that they might never catch the man responsible for this horrific killing.

"I hope it's no-one we know," he said darkly.

"Know?" Mode said doubtfully. "It couldn't be someone local. Who would it be?"

"Well, I'm sure I don't know," Gunwald said, turning away.

Mode munched his bun. "They're splitting up in the posh villa," he said.

Gunwald's eyes widened. "Who says?"

"Common knowledge. Lillian has started packing. I expect Einar will have to sell the house and live at the café. He'll need to stay open all hours if he's to survive. I imagine him in a sleeping bag in the back room. That bitch is no good," he said.

"Well, I don't suppose Einar was the life and soul of the party either," Gunwald said, wondering all the time what this might mean. "Perhaps he'll sell the café and move away. And it'll become a Chinese take-away."

"Fine by me," Mode said.

He took another bun from the bag. It was sponge-like and could be squeezed into different shapes. "Heard any news about Jomann?"

"On sick leave," Gunwald said. "Imagine everything he's been through recently. He spends most of his time at the hospital, I gather. Terrible business about his sister. There's a risk she could wake up and have the mental age of a two-year-old. Her husband can't cope with it. He goes to work as before and waits for them to call him."

"I dare say that's all he can do," Mode said. "But she probably won't wake up after such a long time. Either they wake up right away or they never do."

"I've heard of people who were in a coma for years," Gunwald objected.

"That only happens in America," Mode said and winked.

Then he trotted back to his petrol station. Gunwald sat thinking. It felt as if their community had been taken over. A foreign presence had seeped in and shaken them out of their everyday life. It made them elated, but at the same time anxious; at best it united them and gave them a feeling of belonging and at worst the fear took hold of them at night, in the darkness, under their duvets. All the while life went on, but in a new light. So they took more notice than they used to, as if they were seeing everything for the first time. Thus Gunwald felt that he was seeing Einar for the first time. And asking himself who he was. Gøran. And Jomann. Who had gone off by himself to a foreign country and found a wife. Linda on her bike, whom everyone looked at differently now and this was beginning to unsettle her. She had always been somewhat manic, but now her eyes flittered about nervously. It was clear what people were thinking. She should have kept her mouth shut. Gunwald shifted uneasily. It was the police's job to solve this case, with or without his help. He went out into the yard at the back to check the dog's water bowl. It was almost empty. He refilled it and put it back on the ground.

"Sometimes I think of you," he said. "You were in the yard after all. You must have seen what happened in the meadow. If only you could talk. If only you could whisper in my ear and say, I know him. I know the smell of him. Next time I meet him I will bark loudly, then you'll know who he is. That's how they do it in the movies," Gunwald said and stroked the silky fur. "But this is no movie. And you aren't very bright."

When did you grow old? Sejer wondered, watching Kollberg. You always used to be ten metres ahead. Run down the stairs like a puppy.

The dog stood on the examination table, whimpering. The thin paper tore under its claws. The vet. examined it for lumps and found four. Sejer tried to read his neutral expression.

"They appear solid, not filled with fluid. Clearly delineated tumours." His fingers dug into the red coat.

"I see," Sejer said. Detective inspector and investigator of murders in the prime of his life. Almost two metres tall with reasonably broad shoulders. He was as nervous as a child.

"If I'm to know for sure, I'll have to operate."

"That's decided then," Sejer said.

"The problem is that this dog is big and heavy and old. Ten years is a great age for a Leonberger. Anaesthetising such a dog carries certain risks."

"Anaesthetics always carry a risk, I suppose," Sejer mumbled.

"Yes, to some extent. However, in this case perhaps we should discuss whether he ought to be spared such an operation."

"Why?" Sejer said.

"I don't know that he'll recover afterwards. On the one hand, the tumours do need to be removed whether benign or not. They're pressing on the nerves in his lower back and will cause him to lose mobility. It's a major operation for such an animal. Furthermore, there's a risk that I might damage some nerves, and that could result in paralysis and he'll be worse off than he is now. Then again he might never recover, never be able to stand again. In some cases it can be kinder to the dog to let nature take its course."

The words came at him like hailstones. Sejer tried to buy time so that the lump in his throat would dissolve and free up his vocal cords. Slowly he understood what he had been told. He could not imagine life without his dog. The wordless conversations they had. The black eyes. The smell of wet fur. The warmth from its snout when he sat in his armchair and the dog put its heavy head on his feet. The vet. was silent.

Kollberg had lain down. He took up the whole table.

"You don't have to make the decision now," the vet. said. "Go home and discuss it with yourself and the dog. Then let me know. And just so you know: there's no right decision here, only a choice between two difficult ones. It happens."

Sejer stroked Kollberg's abdomen.

"But in your experience are such tumours often malign?"

"The question really is: can the dog deal with the strain."

"He's always been strong," Sejer said with childlike defiance.

"Take your time," the vet. said. "He's had them for quite a time already."

Later on Sejer sat in the car thinking, "He's had them for quite a time already." Was that a rebuke? Was he so caught up in his job that he no longer noticed those he was responsible for? Why hadn't he noticed? He felt weighed down by guilt and had to sit there for a while to recover. They he drove slowly home. Whose interest am I considering if I ask for the operation, he wondered, Kollberg's or mine? It's acceptable, isn't it, to keep alive those you are fond of. Am I expected to ignore that and treat him strictly as the animal he in fact is? Do what's best for him and not for me? Still, he felt loved by this scruffy animal. Although animals can't love. He had assigned these feelings to the dog. But devotion? That he did have. The shaggy body shook with excitement when he unlocked the door to the flat. Its vigilance, its eagerness and its animal heart, which beat only for him. Which beat regardless. He looked in the mirror. Kollberg did not move.

"What's your heart telling you?" Sara said.

"To go ahead, I think," he said unhappily. "I'm willing to subject him to more or less anything if it means that I get to keep him for a few more years."

"Then you take the risks of the operation," she said simply. "And you have to stand by your decision whatever the outcome."

"Am I allowed to indulge my own wishes and needs?" he said sheepishly.

"Yes, you are. He's your dog. You're in charge."

He called the vet. Listening to his voice he tried to detect nuances in his tone, to see if they might reveal whether he approved the decision. He was persuaded that the vet. was pleased. A time was fixed for the operation. Then he knelt beside the dog and began brushing the long coat. He brushed and brushed, with long strokes, and felt the lumps easily. It gnawed at him that he had not felt them before. Sara gave him a comforting smile.

"Kollberg has no notion of your sense of guilt," she said. "He loves being brushed. He loves you. Right now he's feeling good: he has a loving owner who's brushing his coat. Don't feel sorry for him."

"No. I only feel sorry for me," he whispered.

*

166

Linda had been trying for days to reach Karen. Karen wasn't in, her mum said. No, she was just about to go out. I don't know when she'll be back. Something was going on. She felt a deep anxiety. The two of them had always been together. Now she was avoiding her and hung out with other people. With Ulla and Nudel and the rest of them at the café. Linda was confused and scared, but held on to the last remnant of her anger. Everywhere she was conscious of people staring at her. What had she done wrong? Everything had been fine until she saw the red car. But mentioning Gøran's name was going too far. As if the police wouldn't have checked out all the red cars in the area anyway. Eventually they would have found out that he'd passed the meadow at the crucial time. So he had been caught in the net and now he was struggling to free himself. But Gøran was probably innocent and so he had nothing to fear. Linda reckoned his lying to the police was pretty stupid. He had only himself to blame.

She spent her time thinking up a plan for how to get Jacob. Twice she had gone into town and stood in front of his flat in Nedre Storgate. He lived on the second floor. She had stared up at his windows. There was a statuette in the window, but she couldn't see what it was and had not dared to bring her mother's binoculars. Standing in a street in town didn't attract special attention, but standing there with a pair of binoculars was out of the question. It might be the nude body of a woman and she didn't like that idea. It was white and smooth and glowed when the sun shone through the windows. Of course, she was really hurt not to have been taken seriously over the man in the garden that night. She said nothing to her mum. It was bad enough as it was. Her expression told her plainly enough that she had gone too far. Instead they snapped at each other and Linda screamed that if you'd seen the murder taking place with your own eyes I suppose you'd have thought it best to keep your mouth shut, not get involved. People are cowards! she screamed and stamped her foot. Her mum pressed her lips together tightly. She was, in fact, very concerned.

It was late in the evening. Linda sat brooding. Karen ought to be home by now. It was cold and raw outside and a vicious wind swept round the corners of the house in long, threatening gusts. She liked this weather because she was inside where it was bright and warm.

The curtains were drawn. Nothing would make her look out into the garden. But there was this business with Jacob. It was a matter of finding out when he was at work and when he would be at home. She would be ready and waiting behind a corner and see him walk down the street, pushing forward with his head bowed. Run straight into him. Perhaps she had something in her hands that she would drop when they collided, so that he would have to kneel down to help her pick it up. A bag of apples perhaps. They would roll off in all directions. She imagined Jacob and her crawling around on the pavement, chasing after the shiny red apples. His mouth and eyes. His hands which would caress her, they were probably warm and strong. He was a police officer, after all.

Hi, Linda, he would say, what are you doing here? Oh, I have a dentist's appointment. Or something like that. Then he would apologise for not believing her that night on the telephone. She would look into his blue eyes and make him realise that he had underestimated her. She was no highly strung teenager, as he seemed to suppose. She was deep in thought when suddenly she heard a thumping sound outside. A second later she stood in the hall. She remained standing, breathlessly listening. But she only heard the wind. It shook the trees with terrible force. Then another thump. She ran into the kitchen. Where was it coming from? Was it the same sound as the other night or something else? She looked at the telephone, but thought better of it. It was impossible to call Jacob. One more thump, it was more violent now and was followed by a shuddering crash. As if someone was banging a sledgehammer against something. She stared, terrified, at the windows. The thumping resumed in an uneven rhythm. It was at its strongest when she stood in the hall, so it was coming from the front of the house. Fortunately the door was double locked. Her senses were heightened. It sounded very much like the doors to the outhouse, the way they used to slam when they forgot to bolt them. Was it that simple? More thumping. She ran into the living room and pulled back the edge of the curtain a very little. In the light of the front door lamp she could see the silhouette of the red outhouse with the white doors. Quite right. They were swinging violently in the strong wind.

She sank down from relief. Just as well she had not cried wolf to Jacob. But surely she had bolted them when she put her bike away? In fact, she was absolutely convinced she had.

She decided to put it out of her mind and went to get the newspapers from the stairs to the basement. Sat in the living room and cut out anything more about the case. The cuttings were becoming rarer and rarer, but everything had to be included. She was going to keep them forever. One day, when she and Jacob were married, she would take them out and remember how it all happened when they met each other. The doors were banging. They irritated her, but she was not going to go out in this awful weather and shut them. She went on cutting. Even though she knew what was causing the noise, it still bothered her. Was she going to have to lie awake half the night because of those stupid doors? She put down the scissors, sighing heavily. How long would it take to pull on her boots, run across the yard, fasten the bolts, lock up and run back again? A minute at the most. It was sixty seconds in the darkness. She got up and went into the hall. Hesitated, then put on her mum's boots because they were the nearest. They were way too big. She unlocked one of the locks. Listened to the rain like a steady murmur. Then she undid the safety catch. She inhaled three times, tore open the door and ran down the steps. Nothing to make such a fuss about, she thought, struggling across the yard in the too-big boots. The doors were wide open. Inside was only pitch-black darkness. She got hold of the doors and pulled them shut. The bolt was high up at the top of the doors on the inside. There was no light – they had never put electricity in the outhouse. So she reached up and grabbed the bolt and at that very second she was gripped by panic because she heard a sound, from inside the shed. She spun round, gasping. Was someone watching her? She thought she saw the glinting of an eye in the far corner. Horror and anger alternated inside her as she made a final effort to reach the bolt. Then she felt a violent tug backward and hands squeezing around her neck. All her strength left her. At the edge of her field of vision she saw her own arms flail in desperation. Someone snarled something into her ear and her eyes darkened. She could no longer feel her body, but instead a violent pain in her neck.

169

Something warm and wet soaked through her clothes. Her legs wobbled underneath her like a rag doll's.

From now on you'll keep your mouth shut!

She collapsed and shielded her head with her hands while she felt his arms flip her over and place her on her stomach. Mum! a voice inside her head screamed, Mum, I'm going to die!

He put a boot against her back and forced her down, but released his grip on her neck. She felt a sharp pain in her larynx and clawed at the gravel helplessly. Is that Gøran? she thought. Is he going to kill me too? She didn't cry. She didn't even dare to breathe. He had let go of her and was busy with something else. He'll pour petrol over me, she thought, because there was a can of petrol somewhere which they used for the lawn mower. He's going to pour petrol over me and set me alight. Afterwards they would find her blackened and rigid with only her teeth intact. Then suddenly the doors slammed from the outside. Everything fell silent. He had locked the doors from the outside. She lay motionless and listened. He's going to torch the outhouse with me inside it, she thought. Her body was shaking uncontrollably. She didn't believe it was all over. She stank and she thought she might have wet herself. She was overwhelmed by the enormity of what she was now experiencing. She lay rigid. Couldn't hear footsteps or engine noise, nothing, just the wind in the trees and the rain a torrential roar.

She lay in this position for an eternity, with her face in the sand and the dirt. Couldn't bear to lie still like this and yet didn't dare to get up, she was like an animal caught in the headlights of a car. At last she relaxed. Got up cautiously, staggering on wobbly legs. It was pitch black everywhere. She raised her hands, they were shaking still and twitching. Pushed the door. It moved a tiny bit. It was an old door with a simple lock on the outside. After all, that was why it'd blown open. Or perhaps he had opened it to make the doors slam so she'd come out? How did he know she was on her own? She was often on her own, it occurred to her, and everyone knew it. She pushed and pushed against the door. Perhaps the lock would simply loosen and fall off. It was a short metal pin which went into an eye. If she could make the door move sufficiently it would glide out on its own. Suddenly the doors flew open and she stepped back shocked. She was looking straight at the house. The front door was wide open. Was he in the house? She tiptoed out on to the gravel and listened. Closed the doors behind her. Reluctantly she went up the steps, crouching like an old woman. Peered into the hall. No, he couldn't be in there. She grabbed an umbrella from the shelf and bumped it against the floor a few times. If he were in the house he'd come running out at the sound. But no-one came. She locked the door and went into the living room. There was no-one. How about upstairs? Slowly she went up the stairs. Opened the doors to all the rooms. No-one. She went downstairs like a sleepwalker and into the bathroom. Pulled off her clothes. She whimpered as she put them straight into the washing machine and started the boil-wash cycle. She liked the sound of the machine and the smell of soap powder and conditioner. Then she took a long shower. Closed her eyes in the warm water. Found a dressing gown. Looked in the mirror. She was white as a sheet. There were scarlet marks on her throat.

From now on you'll keep your mouth shut! Who did the voice belong to? It sounded distorted, hoarse and unrecognisable. He was taller than her. Much taller. Gøran isn't that tall, she thought. She wanted to call Jacob. She wanted protection. She was no longer safe. What would Jacob say if she called? Perhaps he wouldn't believe her this time either. Confused, she went to her bedroom and lay down on her bed, leaving the light on. Lay still with her eyes closed. She had been attacked and knew she had to tell someone, but he had told her to keep her mouth shut. If she said anything else he might kill her. This was just a warning. She stared up at the ceiling. Thought about when her mum and her had been decorating the bedroom and were just getting to the ceiling, which was going to be painted eggshell white. They stood on separate chairs with their rollers held high, painting and painting. She had spotted a spider and stood for a while admiring it. Her initial thought was to flick it away. But then she decided to let it stay. It wasn't very big, but it had a round chubby body and long black legs. It had sat as motionless as she herself now did as she lay on the bed. And then she had run the roller over it. At first she couldn't see anything while the paint was still wet. Her mum and her had laughed hysterically at the thought of the spider. But when the paint dried the insect was clearly visible underneath the white paint, perfectly fixed with spiky legs. She wondered what it would be like to die like that. She was staring at the spider and these were the things on her mind while she waited for sleep to come.

But it eluded her. Every time she closed her eyes, she couldn't breathe. From time to time she sobbed silently into the pillow. Her neck hurt. Soon her mum would be back from Copenhagen. Or was it Gothenburg? She couldn't remember. Finally she got up. She put on her dressing gown and went downstairs. Looked defiantly at the telephone. Why should she spare Jacob? She dialled his number without thinking. As he picked up she noticed the clock on the wall which said 2 a.m. He sounded sleepy.

"Linda?" she heard him say. There was obvious annoyance in his voice, but she was prepared for that. It was, after all, the middle of the night.

"I didn't imagine it," she said breathlessly into the handset. Relieved finally to be telling someone. "He attacked me. Just now. Tonight!"

It went very quiet at the other end.

"At home? In your house?"

"Yes! No, in the outhouse."

Again silence.

"In the outhouse?" His voice sounded doubtful. "Linda," she heard him say, "it's the middle of the night and I'm not on duty now."

"I know!" she said.

"When did it happen?"

Linda looked at the clock.

"I'm not quite sure. Perhaps around midnight."

"And you're calling me *now*?"

She cursed herself for not calling right away. But she needed to change her clothes. In case someone should come.

"If you really have something to report, you need to use the emergency number for the police," Skarre said. "However, since you've called me you might as well tell me what happened."

He was awake now. His voice was clear. She started telling him about the doors that banged and how she had gone out to close them. About the man who had jumped out of the darkness trying to suffocate her and how he had put her on the ground and held her down. And the warning. That she wasn't to say anything else. She started crying while she was talking. Kept stroking her aching neck.

"Are you hurt?" Skarre wanted to know. She thought his voice sounded so kind.

"No," she said. "Not really. But if he'd wanted to he could have killed me on the spot. He was very strong."

"How about your mother?" he said. "Where is she?"

"Working," Linda whispered.

"She's not back yet?"

"She'll be back in the early morning."

"But you've called her and told her?"

"No," Linda said.

Skarre went quiet again. Linda could hear his breathing down the receiver.

"How much of this man did you see?"

"Nothing. It's pitch black in that outhouse. But he was tall, I think. Very tall. I think I need protection," she said. "He's out to get me. He's going to do whatever it takes to stop me from giving evidence."

"But you're unlikely to be giving evidence," Jacob said. "Your testimonies aren't that important."

"Obviously he doesn't know that!"

She bit her lip and was silent once more, scared that he would become more dismissive than he already was.

"Why didn't you call your mother?" Skarre said.

Linda sniffed. "She's always telling me that I'm exaggerating."

"Are you?"

"No!"

"Then you have to call her at once and tell her what has happened. Does she have a mobile?"

173

"Yes. Can't you come over?"

"Linda. You've called my home number again and there's nothing I can do. However, I can send someone else—"

"That's not what I want!"

Skarre sighed a long sigh. "Try to get hold of your mother. I'm sure you can manage that. Talk to her and together the two of you can decide if you want to report it."

Linda felt something big and heavy sink inside her. "You don't believe me," she said weakly.

"I understand that you're afraid," Skarre said diplomatically. "What happened in Elvestad was terrible. Everyone's afraid. It's normal."

Linda had a lump in her throat so big that she could no longer speak. He didn't believe her. She could hear it in his voice. He was annoyed, he talked to her the way you talk to a lying child, whilst at the same time trying not to upset her. She felt dizzy and supported herself against the table. Her knees began to tremble. Everything was going wrong, no matter what she did. She'd described it just like it happened: that she'd seen two people in the meadow, she'd said it looked as though they were playing. She had never said that she saw a murder. She had said the car looked like the one Gøran had. Not that it was the one. She had reckoned it was important since they went on and on about it on the radio and on the TV. Now everyone was turning against her. And now, when things were starting to happen, they didn't believe her. Skarre made one last effort. "I suggest you call your mother and explain everything to her. Then you go to bed and wait for her. Your mother can call the police later if she thinks it's necessary."

Linda hung up and went upstairs. She felt lethargic. She stayed in bed staring at the bump that was the spider. Everywhere she looked she saw only enemies. They treated her like a brat. Then again she was seized by fear and she felt very cold. She wrapped her duvet round her and shut her eyes tight. She didn't want to call her mum. She wanted to be alone. Become invisible. Not bother anyone any more. Not accuse anyone, not give evidence, not say hello, not be in anyone's way. They wanted her out of the way. She understood it

174

now. There was a ringing sound in her ears. She didn't understand it. Just lay still, waiting for the light. At 4 a.m. she heard the key in the lock and shortly afterwards footsteps on the stairs. Her door was opened a chink. She said nothing, pretended to be asleep. Then her mum went to bed. Linda turned on the light and went over to the mirror. The marks on her throat were already fading. Could it really have been Gøran? It had not sounded like his voice. She was convinced that the man in the outhouse was taller. How would she ever dare go out again? Take the bus to college or cycle along the road? Perhaps he was watching her, spying on her. She went back to bed and lay down. The hours passed. Light began seeping through the curtains and she heard the birds in the garden outside. Now that her mum was in the house she finally began to relax. She fell asleep and woke up because someone was standing by the side of her bed. It was close to noon.

"Are you ill?" her mum said, baffled. Linda turned her back on her.

"Aren't you going to college?"

"No."

"So what's wrong?"

"Headache."

"Why did you start a boil wash and leave the clothes in the machine?" her mum wanted to know. "You could at least answer me," her mum said.

But Linda said nothing. It felt good to lie quite still and not speak. She would never speak again.

CHAPTER 18

According to the forensic report the murder weapon had a smooth surface. As a result, a hammer was eliminated. The weapon was either very heavy or the killer very strong, or both. Sejer turned the pages one by one and pondered. The audacity of the case bewildered him. In a meadow, while it was still light. Only a few metres from Gunwald's house. Mind you, if the killer was from outside the area he might not know of the house and in the heat of the moment he might not have seen it. Attacks of this sort generally happened under cover of darkness. The man had not turned off the road and driven Poona to a grove. He had acted on impulse, it had happened suddenly. For some reason he had been overcome by the need to destroy, with a force rarely seen. If this was the first time it had happened to him, he must now be truly frightened of himself and of his rage. It was going to show in some way. But that might take time. Possibly he would start drinking. Or he might develop an irascible and argumentative pattern of behaviour, or he might become withdrawn and walk around silently with his hideous secret.

Jacob Skarre appeared in the doorway. He looked tired, which was unusual for him.

"Late night?" Sejer said.

"Linda Carling called in the night. It was nearly 2 a.m."

Sejer looked at him in surprise.

Skarre closed the door behind him. "I'm concerned," he said.

"You don't have to think of her as your daughter," Sejer said.

"No. I'm concerned for myself."

Sejer gestured towards a chair.

"This is the second time she's called. The first time she reported there had been a man in the garden staring at her. She was home alone, she often is. Then she called just after 2 a.m. last night and told me she'd been attacked. In the outhouse. By a man she thought was the killer. And who had come to warn her against saying anything else about the Hvitemoen case."

Sejer raised one brow several millimetres. This was an indication that he was now very much surprised. "And you're telling me this now?"

Skarre nodded wearily. "The thing is, she's making it up," he said. "It's me she wants."

"The confidence of the young is so refreshing," Sejer said, narrowing his eyes. "Are you quite sure?"

"I was sure last night," Skarre said heavily. "She claimed the attack took place around midnight. She called no-one. She took a shower and went to bed. She didn't even call her mother, who was away somewhere in her truck. She didn't get up until 2 a.m. to call me. I don't understand it. She should have called right away. The emergency services. Not my home number. And there's something else. I've seen her – twice – outside my flat. She stood on the pavement staring at my windows. Obviously, she doesn't know that I saw her."

"But you say you're concerned?"

"What if she's telling the truth," he said. "What if the killer really did come to her house?"

"I agree, it sounds like a fantasy," Sejer said decisively.

"I'm worried that I might be wrong."

"But apart from that?" Sejer said. "What could she tell us about her attacker?"

"Nothing. But she thought he was tall."

Sejer remained at his desk, resting his chin in his hand.

"It's highly unlikely that he would stick his neck out like that."

"True," Skarre said. "Highly unlikely. However, it's best that I don't have anything to do with her. Then it'll pass of its own accord. He ran his hand through his curls. They still stuck out. "You're going to see Gøran Seter?"

"I'm going to lean on him hard. If I get a reprimand from above afterwards, I'm prepared to accept it if it gets the case moving. If nothing else then I want to eliminate him."

"He's not our man," Skarre said. "We're not that lucky."

"I understand what you're saying. Besides, there's Kolding. Although his astonishment was genuine when I confronted him with the statement from Torill at the petrol station. He insisted that he drove straight back to town. Didn't understand it. Said she had to be mistaken. But, if you look at what we've got on Gøran, then think about it. He's lying about where he was that evening. He drives a car matching Linda's description."

"We can't trust Linda."

"But nevertheless. A car was mentioned. He drives one like it. He passed the scene at the crucial time. He was seen with scratches to his face."

"From the dog."

"So Gøran says. He's wearing brand-new trainers. He was dressed in a white shirt and dark trousers, as Linda described the man in the meadow. But when he got home he was wearing something else. Why did he change? He works out a lot. He is strong. And for all we know he could be taking steroids. Which destabilises a man. Finally, according to Ulla, the last thing he did at Adonis was to take a shower. What did he need to wash off?"

Skarre went to the window. Stood there for a while, watching the river and the boats.

"If I'm wrong about Linda, I'll no doubt pay for it later," he said glumly.

"How about talking to her mother?" Sejer said. "If Linda really was attacked her mother will get to the truth of it somehow."

Skarre nodded. "She also has a friend. Karen. She'd probably tell her."

"You deal with the ladies," Sejer said. "You're good at that."

Skarre breathed through his nose. "Kollberg," he said. "When is his ordeal?"

"Tomorrow evening," Sejer said. "Don't talk about it. I'll let you know in my own time."

"Give him my best," Skarre said.

*

Once upon a time Gøran had been a child. A little, blond boy running around in the big yard. His mum would watch him from the window, Sejer thought, admiring the boy. She would tuck him in every night. The moments follow each other and make up a life. Perhaps they had been mostly good ones. Still, you could end up with this one thing, evil. Life is more than thoughts and dreams. Life is the body, muscles and a pulse. Gøran had been working out for years. Pumped iron so his muscles bulged like thick ropes under the skin. What did he need them for – apart from lifting even heavier weights? Was it a question of vanity or perhaps an obsession? What was he afraid of? What was he trying to hide by wearing an armour of rock-hard muscles? A dog barked inside the house and he glimpsed a face in the window. A man appeared on the doorstep, his arms folded across his chest. Ran his eyes up and down Sejer disrespectfully. He was not as heavy-set or well-built as his son; his strength lay in the hard stare and the arrogant attitude.

"I see. It's you again. Gøran's in his room."

Torstein Seter led the way in and up the stairs to the first floor. Opened the door without knocking. Gøran sat in a chair on the floor wearing a sleeveless blue vest. His feet were bare. In each hand he held a dumbbell. They were round and smooth, slim in the middle with a ball at each end. He lifted them alternately in a regular rhythm. A tendon in his neck twitched with each raise. He looked straight at Sejer, but carried on lifting. Sejer remained standing as if spellbound. He followed the dumbbell with his eyes, up and down, in steady movements. Gøran put them on the floor.

"How much do they weigh?" Skarre asked him lightly. Gøran looked down on the dumbbells.

"Ten kilos each. They're just the warm-up."

"And when you've warmed up?"

"Then they weigh 40."

"So you have several sets?"

"In all weights."

He got up from the chair. His father was lingering in the doorway.

"You're a busy man these days," Gøran said, tossing his head. However, he was smiling. If he felt at all afraid, he was good at hiding

179

it. By standing up he was showing off his body which instantly made him bubble with confidence.

Sejer looked at his father. "You can stay if you want to, but it would be best if you sat down."

Seter sat down demonstratively on the bed. Gøran went over to the window.

"I have a question," Sejer said, still looking at the dumbbells. "On August 20th when you left Adonis you were wearing a white tennis shirt and black jeans. Are we agreed so far?"

"Yes," Gøran said.

"I want you to find these clothes."

Silence. Gøran lifted the dumbbells once more as if he felt safer holding them in his hands. He held them in front of him, his palms turned upwards as he flicked his wrists in short movements.

"I've no idea where those clothes are," he said casually.

"Then you'll have to look," Sejer said.

"My mum does my clothes," Gøran said. "They could be in the washing machine or out on the line, or whatever."

He shrugged. His face was impassive.

His father was watching them warily from the bed. The terrible impact of the question had just dawned on him.

"You can start by looking in the wardrobe," Sejer said pointing to a wardrobe in the room, which was obviously Gøran's.

"Tell me one thing," Gøran said. "Can you really turn up like this and demand that people empty their wardrobes? No papers or anything?"

"No," Sejer admitted and smiled. "But I'm entitled to try."

Gøran smiled too. Then he put the dumbbells on the floor. They landed at the same time and you could tell from the sound how heavy they were. He opened the door to his wardrobe and started rummaging around half-heartedly.

"Can't see them," he said petulantly. "Must be in the wash."

"Then we'll go and look in the washing basket," Sejer suggested.

"Not much use," Gøran said. "I have several white tennis shirts and several pairs of black jeans."

"How many?"

He groaned. "What I'm saying is," Gøran said wearily, "that I won't know exactly which tennis shirt or which jeans I wore that night."

"Then find me all of them," Sejer said.

"But why all this fuss about my clothes? Why do you care about them?" Gøran's face was flushed. He started pulling clothes out of the wardrobe. They landed in a heap on the floor, covering the dumbbells. Underpants, socks, and T-shirts. Two pairs of blue jeans. A jumper and a small box made from clear plastic. Inside was an atrociously garish bow tie.

"They're not here," he said, standing with his back to him.

"What does that mean, Gøran?" Sejer said calmly.

"No idea," he grumbled.

"The washing basket," Sejer said. "Let's look in there. Or in the washing machine. And on the washing line."

"Is this a joke?" he said, angry now.

His father sat watching them tensely.

"This isn't legal," Gøran said in a strained voice.

"No. You're right. But I'm only asking for a small thing. It should be in everyone's interest to resolve this."

"And if I refuse?"

"Then there's nothing I can do. On the other hand, clearly I'll be wondering what this means: that you're making difficulties rather than cooperating."

His father was restless, his suppressed fury was undisguisable.

Sejer rooted around the clothes and found one of the dumbbells.

Gøran gave him a stiff look. "What is your point?"

"I've come to clear you from the investigation," he said. "To eliminate you. That's what you want, isn't it?"

Gøran's eyes flickered with uncertainty. "Of course."

"Then you'll have to find the clothes. It's a perfectly simple request."

Gøran gulped. "We'll have to ask my mum. She does all the washing."

"Will she be able to find them?"

"Well, I don't know!"

181

"So you're scared that she won't find them?"

Gøran went to the window again. Stood there looking at the garden.

"Tell me where you were on the evening of the 20th."

Gøran spun round. "Just because I tell a white lie," he spat out, "that doesn't make me a murderer!"

On the bed his father blinked with fear.

"I know, Gøran, because I get told a lot of them. But if you know what's good for you, you'll tell me the truth now however unpalatable it is."

"It's no-one's business," he said fiercely. "Bloody hell, why is this happening to me!" He was boiling with rage now.

His father had got up. "What are you talking about, Gøran?"

"You can go now," Gøran said.

His father gave him a searching look and reluctantly left the room. He left the door open behind him. Gøran closed it with a kick and sank on to his bed.

"I was with a woman."

"That happens," Sejer said. All the time, he was watching him. Somehow he felt a grain of sympathy. It crept up on him as it always did when someone sat sweating like that, writhing in despair. But this house, this room, did not appeal to him. It was a grim house, devoid of warmth.

"What's her name?"

"There'll only be more trouble if I tell you."

"It's better than having something far more serious pinned on you."

Gøran gestured helplessly. "I don't deserve this, for Christ's sake."

"We don't always get what we deserve," Sejer said. "Being with a woman is not a criminal offence. It happens all the time. Is she married?"

"Yes."

"Are you scared of her husband?"

"Hell no! Scared of *him*? They're getting a divorce anyway."

"So what's the problem?" Sejer scrutinised him. His young face struggled with a difficult decision. "She's somewhat older than me."

"That happens too," said Sejer gently. "It's not as weird as you'd think."

"For God's sake, I'm not saying it's weird! But I'll be a laughing stock. So will she."

"You'll get by. You are adults. Compared to what else is happening in your village, this would be a trifle."

"She's forty-five years old," Gøran said, staring down at the floor.

"How long have you been seeing her?"

"Almost a year."

"And Ulla, does she know?"

"No, for heaven's sake!"

"You've been with Ulla and also had a relationship with a married woman?"

"Yes."

"Where do you meet?"

"Her house. She's alone a lot."

"Her name, Gøran."

There followed a long pause. He ran his hands through his hair and groaned. "She'll go crazy."

"This is serious. She'll understand."

"There's not much to be had from Ulla," Gøran said bitterly. "It just looks that way. So those other things – well, you know what I mean – I have to get from somewhere else."

"What other things?"

"Don't pretend you don't understand!"

"I only want to be sure I've understood you correctly. You're entitled to that. The relationship is about sex and not a lot else?"

"Yes." His face was a deep red now. Sejer could still see faint marks from the scratches.

"Her name's Lillian. She lives in the chalet-style villa, the one everybody despises. She's married to Einar Sunde. Who runs the café." He wiped the sweat from his brow.

"She was the one you called from the car?"

"Right."

"What time did you arrive at her house?"

183

"No idea. I went straight from Adonis. And I drove fast." He looked unhappy. And embarrassed.

"So if you left at 8 p.m., as Ulla said, then you'd have got to Lillian's before 8.30 p.m.?"

"I didn't look."

"You should be happy," Sejer said. The shift in his tone of voice confused Gøran. He raised his head.

"You've just given me an excellent alibi. Assuming she confirms your story."

Gøran bit his lip. "If she doesn't she's lying. We're talking about a married woman here. What if she won't admit to it?"

"I'll ask her."

Gøran shivered. Sejer took a last look at the dumbbells. They were heavy and round and smooth. He clearly wanted to take them for examination, but to do that he would first have to charge Gøran and it was too early for that. He left the room and Gøran followed him down the stairs. His mum appeared in the doorway to the kitchen; she gave them a frightened look. At the same time Sejer heard the dog scratching from the other side of a closed door. It was whining.

"Is something wrong?" she said anxiously.

"Probably not," Sejer said and took his leave. Gøran's mother went over and patted her son, brushing his shoulders. Then she noticed his bare feet. She fetched a pair of slippers from the hall. Gøran stuck his feet in them obediently. Sejer was reminded of curling. The mother was like a broom the way she swept potential obstacles away from her son's path so that he would slide effortlessly straight into the goal. He had seen it many times.

He went out to the car. Gøran's father was chopping firewood. He looked up as Sejer appeared, and elaborately turned his back.

"Hello, Marie," Gunder said.

He studied the lifeless face. "I'm cross today. Let me tell you one thing. Journalists are vermin. If they find a tiny crack they'll squeeze through. Yesterday they called eight times. Imagine! Most of them women and they were ever so concerned, oh yes! Their voices soft like beggars. They all know about Poona, that she was coming to me. It's in your own interest, they say, that you talk to us. Tell us your side of the story. We'll write about it anyway. Not because we'll sell more papers, but because it's our job. People really care about you, you and your Indian wife. They want to know who she was and where she was going. They're worried about you and they want to know what's going on. They say things like that, Marie. We're right outside your house, can we come in? they said. I hung up. Then another paper calls. And so on it went. And then they started ringing the doorbell. When I opened the door there was a lady there with a bouquet of flowers and a huge camera. I couldn't believe my eyes. I think you're stupid, I said. Plain stupid. Then I slammed the door. I turned the lights off and drew the curtains. It's not like me to slam the door, but I'm not quite myself.

"The weather today's awful. I'm glad the house is on high ground. The basement is damp, but there are no other problems. I haven't spoken to Karsten, so I don't know how he's doing. But I have much more important things to tell you. I've finally met Poona's brother. My brother-in-law, Shiraz Bai. Quite a character, believe you me. A lean, skinny stick of a man with pitch-black hair. Very like Poona. But not as pretty, obviously. He said I could keep her here in Elvestad. I was so relieved, Marie, you can't begin to imagine. It was I who talked her into coming to Norway and right into this awful business. So now I'm going to tend to her grave for all the years I have left. I suspect that her brother is pleased, too. He was keen that I should pay. But that's easy for us to say. We live in one of the richest countries in the world. Shiraz works at a cotton mill, they probably aren't paid much. Incidentally, there are rumours that the police are about to arrest someone. A young man from Elvestad, I don't know if you know of him. Gøran, Torstein and Helga's son. He is nineteen. I don't understand why they're arresting him. He's seeing a nice young woman and his parents are decent people. But the truth is, I'm not interested any more. I would like to see him punished, that's all. But I don't need to know who he is. I don't want to know what he looks like. It will only give me nightmares. Seeing his face in the darkness. Things like that. I just want to have Poona buried. Plant flowers. Autumn comes so quickly. I'm worried that the investigation is taking so long that we'll have frost before then. What do you think the vicar will say? Poona is a Hindu. There must be rules and regulations in such cases. I'll bury her next to Mum. Once you get away from this noisy machine I'll take you up there and show you, even if I have to push you in a wheelchair. I won't mind pushing you around if it comes to that. As far as Karsten is concerned, well, I'm not so sure. Please forgive me for being so blunt, but you deserved better. I'm saying this out loud even though you can't hear me. What if there was just a tiny chance that some of it filtered through to you? What if you felt so outraged that you woke up?"

Skarre was driving. Sejer was thinking out loud.

"If Gøran really did visit this woman, then Linda's sighting of the red car isn't worth a whole lot."

"Could he have managed to be in both places?"

Sejer hesitated. "Possibly. But would he have gone to see someone after committing such an act? He would have wanted to be on his own. In a dark place."

"But is a married woman of forty-five going to admit to a relationship with a nineteen-year-old?"

"Perhaps not, to begin with."

"Don't spare anyone, wasn't that what you said? You're not all that tough, Konrad."

"I can learn," he said.

Lillian Sunde appeared in all her glory. Something about her appearance made Sejer suspect that she had seen them from the window and that she had prepared herself well. Her reaction was theatrical, when she tried to express surprise. She put her hand over her mouth.

"Oh God! You're here because of the murder?"

They nodded. She was definitely attractive, a bit affected perhaps, there was too much of everything: make-up, jewellery and a whole range of fragrances with no common theme that wafted through the open door. Even Ulla has more style than this, Skarre thought, looking down at the steps for a moment. She ushered them into a hall with black and white chequered tiles that was bigger than Sejer's living room. A broad staircase up to the first floor. Lillian Sunde wore shoes that clattered with each step.

"You must be desperate for clues if you've come to see me," she said coyly.

Sejer coughed. "I won't waste your time," he said. "Or my own. I just need to know where you spent the evening of August 20th."

They had reached the living room. It was vast, with something as exotic as a sunken sofa. Sejer had never seen anything like it in all his life and was instantly attracted to it. Like stepping into a sandpit. A small hollow in the floor.

Lillian Sunde's eyes widened.

"Me? The 20th? Was that the day it happened?"

"Yes."

He forced himself to look away from the sofa and look instead at her.

She frowned. "I'll have to think about that. What day of the week was it?"

"A Friday."

"Ah. On Fridays I go into town for acupuncture. I have, no, it's irrelevant what I've got, but it helps me. Then I go shopping, food and so forth. I might have been at the hairdresser's that day. I have my hair dyed every six weeks," she said smiling. "And then," she went on, and it was as if she suddenly remembered because she became quiet and her smile vanished. "That was the evening I watched that film on TV." She contemplated this and avoided their eyes by resting her forehead in her hands. "An American film, I don't recall exactly which one. I think it started round about 9 p.m. It was long. I watched all of it."

"Who was with you?" Sejer said.

She glared at him. "With me? No-one. The kids have grown up, they're never at home in the evenings now. And as far as my husband is concerned . . ."

"He works at the café."

"Yes. He's rarely home before midnight. And it's 2 a.m. on Saturdays."

"I need to confront you with something," Sejer said, and recognised the familiar unease. He liked her. She was a nice and pleasant woman who possibly had no reason in the world to have a bad conscience. Yet.

"Do you know Gøran Seter?"

Her eyes widened again. "Gøran Seter? I know who he is. But I don't know him."

"He says he spent the evening with you. Here, in this house."

Her eyes were huge now, like a child's who has seen something appalling. "Gøran Seter? Here, with me?"

"He says you have a sexual relationship and that it has been going on for about a year."

She shook her head in disbelief. Started pacing up and down. Flung out her hands dramatically. "What on earth are you talking about?"

Sejer said: "Is it true, yes or no?" giving her short quarter, because he was busy with the questions, he hoped that Skarre was keeping his eyes open. That he was taking in every detail.

"He's never been in this house! Unless he's been here with one of the kids, but I doubt that. Why would he?"

"I just told you. Are you seeing him?"

She fidgeted. Ran her hands through her hair. It was dark copper and piled up on the top of her head. A few long tresses had come loose. The piled-up hair made her seem formal, Sejer thought, but the loose tresses suggested frivolity.

"Honestly! Why is he saying this? I'm a married woman."

"But I understand you are shortly to be getting a divorce? Am I right?"

She rolled her eyes at how much he knew. "Yes! But that doesn't mean I run after younger men."

"He's nineteen," Sejer said.

"Do you know how old I am?" she said irritably.

"Forty-five, I believe," Sejer said.

She began her pacing again. "I don't understand this," she said, stressed. "Why would Gøran say such a thing?"

"Perhaps because it's true?" Again he thought he could see a number of competing emotions flash through her mind. "This is the situation," he said coldly. "There are certain aspects of Gøran's statement concerning that evening which have led us here. If it is the case that you're able to confirm that he was here with you and you can tell us anything about how he acted, then you'll be helping us to move our enquiries forward. Think carefully before you answer. What you say may have a significant effect on how we proceed."

She stared at them in turn and started walking up and down.

"So, I'm to save Gøran's skin?" she said. "But surely he doesn't have anything to do with the murder?"

"Well, you told us that you didn't know him, did you not?"

"No . . . But all the same."

Sejer studied her evident dismay, and then said: "Is it the case here that you have a choice between saving Gøran's skin and your own reputation?"

She walked out to the kitchen. Came back with a glass of water which she drank while still standing.

"Once, I'll admit to that, I went to a disco in town. Myself and a girlfriend. Gøran was there along with some other young people. We danced and flirted a bit. That sort of thing. He must have got some ideas into his head that he's still fantasising about. Maybe he's oversexed. He works out a lot. Bulges everywhere."

"You're aware of that?" Sejer said.

She blushed and turned away.

"So there's no truth at all in his story?" he said.

She turned and stared at him. "Absolutely not."

He handed her his card. "My number. If you wanted to get in touch. What was the film about, by the way, the American film?"

"Unrequited love. What else?" she said sulkily.

CHAPTER 19

The news of Gøran Seter's arrest came to Gunwald almost as a physical shock. The name was not mentioned, but he guessed it from the description of a young man, nineteen years of age, who lived with his parents within a few kilometres of the crime scene. A young man who worked out, who worked for a carpenter and who drove a car similar to the one seen by the witness who had cycled past. He slurped his coffee and clenched the newspaper tight in his other hand. It could not be true. Not the Gøran he knew, who was a bright young man with a great deal of energy, a steady girlfriend and proud parents, a good job and nice friends. Nor was it Gøran who had thrown the suitcase into the lake.

The article amazed him. He stared at the fat dog under the table. "Did Gøran do it?" he said out loud. The dog raised its head and listened.

"Because it was Einar Sunde who threw the suitcase into the lake." Gunwald was startled. He had said it out loud and he looked over his shoulder. He could just see the meadow between the dark spruce trunks. It lay there as though nothing had happened, a pretty little corner of Eden. The rain had washed away every trace. The blood from the woman's catastrophically wounded body had seeped into the ground and vanished. I have to call, he thought. If only to say that the suitcase has a different story. I don't need to say it was Einar, only that it wasn't Gøran. I don't understand it, he thought, staring in bewilderment at the newspaper. He read the story through again. Several conflicting explanations as to where Gøran had spent the evening and problems corroborating certain things had put him under suspicion. In addition, there was forensic evidence which needed further examination. The bit about the forensic evidence was pretty awful. Poor Torstein and Helga, he thought. And how the rumours would fly. Personally he never sat gossiping at the café. He was too old for that and preferred to sit alone in front of the TV with an Eau de Vie. But Gøran was probably innocent and the police would discover this without his help. Or maybe they wouldn't? He didn't have to call right away. He had first to think. About how he should say what he had to say. It was important that everything was correctly done. He wasn't going to give his name, not under any circumstances. He carried his cup and saucer to the kitchen table and put the dog on the leash. Once again it was time to get ready to sell four cartons of milk, a loaf of bread and, if he was lucky, a crate of beer. He drove off and opened up his shop. Shifted the bundle of newspapers inside. Stared once more at the headlines. It felt strange to know that it wasn't Gøran when everyone else would be thinking it was. A mixture of self-importance and anxiety waged war inside him. If I were young I would have called a long time ago, he thought. But I can't risk exposing myself. I'll be retiring soon.

Linda heard the news on the radio as she sat in her dressing gown at the kitchen table. She shook her head at the news. It couldn't be Gøran. Or did they know something she didn't? She rubbed her neck. It was still aching. She had been taking painkillers, but they didn't help. She felt enveloped in a strange mist where no-one could reach her. Inside the mist there was only room for Jacob with the blue eyes. The world became blurred, but Jacob was crystal clear. Sometimes she had long conversations with him. His voice was so real.

Gunder saw the headline as he took the newspaper out of his letterbox. For a while he stood staring into space. He didn't feel anything, merely exhaustion. There's so much noise, he thought. Perhaps we should all shut down and go to bed once and for all. He dragged himself back to the house and sat down to read.

Mode at the petrol station took his time with the customers that day as everyone had an opinion about the case. The community was soon divided into two camps. Those who thought Gøran was innocent and those who condemned him out of hand. There was also a modest don't-know contingent who shrugged and looked away. Smart enough to shut up and with enough foresight to know that there would have to be a verdict one day.

Preparations were made at the police station for the first interrogation. Gøran walked with his head held high. He remembered his mother's face in the window. His father, completely silent, his black eyes filled with doubt. His father had never been good with words. His mother cried like a baby. The inspector walked ahead of him, silent and grey like a wall. It was all very strange, Gøran thought. It all seemed so unreal. However, the police officers were friendly enough. No-one was going to beat him up, he was sure of that. A horde of journalists followed them down the corridor. He didn't hide from them. Walked calmly with firm steps. Your lawyer is on his way, he's in a taxi with the case documents on his lap, they said. He'll argue your case. It's important that you trust him.

Why did they say that? Gøran tried to work out what was the clever or the right thing to do in this unreal situation. What had they found which had caused him to be brought here? They walked along, a purposeful and busy group of people. From time to time they would stop, as when someone leapt out from an office with even more papers. Then he would stand still and wait. Started walking again when they did. His mouth felt dry. What kind of room were they making for? A bare room with a blinding light? Would he be sitting with just one other person or would there be witnesses present? He had seen so many films. Fragments of images flashed by: men shouting and banging their fists on the table, exhaustion, no food, no sleep, the same questions for hours. Once more. Let's start at the beginning. What happened, Gøran?

His knees threatened to buckle. He turned and looked back. More police officers. I bet they're busy, he thought. Phones were ringing. Soon the whole country would know what had happened. It would be discussed in the news on the radio and on TV. When that night's programmes were over, it would remain in the news headline summary box under the test pattern. Gøran didn't know that at this very moment three officers were in his room turning his drawers and wardrobe inside out. Every single article of clothing, every single pair of boots and shoes were carried off in white plastic bags. His whole life disappeared out through the door of his childhood home. His mother had run round to the back of the house where she stood by the trunk of an oak tree, looking as though she was praying. His father stood like a soldier glowering at them all as they passed. They were in the basement looking through the washing basket. They went through the post in the kitchen even though he never received any letters. Apart from his pay cheque on the first of every month. He tried to identify his lawyer, but didn't know what he looked like. When finally he turned up, Gøran lost all hope. A frail man with tufts of grey hair and spectacles with an old-fashioned frame. A drab grey suit. A bulging briefcase under his arm. He looked as though he had too much to do and probably didn't get enough to eat or enough sleep. Clearly he never had time to work out – as he pulled off his jacket his biceps were smaller even than Ulla's, Gøran thought. They were given a room to themselves. Gøran tried to relax.

"Are you all right, given the circumstances?" the lawyer asked, opening a folder.

"Yes," Gøran said.

"Do you need anything? Food? A drink?"

"A Coke would be nice."

The lawyer popped his head out into the corridor and sent for a Coke.

"Nice and cold," he added.

"My name's Robert Friis," he said. "Call me Robert."

His handshake was dry and businesslike.

"Now. Before we start. You've denied any involvement in the murder of Poona Bai. Am I right?"

"What's that?" Gøran said, not catching the foreign name.

"The woman found dead at Hvitemoen was Indian. Her name was Poona Bai."

"I'm innocent," Gøran said quickly.

"Do you know anything about the murder at all, such as who might have done it?"

"No."

193

"Have you otherwise been near the crime scene on another occasion and possibly left behind personal belongings or other such items?"

Gøran ran his hand over his forehead. "No," he said.

Friis kept looking directly into his eyes.

"Then it is my job to prevent you from being convicted," he said briskly. "That's why it's of the utmost importance that you tell me everything and that you hide from me nothing which the prosecutor can spring on me later."

Gøran gave him an uncertain look. "I have nothing to hide," he said.

"That's good," Friis said. "However, there may be things you don't remember right at this moment, which may come back to you later. Be sure to tell me those things as soon as you remember them. You are entitled to speak to me whenever you want. Make sure you do do that. Naturally I'm working on other cases, but I will do whatever is necessary for you."

"I told them everything already," he said.

"Good," Friis said.

Gøran's Coke arrived. It was cold and it pricked his tongue.

"Then I need to ask you if you understand the seriousness of the situation. You're charged with murder. With particularly aggravating circumstances."

"Yes," Gøran said. He hesitated slightly. Nothing like this had happened to him before, so he was stumbling into unknown territory.

"Aggravating circumstances means that you might receive an additional punishment of up to two years for the battery of the deceased. Such acts make the police especially angry. They will now petition that you be remanded in custody and while you are on remand they will obtain as much evidence as they can to bring a case against you. Meanwhile you'll stay here with restraints on correspondence and visits."

"I have to stay here?" Gøran stammered. He had imagined that they would interview him, perhaps for hours, but he had hoped that he would be allowed to leave later in the day. Einar's Café would be packed with people. He had to go there and be with them. Listen to what they said. He was stricken by some sort of panic. He drank his Coke nervously.

"They'll try to wear you down," Friis said. "Remember that. Always count to three before you answer any questions."

Gøran looked at him blankly.

"They want you to lose control. It's important that you don't. Even though you might be worn out, tired, even exhausted. Do you lose control easily?"

"I can take a lot," Gøran said, leaning forward demonstratively across the table. Friis could see the powerful arms. He took note of them.

"I'm not talking about physical strength," he said. "Rather about what goes on up here." He pointed to his own head. "The officer who'll be interrogating you isn't allowed to hit you. And he won't, I know him. However, he will be doing everything else not covered by the law to force a confession out of you. That's his only aim. A confession. Not whether you're guilty or not."

Gøran gave Friis a horrified look. "I've nothing to fear," he said, but his voice broke at the end of the sentence and he gripped his glass of Coke so tightly that it looked as if it might crack. "After all, I've an alibi," he added. "She's reliable, too. Unless she pulls out. That's why I don't understand why I'm here at all."

"You're speaking of Lillian Sunde?" Friis said gravely.

"Yes," Gøran said, surprised at how much they all knew in such a short space of time.

"She denies that you were at her house," Friis said. Gøran's eyes widened. His face drained of colour. With a jolt he got up from the chair and banged his fists on the table.

"For fuck's sake!" he screamed. "What a bitch! Bring her here and then I'll tell you what's really going on here. I've known that woman for over a year and then she goes and—"

Friis got up and pushed Gøran back on to his chair. A shocked silence followed.

"You forgot to count," he said quietly. "One outburst like that in court and you'll be branded a killer. Do you understand the seriousness?"

Gøran breathed heavily. He clutched the edge of the table with both hands. "I was with Lillian," he whispered. "If she says I wasn't, then she's lying. If you only knew what I know about her! What she likes and doesn't like. How she wants it! What she looks like. All over. I know!"

"She has much to lose," Friis said. "Her own reputation, for example."

"She never had one," Gøran said angrily. A tear ran treacherously down his cheek.

"It might be hard for people to understand why you were going out with Ulla Mørk while also visiting Lillian at her house over a period of a whole year."

"But it's not a crime," Gøran said.

"Indeed it isn't. But people need to understand who you are and how you think and act. At least you need to be able to explain it if they ask, and they most certainly will ask. So you can start by explaining it to me."

Gøran looked at Friis in surprise. It was blindingly obvious. Two women were better than one. Besides, they were different. Ulla looked good next to him, but always wanted to be in control. Something was always not right for her. Lillian was always up for it. Lillian didn't need him to hold her hand or take her to restaurants. Ulla was high maintenance, she needed pleasing before she would give him what he needed. This burning desire which all men had and which was the real reason they had girlfriends at all.

"A girlfriend means more than just sex, doesn't she?"

Gøran looked at him somewhat exasperated. "You fall out of love," he said wearily. "Often quite quickly."

"What about love?" Friis said.

Gøran smiled incredulously.

"Gøran," Friis said sternly. "There will be adults on the jury who'll assume that you and Ulla were a couple. And all that entails. Just because you have never experienced love does not mean it doesn't exist."

Gøran glared despondently at the table.

"The jury needs to hear that you love Ulla. And that Lillian was an

196

affair that you wish you'd never ever started. However, it was the worst possible bad luck that you happened to be there on the evening of the 20th. That's what you've told the police and you have to stick to that."

"Of course," Gøran said. "Because it's true."

"Ulla broke up with you after you'd been to the gym. Outside Adonis. And you went straight to Lillian's. Am I right?"

"Yes," Gøran said. "I called her first."

"Were you angry with Ulla?"

"More annoyed. She kept breaking up with me. I didn't really know what to think. Bloody women, they say one thing and—"

"Calm down, Gøran, calm down!"

He crumpled once again. "I didn't kill that woman at Hvitemoen. My head feels all messed up, I feel dizzy when they ask me about times and dates, but I'm sure of this one thing: I did not kill that woman! I didn't see a living soul," he said. He felt dizzy. It was a rare and strange feeling for him.

"Konrad Sejer is heading the interrogation," Friis said. "He'll be here soon to fetch you. You'll be spending quite a lot of time with him. The first few days he'll probably spend building trust between you."

"The first few days?"

"Don't forget to breathe. Don't give them anything, Gøran, play your cards calmly and with dignity. If you lose control, he'll attack you at once. He looks kind and mild-mannered, but he's out to get you. He believes you killed this woman. That you smashed her head out of pure fury because something else in your life, something she wasn't a part of, had gone wrong. You don't like being rejected, do you?"

"Well, I don't suppose you'd bloody like it either," Gøran flared up. Then he closed his eyes. "I spent loads of money on Ulla. Went wherever she wanted to go, bought her presents. Paid for everything, the cinema and the café, though she earns her own money. And then all of a sudden she can't be bothered any more."

"Well, we don't send bills to our ex-lovers, do we?"

"I would if I could!" he said angrily.

"Were you fond of her?"

Gøran remembered to count to three. "You get used to people. After such a long time."

Friis looked out of the window as though hoping that someone there might be able to help him.

"Yes. Used to. You were used to her being there for you. When she left, you felt deserted. Am I right?"

"I still had Lillian."

"Did you want to hit someone?"

"I've never hit Ulla," he shouted. "Not ever. Has she said so?"

"No. But the police will claim that you hit someone else in an attempt to relieve your aggression. That you happened to meet Poona and that you destroyed her. Alone in a foreign country. Small and delicate." Friis took out his notebook and his pen. "Let's go through that day, the 20th, from when you got up in the morning till you went to bed that night. Every hour of the day. I need a full account. Take your time, and don't leave anything out."

"I thought this was what the police did?"

"They'll do that as well. And let me add: it is essential that the two stories add up. Do you understand me?"

"I was with Lillian," Gøran said.

Is it my fault? Linda thought. It didn't trouble her too much. They could lock up Gøran, or Nudel or Mode, or anyone, she didn't care. She went to bed saying she had a bad migraine, her mum couldn't make her go to college. She lay staring at the spider in the ceiling and had practically stopped eating. She felt wonderfully light and weak, almost dreamy. Her mum got in her truck and left. She didn't know that Linda got up then and cycled to Gunwald's shop to buy the papers. They still wrote about the case, especially since Gøran's arrest. But Gøran had not done it. The man in the outhouse was much taller. His voice was different, too. So they would have to let him go. Perhaps he wanted to take revenge on her for what she had said about the car. But she didn't even have the strength to be afraid. She fantasised during the long hours she spent in bed. In her mind she had been kidnapped by a cruel and cynical criminal. She was kept hostage in a sinister house, while Jacob crept in through the back door with a loaded gun and freed her, risking his own life in the process. There were several variations of this fantasy. Sometimes Jacob was shot and then she would put his head in her lap and wipe the blood from his temple. Sometimes she herself was shot. Then he would call out her name over and over. Cradle her. Put his hand on her heart and call out, trying to reach her. The variations were endless and she never tired of it. She wondered if Jacob had his own gun or whether they were all kept at the station and had to be signed in and out. If it was possible to get a weapon for self-defence. You could never be too careful. And when Gøran came out ... She closed her eyes. Her neck ached. Her back, too, she had been lying down too long. She almost enjoyed this aching, liked being tormented by something. She lay very still and suffered for her great love.

CHAPTER 20

There's a way through to every human being. That's what I'm looking for, Sejer thought. The vulnerable soul hiding beyond the steely body. He couldn't go wading in. It was a case of reaching a point where Gøran would invite him in himself. That would take time.

As he approached the room where Gøran was waiting, he thought of Kollberg. The operation finished and coming round from the anaesthetic. He wouldn't be able to stand up yet.

Gøran sat behind the table, looking tense.

"Now it's our turn," Sejer said, smiling. He rarely smiled, but Gøran was not to know that. There were bottles of Farris mineral water and Coca-Cola on the table. It was actually a nice room, with cosy lighting and comfortable chairs.

"Before we begin you need to know the following . . ." Sejer looked at him. "You have the right to have someone present throughout the interrogation. Such as Friis. You have the right to rest whenever you're tired. Food and drink when you're hungry. If you want to break off the interrogation, you can leave the room at any time and return to your cell. Is what I'm saying quite clear?"

"Yes," Gøran said, surprised at all the things he was entitled to.

"Did you get on well with Friis?" Sejer asked. Friendly, Gøran thought, almost paternal. Trying to build trust. He is the enemy. Breathe, he thought. One, two, three.

"I don't have much to compare with. I've never needed a lawyer before."

"Friis is good, just so you know. You're a young man full of energy, so you'll get the best. It won't even cost you anything. Others will be picking up the bill."

"You mean taxpayers?" Gøran said with sudden irony. He forgot to breathe.

"Correct," Sejer said. "That's what it means to live in a democracy."

"If this really is a democracy, then I'll be out before the day is over," Gøran said. "Just because I had something to hide from you doesn't mean that I killed this woman."

"Tell me what it means," Sejer said.

Gøran thought of Lillian. "I was stupid trying to protect a married woman," he said bitterly. "I should have told you straightaway that I was with Lillian."

"Lillian says you weren't," Sejer said.

"Lillian is a cunt!" He got halfway up from the chair, but slumped down again. "I don't understand why women won't own up to what they do in bed," he said, exasperated. "They get horny too. They just won't admit it."

"It's harder for a woman," Sejer said. "For all sorts of reasons. Sometimes it's used against them. However, as you're a man then it's quite all right."

He poured drinks into two glasses and pushed one towards him.

"Let it go, Gøran. Let's talk about something else. We've got plenty of time. The house you live in, it's a lovely place. Have you lived there all your life?"

"Yes."

"How was it to grow up in Elvestad?"

"Well, it's not exactly Las Vegas." Gøran smiled without meaning to. Friis had told him to answer the questions, and nothing beyond that, but chatting was easier.

"Perhaps you dreamed of being somewhere else?"

"Sometimes," he said. "A flat in Oslo, maybe. But the rent would eat up my wages."

"But you're good at finding things to do. You're busy, aren't you? You've got your job and you work out a lot. You spend time with your friends. Have you always been doing that well?"

Gøran was not used to being told that he was successful. Now that he thought about it, it was entirely justified. "I've been working out since I was fifteen."

"I do a fair bit of running myself," Sejer told him. "So my stamina's good. But I'm probably not very strong."

"That's interesting," Gøran said. "Most people live in complete ignorance of their own strength. Because they never use it. If I was to ask you: how much can you lift? I'd bet you wouldn't know."

"You're right," Sejer said, and smiled shamefacedly. "I have no idea. Should I know?"

"Hell, yes! It's important to know what you're capable of."

"You're saying that it's important to know yourself."

"I think so. I know what I'm capable of. One hundred and fifty bench presses," he said with ill-concealed pride.

"That doesn't mean a great deal to me, I'm sorry to say," Sejer said. "You could have said one hundred or two hundred. I wouldn't have known the difference."

"Exactly. That's what I think is strange."

Sejer made a note.

"What's that you're writing?" Gøran said.

"I'm making a note of what we're talking about. You've got a handsome dog. Does it mean a lot to you?"

"I'm used to it now. I've had it for four years."

"Then you'll have it for many years to come," Sejer said. "Me, I have a Leonberger. He's just had surgery for tumours on his back. I'm not sure he'll ever walk again. He looks like Bambi on ice, poor chap."

"How old?" Gøran said, interested.

"Ten. His name is Kollberg."

"What sort of name is that?"

"Thank you," Sejer said cheerfully. "That's the reaction I usually get. What's yours called?"

"Cairo. You know, dark and hot."

"Mm. Good name. Unfortunately my imagination is not as sophisticated as yours."

Gøran had now received two compliments in a short space of time, more than normally he got in a year.

"Tell me about some of your girlfriends," Sejer said. He was still smiling, a big trustworthy smile as wide as an ocean.

Gøran squirmed. "Don't have girlfriends," he said. "I'm with a woman or I'm not."

"I see," Sejer said. "You're with women. But you're not fond of them."

"I suppose I like some of them better than others," he said reluctantly.

"Was Ulla one of them?"

Silence. Gøran drank his Coke and caught himself checking the clock. Five minutes had passed.

"How many girls are we talking about?" Sejer looked at Gøran. His skin was smooth and pale, his neck muscular from years of weightlifting, his fists were powerful with short fingers.

Gøran counted in his head. "Let's say twelve to fifteen."

"In how many cases did the girl end the relationship?"

"Hell, never," Gøran said, "it's always me. I get bored easily," he said. "Girls get upset over nothing. There's so much fuss with them."

"Yes. Absolutely. We can agree that they're different. But if they weren't, it wouldn't be any fun chasing them."

"No, ha-ha. You're right about that." Gøran chuckled good-humouredly to himself.

"And Ulla?" Sejer said, cautiously.

Gøran scratched his head. "Ulla is attractive. Fit. The only thing that sags on her is her head from time to time."

"So it was tough when she broke up with you? When you're used to being the one who ends it?"

"The thing is," Gøran said, "that she changes her mind like a kid. She's always breaking up."

"Do you think she'll come back to you?"

"I expect so," he said. For a moment he looked straight at Sejer. "And that moron who identified my car, she couldn't tell the difference between a bus and a truck. That Linda's not all there. It's crap that you take that stuff seriously."

"Let's take it easy. We're in no hurry."

Gøran bit his lip. "You should be out there looking for the bastard who actually did this. You're wasting your time with me here. I hope you've ensured that there are others still looking for him, otherwise

203

I can tell you that you're squandering taxpayers' money in a big way."

Sejer leaned back in his chair.

"Did you like school? You went to school in Elvestad."

"Yes. I liked it."

"The teachers too?"

"Some of them. The one who taught woodwork. And the PE teacher."

"Yes," Sejer said. "You work for a carpenter. What do you do there?"

"I'm an apprentice. Make everything from shelves to flower boxes. To order."

"Do you like it?"

"The boss's all right. Yes, it's fine."

"And there's a pretty nice smell in the workshop, am I right?"

Gøran nodded. "Yes. There's a good smell of wood. And they don't all smell the same. You learn that after a while."

Time passed. The men talked. Gøran's shoulders relaxed. He smiled more often. Helped himself to Coke. Asked Sejer if he was going to get himself a new dog if it turned out to be bad news about what's-his-name again? Kollberg. A ridiculous name for an animal!

"I don't know yet," Sejer said, expressing both exaggerated and genuine sadness at the same time.

He made notes all the time. Did Gøran have any good advice to give when it came to training dogs? I haven't been very lucky with mine, he admitted. Somewhat embarrassed by this admission, he looked at the master like a guilty schoolboy. Oh well, Gøran had that totally under control and, warming to his subject, talked about Cairo, who obeyed his every command. "But if you don't have an obedient dog, it could be that you never really wanted one."

"That was a very insightful comment," Sejer said. And Gøran received his third compliment. Two hours flew by. Sejer wrote up his notes.

"Read this through carefully. You have to sign it, agreeing that this was the conversation we have had. You need to do this every time we've talked. That way it's you who decides what it should say here."

Gøran nodded, read the statement and signed it. Sejer got up and stood next to him.

"Hell," Gøran smiled, looking up from his chair; despite all his strength he felt small next to Sejer. "You're nearly two metres tall!"

He was led back to his cell. No-one had mentioned the murder. He didn't understand that. However, it was lunchtime now. Bacon and eggs. While he ate, he thought about Sejer. It was really very sad about his dog.

"Hello, Marie," Gunder said. He pulled the chair over to her bed. She had been disconnected from the respirator and was breathing on her own, but she had not regained consciousness. He was alarmed by the unaccustomed quiet in the room. She was breathing, but not as regularly as with the machine. It made him nervous and he wanted to help her.

"Today I was looking at that photograph of you and Karsten. From your wedding. How you've changed. Your face has lost its shape. The doctor says it's because you aren't using your muscles. And it won't help if I say something funny, you won't laugh anyway. I can't bear to think about the future, and that really worries me. Poona would have been getting to know Elvestad and the house and the garden by now. She would have learned to use the washing machine and the microwave and the video recorder. We would have sat together on the sofa watching Indian films. They make a lot of films in India. Love stories with tough heroes and beautiful women. Not the gritty real-life films we make about ordinary people. They dream a lot, Indian people. They have to. They are so poor.

"Do you know what? I've had several letters. From foreign women. Russian and Philippine, and they are offering themselves. They say they feel sorry for me. Would you believe it? Poona's not even buried yet. I don't know what to think.

"They are questioning Gøran now. He's denying everything. What else would you expect? Either he did it or he didn't, so he'll never own up to it. It is hard to understand why a young man with his life in front of him would go and do something like this. It said in the paper that he's been remanded in custody for four weeks. I think about his parents a great deal. They're ordinary, hard-working people. Did everything they could for him, I hear. They've had their worries about him and hopes too. Now evidence will have to be found. Evidence beyond reasonable doubt that Gøran is the guilty one. Sometimes I think about what it must have been like for Poona. When she stood there waiting at the airport. When she travelled alone with a strange man right to her death. What about the taxi driver, by the way? What if he did it? And all this because you crashed your car. I'm not blaming you, Marie, but you were never a good driver. Maybe you never should have driven at all.

"I've been thinking of the winter of '59, when we had so much snow. You and Kristine were playing behind the house. I could see you through the window. I had measles and had to stay indoors. You were so overexcited and screaming and giggling, I could hear you all the way to the living room. The weather was mild and you did the most awful things in that wet snow. Do you remember? I daren't say it aloud even if you can't hear me. I said nothing to Mum. She would have had a fit. People do so many strange things, Marie. I'm still thinking about Poona's brother. He's sent me a pretty photograph of her. It's bigger than the one I took and I've bought a fine frame for it. I've promised to get in touch with Shiraz when the date for the funeral has been set. But I don't suppose he'll come back. Possibly he thinks it's a sin to bury her in our consecrated earth. Consecrated earth, now what is that? Earth is earth, surely. I've spoken to Pastor Berg. I gave him something to think about, I can tell you. Has her brother really approved this, he kept fussing. Are you quite sure? We can't risk there being any repercussions. And a Hindu, too. I can't mention that in church, Jomann, I hope you understand. He's nice, the vicar, but terrified of getting into trouble. Nevertheless, I was given permission to play Indian music at the start of the service. Have to look for some in town. Mode has some CDs at the petrol station, but I don't suppose he'll have what I'm looking for. I do hope Karsten will come, but I'm not sure he will. Do you know what? In some ways I think it's a miracle you're still alive. When your body isn't able to feed itself. I don't think you ought to drive again. You can call me if you're going somewhere, I'll take you. Karsten is always so busy. But we can talk about that later. When you wake up."

Mode took a coin from the bowl and put it in the Wurlitzer. The music's as old as Einar, so help me God, it crossed his mind. The café was busy. Einar was drying glasses. He wasn't very talkative these days. Rumour had it that Lillian had started packing. Wicked tongues thought it a bit odd that the break-up had happened so soon after the murder at Hvitemoen and the arrest of Gøran Seter. Imaginations were working overtime.

Nudel, Karen and Frank sat chatting in a corner. They ordered more beer and looked across to Mode's petrol station where Torill was working behind the counter. Mode came over to their table and sat down. He was a quiet man with a calm face. His hair was blond and thin and combed straight back from his forehead. He looked older than his twenty-eight years.

"Of course, we can sit here saying Gøran is innocent," Frank said. "But the truth is that if they'd nicked someone else other people would be sitting at some other table saying exactly the same thing. That's what I think."

They all looked down at their glasses.

"Another thing is . . ." Nudel said anxiously. "All the stuff the cops know that they haven't said. When they go as far as bringing him in, they have to know a lot more."

"Yes, but for goodness' sake!" Frank said, shaking his head. "Has Gøran ever hit anyone?"

"There's always a first time," Mode said, lighting a cigarette.

"I wonder if we're allowed to visit him?"

Einar coughed from behind the counter. "There are restraints on his letters and visits. None of us would get in. His parents, perhaps. No-one else."

"Imagine sitting alone in a cell, no radio, TV or newspapers. Not being able to control what they write about him."

"Does anyone know what sort of chap this defence lawyer is?" Nudel said.

"Thin, grey fellow," Mode said. "Doesn't look very tough."

"Well, it's not exactly muscles that lawyers need most of in court," Frank said. He rocked his heavy head from side to side. "They're talking about forensic evidence. I'd like to know what they mean by that."

"Hair, stuff like that," Nudel said. "It would be bad news for Gøran if he's left any hairs behind."

"You talk as if Gøran did it!" Frank said heatedly.

"But, for fuck's sake," Nudel said. "He's in there! They're putting together a case against him. They must have something on him."

"But I don't understand," said Frank, as if he could not grasp even the possibility that he might be so mistaken about another human being. "They'll probably have him examined by a psychiatrist to decide if he is sane."

"Well, he is. At least we know that."

Frank took several gulps of his beer and burped. "Whoever smashed that woman's head in certainly isn't."

"He could be sane otherwise," Einar said. "Just not at that very moment."

A new comment which needed digesting. It was quiet for a while. Everyone had a picture of Gøran in their minds. They imagined him sitting at one of the tables, drinking from a plastic cup. They imagined his face desperate and lost, with beads of sweat on his forehead. Crouched in a chair, a hard chair perhaps. He'd been sitting there for a long time and was starting to jerk from side to side. His back ached. He kept looking at the clock. A gruff interrogation leader in front of him who decided how long they were going to sit there. The image was very vivid to them, but incorrect.

At that very moment Gøran was sinking his teeth into a fresh-baked pepperoni pizza. The cheese formed fine strings which he gathered up with his fingers.

"You were used to Ulla," Sejer said quietly, "and when she said she was breaking up with you, you didn't take it seriously?"

"No," Gøran said, munching greedily. The pizza was good, he had asked for extra seasoning.

"So it didn't upset you?"

He swallowed and washed the mouthful down with Coke. Ran a hand through his coarse hair. "No," he said.

"Ulla said you were angry. Strange how people are. We see things differently. Perhaps you weren't sad either?"

"Sad?" said Gøran blankly.

"Tell me something that would make you sad," Sejer said.

Gøran thought hard. He took another bite.

"Can't you think of anything?"

"I'm never sad."

"But what if you're not happy? You're a nice guy, but surely you're not always happy?"

"Of course not."

"So?"

Gøran wiped his mouth. "If I'm not happy, then I'm angry, of course."

"Ah . . . I get it. But you can't possibly have been happy when Ulla broke up with you?"

Long pause. "I understand what you're getting at."

"You were angry. Can we agree on that?"

"We can agree on that."

Another pause.

"So you called Lillian. You asked if you could come over?"

"Yes. She said it was fine."

"She's saying that you never came to her house. Did something happen?"

"No! I was with Lillian."

He took a fresh napkin and wiped his mouth again.

"Did you need comforting?"

Gøran snorted. "I never need comforting."

"So what did you need?"

"For Christ's sake, man. Use your imagination!"

"You needed a woman's company?"

Gøran gawped at him and leaned forward across the table. He was grinning so heartily that Sejer frowned.

"Please explain to me what's so funny. You're too quick for me, Gøran."

Gøran digested the compliment and mimicked Sejer. "'You needed a woman's company.' Good God, when did you grow up? In World War One?"

Sejer smiled. "I'm old-fashioned. So you've found me out. But anyway. What *did* you need?"

"To come," Gøran said curtly. He sank his teeth into the pizza once again.

"Did you?"

"I've already told you."

"No. You called Lillian. She said you could come over. Let's do this one step at a time. Just what were her exact words?"

"Eh?"

"Can you remember exactly what she said?"

"She said it was fine."

"Just 'That's fine'?"

"Right."

"Did you notice a foreign woman walking along the road as you came driving?"

"I didn't see anyone."

"Was she carrying a suitcase?"

"I didn't see any suitcase."

"What colour was it?"

"I don't know. I didn't see anyone."

"She was only carrying a handbag? Red fabric. Shaped like a strawberry," Sejer said. "Do you remember it?"

"No," Gøran said, wondering. Suddenly he looked unsure.

"You've forgotten it among all the other things?"

"There's nothing to remember," Gøran said. He put the pizza slice down again.

"Perhaps you've suppressed it?"

"I would've remembered something like that."

"Something like what?"

Silence.

"Perhaps you were far away when it happened. Only your body was present," Sejer said.

"It was with Lillian. In action. I even remember her bed linen. It was green with water lilies. Let me tell you something," he said confidentially. "Older women are much better than young ones. They open up a lot more. Literally. The young ones tend to tense up."

He pushed off his shoes and kicked them away. Sejer said nothing and scribbled for a long time. Gøran was silent. The mood was calm, almost peaceful. The light in the room grew softer and the glow from the lamps became more yellow as the evening proceeded. Gøran was tired, but not from everything that was happening to him. His head was clear. In control. He counted to three. But he hadn't been able to work out. A restlessness was building up in him. It was impossible to fight.

"Kollberg's lying in my living room, he can hardly move," Sejer said and sighed. He put his pen down. "I don't know yet if he will recover. If he doesn't, I'll have to have him put down."

He looked across to Gøran for a long time. Gøran stayed cool.

"No," Sejer said, as though he could read his mind. "I'm just mentioning it. I'm at work, but every now and then my thoughts fly away. Sometimes I wish I were somewhere else. Even though I like my job, being here, with you. Where are your thoughts?"

"Here," Gøran said, looking at Sejer. Then down at his hands.

"Did you follow the story in the newspapers?" Sejer said. He put a Fisherman's Friend in his mouth and pushed the bag towards Gøran.

"Yes, I did," he said.

"What was your reaction to what had happened?"

Gøran breathed in. "Nothing much. It was bad, of course. But I prefer the sports pages."

Sejer buried his face in his hands as though he was tired. He was in fact alert and watchful, but that small movement might suggest that he was about to call it a day. Six hours had passed. Just the two of them. No telephones, or footsteps or voices, not a sound from outside could be heard. You would think the huge building was empty. In fact it was teeming with activity.

"What do you think about the man who did this? I've had a lot of thoughts myself. How about you?"

Gøran shook his head. "No thoughts at all," he said.

"You have no opinion about what kind of man he might be?"

"Of course not."

"Can we agree that he would have been in a rage?"

"I've no idea," Gøran said sulkily. "Finding him is your problem."

"And in your interests, too, I'd imagine." Once more this gravity in Sejer's face. The stare was as steady as a camera lens. He ran his hands through the grey hair and pulled off his jacket. He did it slowly and hung it carefully on the back of his chair. He unbuttoned the cuffs of his shirt and started turning up his sleeves.

Gøran looked at him incredulously. He had a bed in his cell, with a blanket and a pillow. He was thinking about it now.

"Once, a long time ago, I was on patrol in the streets of this city," Sejer said. "It was a Saturday night. There were two of us. There was a fight outside the King's Arms. I got out of the car and went over to them. Two young men, your age. I put my hand on the shoulder of one of them. He spun around and looked me straight in the eye. And then, without any warning whatsoever, his hand shot out in the dark and he plunged a knife into my thigh. He drew a long cut which left a scar I have to this day."

Gøran pretended he wasn't listening, but he was engrossed. Any word, any unexpected story was precious to him, something far removed from all this. A kind of break.

"That was all I wanted to say," Sejer said. "We often see stabbings on film and read about them in the papers. Then you stand there with a knife in your thigh, in excruciating pain. I lost my voice. Everything around me seemed to disappear, even the sound of people screaming and shouting. The pain was so fierce. Today I can laugh about it. A simple flesh wound. All that's left is a pale line. But right at that moment it made the rest of the world disappear."

Gøran didn't know where this was going, but for some reason he was worried.

"Have you ever felt great pain?" Sejer said. He was leaning forward now. His face was close to Gøran's.

Gøran moved back a bit. "Don't think so," he said. "Except when I work out."

"You push yourself over your pain threshold when you work out?"

"Of course. All the time. Otherwise you don't progress."

"Where do you need to get to?"

Gøran watched Sejer's tall body. He didn't give the impression of being muscular, but he was probably tough. His eyes were unfathomable. They never flickered. All he wants is a confession, he thought. Breathe in and out. Count to three. I was with Lillian. Suddenly he said: "Do you want to arm-wrestle?"

Sejer said: "Yes. Why not?"

They got settled. Gøran was ready immediately. It came to Sejer that he would have to touch Gøran now, hold his hand. He hesitated.

"Not up for it?" Gøran teased him.

Sejer shook his head. Gøran's hand was warm and sweaty.

Gøran counted to three and pushed violently.

Sejer did not attempt to drive Gøran's fist down. He was only concerned to hold out. And he managed that. Gøran's strength exploded in one violent charge, then it died away. Very slowly, Sejer pushed his fist to the table.

"Too much static training. Don't forget stamina. Remember that in future."

Gøran massaged his shoulders. He didn't feel good.

"Poona weighed 45 kilos," Sejer told him. "Not very strong, in other words. Nothing for a grown man to brag about."

Gøran pressed his lips tight.

"But I don't suppose he goes around bragging about it. I can see him clearly," Sejer said, staring directly into Gøran's eyes. "He's mulling it over, he's trying to digest it. Get it out of his system."

Gøran felt dizzy.

"Do you like Indian food?" Sejer said. He was quite serious. There was no trace of irony in his voice. "You're not answering. Have you ever tasted it?"

"Er, yes." He hesitated. "Once. It was too strong for my liking."

"Mm," Sejer said. He nodded agreement. "You feel like a fire-breathing dragon afterwards." Gøran had to smile at that. It wasn't easy keeping up with Sejer. He caught himself looking at the clock. His body had slumped a little.

"If I have to have Kollberg put down, it will be the worst day of my life," Sejer said. "It really will be the worst day. I'll give him two, three days, then we'll see."

Gøran suddenly felt nauseous. He wiped at his brow. "I feel ill," he said.

CHAPTER 21

Deep down, Linda knew that Jacob was beyond her reach. This fact was like a thorn in her foot, it hurt with every step. At the same time she nurtured a feeling in her heart that he belonged to her. He had come to her door, had stood on the top step with the outside light making his curls shine like gold, had looked at her with his blue eyes. His gaze had pierced her like a ray. It had attached itself to her and become a bond between them. She had a right to pick him up and carry him close to her heart. It was inconceivable to think of him with another girl. She couldn't conjure such an image in her mind. Finally, she was truly able to understand those who killed for love. This understanding had crept up on her, solid and weighty. She felt wise. She imagined herself plunging a knife in Jacob. Then he would collapse in her arms or lie bleeding on the ground. She would be there when he died, she would hear his last words. Afterwards, for the rest of her life, she would visit his grave. Talk to him, say all the things she wanted to and he would never be able to run away.

She got out of bed and dressed. Her mum was gone to Switzerland for a load of chocolate. She took two Paralgin painkillers and washed them down with water. Put on her coat and found the bus timetable in the kitchen drawer. Then she went down the road to wait. The bus was practically empty, just her and one old man. She had a knife in her pocket. A vegetable knife with a serrated edge. When her mum chopped carrots with it they ended up with tiny, fine grooves. She curled up on her seat and felt the knife handle. Her own existence was no longer about college, job, husband and children, or her own salon with its very own smell of hairspray and shampoo. It was a question of her peace of mind. Only Jacob could give her that; dead or alive was irrelevant, she had to have peace of mind!

*

An hour later Skarre's car rolled quietly down Nedre Storgate. He was not thinking of what was going on in the street, his thoughts were far away. He parked alongside the kerb and pulled the handbrake. Sat there deep in thought. His mobile phone played the first few notes of Beethoven's Fifth and it startled him. It was Sejer. After the call, Skarre sat in the car thinking. Sejer had asked him a strange question, in that quaint, bashful manner of his when the subject was women. Imagine you know a woman, you visit her regularly. You have a relationship which is not about love, but about altogether different things.

Sex, Jacob had suggested.

Precisely. She's married to someone else and you're keeping the relationship secret. You come to her house when she's alone. Imagine such a relationship and such a visit.

Happy to, Skarre had grinned.

You know your way around the house, you've been there before. Soon you're on your way to her bedroom. You know that too, the furniture and the wallpaper. Then you make love, as Sejer put it.

Quite so, Jacob had said.

Afterwards you leave her house and you drive home. Now, my question is – and think carefully – would you remember her bed linen afterwards?

Skarre sat at the steering wheel contemplating this question. Tangled up in different bed linens. He thought of an evening with Hilde after they had been to the cinema to see "Eyes Wide Shut" and the lamp by her bedside with the red shade. The sheets were plum red, the sheet a lighter shade than the duvet cover and the pillow with the white flower. He thought of Lene with the golden hair and her bed with the Manila headboard. The duvet with the daisies. Incredible, he thought, and lifted his head. A shadow slipped round the corner. He sat there staring. Someone in a hurry, a sudden flurry and then gone. As if someone had been there watching him. He shook his head and got out of the car. Walked to the hallway looking for the keys to his flat. Again he heard a sound. He stopped and listened. I'm not afraid of the dark, he told himself, and let himself in. Walked up the stairs. Went to the window to look down at the empty street. Was someone there? He looked in the directory and picked up the telephone. It rang twice before she answered.

"Jacob Skarre," he said. "We spoke the other day. I was with Inspector Sejer. Do you remember me?"

Lillian Sunde said yes, how could you forget such a confrontation?

"I've just got one question," he said. "Do you have a set of sheets which is green and is embroidered with water lilies?"

After a long silence she said: "Is this a joke?"

"You are not answering my question," Skarre said.

"I couldn't tell you that. Not off the top of my head."

"Come on," Skarre said aggressively. "You know perfectly well what sort of bed linen you have. Green. With water lilies—"

He heard a click as she hung up. Her reaction troubled him.

Gøran was sitting on the bunk, eating his breakfast with the tray on his lap. It was going slowly. He had hardly slept. He had never thought that he wouldn't be able to sleep when they finally took him back to the cell after all those hours. His body ached and felt heavy like lead as he lay down, still with his clothes on. It was as though he was swallowed up and sinking into the thin mattress. But his eyes were open. He lay like that for most of the night, almost bodiless. Two wide-open eyes staring at the ceiling. From time to time he heard footsteps outside, a few times the jangling of keys.

He washed the bread down with cold milk. The food swelled up in his mouth. The feeling of being let down by his own body was terrifying. He had always been in total control. His body had always obeyed him. He wanted to scream out loud. Punch his fists through the wall. Inside his well-trained body a surplus was building up and it was threatening to blow him to pieces. He sat still on the bunk looking around, trying to find a point he could direct it at. He could throw the tray at the wall, tear the mattress to shreds. But he stayed on the bunk. Quiet as a mouse. In a kind of motor collapse. He stared at the food again. Watched his hands. They seemed unfamiliar. White and limp. The lock slammed. Two officers came in, time for the next interrogation, they said.

The bottles of Farris mineral water and Coca-Cola were in place, but no Sejer. The officers left without locking the door. He was seized by the crazy notion that he could just go. But they were probably right outside the door. Or were they? He sat in the comfortable chair. While he waited he heard the seven-storey building wake up and come alive. There was a gradually increasing humming around him of doors, footsteps and telephones. After a while he stopped hearing it. He wondered why. No-one came. Gøran waited. He smiled bitterly at the idea that this might be a sort of torture to soften him up. But he was ready now, not dizzy like yesterday. He looked at the clock. Changed position in the chair. Tried thinking of Ulla. She was so far out of reach. He felt really upset at the thought of Einar's Café. All of them sitting there gossiping. He couldn't be there to put them right. What were they thinking? What about his mum? She was most likely sitting in a corner of the kitchen snivelling. His dad was probably in the yard with his back to the windows, angrily keeping himself busy with an axe or a hammer. That was how they lived, he realised, with their backs to each other. Then there was Søren at the workshop. He must have an opinion. Perhaps people popped in to talk to him. As though Søren knew anything. However, they were probably everywhere now, all talking about him at Gunwald's and at Mode's petrol station. He would be out of here soon. Would be walking down the street and see all the faces, each with their own private thoughts. Were there pictures of him in the papers? Was that allowed when he hadn't been convicted? He tried to remember what the law said, but he couldn't. He could ask Friis. Not that it made any difference. Elvestad was a small village. Reverend Berg had baptised and confirmed him. An amusing thought struck him that perhaps the vicar was sitting at his breakfast table even now, praying for him. I ask you, Lord, be with Gøran in his hour of need. The door opened and it made him jump.

"Slept well?"

Sejer towered in the doorway.

"Yes, thank you," Gøran lied.

"That's good. Let's get going then."

Sejer sat down at the table. There was something light and effortless about him although he was a tall man. Long-limbed with broad shoulders and a lined face. It was probably true that he was in good shape, as he claimed. Gøran could see it now. A runner, Gøran thought, someone who runs along the road in the evening, mile after mile at a steady pace. A tough, persistent bastard.

"Is that mutt of yours walking?" Gøran said.

Sejer raised an eyebrow. "Dog," he corrected him. "Is that dog of yours walking. I don't have a mutt. No. He lies in front of the fireplace, limp as a bear skin."

"Aha. Then you'll have to have him put down," Gøran said, callously. "No animal should be reduced to that."

"I know, but I'm putting it off. Do you ever think of Cairo? That one day you'll have to have him put down?"

"That's ages off."

"But it'll happen one day. Don't you ever think of the future?"

"The future? No. Why would I?"

"I want you to think of the future now. What do you see when you look ahead?"

Gøran shrugged. "It looks like now. I mean, before all of this." He flung out his hands.

"You think so?"

"Yes."

"But certain things are very different. Your arrest. These conversations. Won't they make a change?"

"It'll be tough when I get out of here. Meeting people again."

"How would you like it to be once you get out?"

"I want it to be like it was."

"Can it be?"

Gøran wrung his hands in his lap.

"Can life ever be the same again?" Sejer asked again.

"Well, nearly the same."

"What will be different?"

"Well, as you say . . . everything that has happened. I'll never forget it."

"So you haven't forgotten? Tell me what you remember."

219

Sejer's voice was very deep and actually quite agreeable, Gøran thought as he pushed his chair back. Opened his mouth and yawned. The silence quivered like a spear in the room; now it turned slowly and pointed at him. His eyes began flickering.

"There's nothing to remember!" he yelled. He forgot to breathe, forgot to count, grabbed a Coke bottle and threw it against the wall. The liquid cascaded down.

Sejer didn't even flinch. "We'll stop here, Gøran," he said quietly. "You're tired."

He was taken to his cell and brought back two hours later. He felt heavy again. Lethargic and slow. Unconcerned in a pleasant sort of way.

"You visit the gym often," Sejer said. "Do you keep your dumb-bells in the car? So that you can use them whenever there's the slightest opportunity? In a traffic jam? Or waiting by a red light?"

"We don't have traffic lights or jams in Elvestad," Gøran said.

"The lab. has found traces of a white powder on her handbag," he continued. "What do you think it might be?"

Silence.

"You know that odd-looking bag of hers. Green. Shaped like a melon."

"A melon?"

"Heroin, perhaps. What do you think?"

"I don't do drugs," Gøran said harshly.

"No?"

"I've tried a bit of everything. Way back. But it's not my thing."

"What is your thing?"

A shrug.

"Going to the gym, isn't it? Muscles like steel, sweat dripping, the agony in your arms and legs when they are deprived of oxygen, the stifled groans from your own throat with each lift, the feeling of raw power, of everything you can overcome, the bars which grow warm beneath your hands. Does that feel good?"

"I like working out," Gøran said impassively.

"After a while the bar gets greasy and slippery. You thrust your hands into a box of magnesium. A fine white powder. Some of it wafts up into the air around you and sticks to your skin, gets in your hair. You took a shower, but some of it found its way on to Poona's bag. Probably because it was made from fabric. A synthetic material to which everything sticks."

Once more Gøran looked blankly at Sejer. It felt as though his thoughts were flying off in all directions. He couldn't get them under control. He could no longer remember what he had said. Could no longer make sense of what the policeman was saying.

"I hardly got any sleep," he said weakly.

"I know," Sejer said. "But we've plenty of time. It's important to get this right. You're saying you were with Lillian. Lillian says no. Perhaps you were out Hvitemoen way, but wished you were with Lillian."

"I was with Lillian. I remember it. We had to hurry."

"I suppose you always had to? Someone might come."

"I don't understand why she's lying."

"You called and asked to come over. Did she say no, Gøran? Were you rejected for the second time the same evening?"

"No!"

Sejer took a few steps. Gøran was overcome by a terrible restlessness, an irrepressible urge to move. He looked at the clock. Eleven minutes had passed.

"When you read about the murder in the paper," Sejer said, "then you must have had a reaction. Formed images in your mind. Would you like to share them with me?"

"Images?" Gøran's red eyes blinked.

"The ones you create in your mind. As we all do when someone explains something to us. We try to visualise it. It's an unconscious reaction. I would like to know what were your images of Poona's murder."

"I have none."

"Let me help you find them."

"But why do you need them?" Gøran said uncertainly. "They're just fantasy."

"To see if they resemble what we've found."

"But that's impossible! I didn't do it!"

"If we find them, you'll sleep better at night. Perhaps they frighten you?"

Gøran buried his face in his hands. For a while they sat in silence.

And then Sejer said: "Have you ever been to see Linda Carling at her house?"

"What? No. Why would I want to do that?"

"I imagine you were quite upset at the thought of her identifying your car."

"Quite upset? I was bloody furious."

"Is that why you went over to scare her?"

Gøran looked at him in amazement. "I don't even know where she lives."

They both jumped as the door opened and Skarre came in.

"Telephone," Skarre said.

"It had better be important," Sejer said. He looked at Gøran and left the room.

"Is it Sara? Has Kollberg got up?"

"Ole Gunwald," Skarre said. "Will speak only to you."

Sejer turned into his office. He answered the telephone standing up.

"This is Gunwald from Elvestad. I live at Hvitemoen."

"I remember you," Sejer said.

"I've left it a bit late, but it's about the murder."

"Yes?" Sejer said impatiently. Skarre held his breath.

"You've arrested Gøran Seter," Gunwald said, obviously uneasy. "I've got something to tell you in connection with that. You've got the wrong man."

"What do you know about it?"

"It was me who called you about the suitcase," Gunwald said. "And I left something out. It wasn't Gøran I saw out at Norevann."

Sejer's eyes widened.

"You saw who it was?"

"I think it's best if you come over," Gunwald said.

Sejer looked at Skarre. "We'll take your Golf."

222

"Not possible," Skarre said grimly. "I woke up to four flat tyres this morning. They'd been slashed."

"And I thought you lived in a nice area."

"So did I. I suppose it was just some kids messing about."

"What are you thinking?" Sejer said as they drove. He didn't like the patrol car and let Skarre take the wheel.

"Gøran is innocent, isn't he?"

"We'll have to wait and see."

"But an elderly shopkeeper wouldn't make up something like this."

"Everyone makes mistakes."

"Including you. Have you considered that?"

"Many times."

Another pause.

"Do you have a problem with people who work out?" Skarre said.

"No. But I question it."

"You question it? Surely that's the same as having a problem with it."

Sejer looked at Skarre. "It's about charging up, isn't it? Training persistently for many years. With heavier and heavier weights. Sooner or later a need for release is created. But it never comes. Only heavier and heavier weights. It would drive me mad."

"Mm," Skarre smiled. "Mad. And very strong."

Nineteen minutes later they pulled up in front of Gunwald's shop. He was unpacking boxes of breakfast cereal when he spotted them through the window. The sight of them made him weak at the knees. There was something ominous about the two men. A migraine started pricking at his temples.

"I'm sorry," he stammered. His words were barely audible. "I should have called you earlier. I'm just so confused. Einar didn't do it, of course, neither did Gøran. That's why I had doubts."

"Einar Sunde?"

"Yes." He bit his lip. "I recognised both him and his car. A green Ford Sierra."

"But it was late. Must have been almost dark."

"I saw it clearly. I'm certain of it. Unfortunately, I suppose I should say."

"How good is your eyesight?" Sejer indicated the thick lenses in the spectacles.

"It's fine when I'm wearing these."

Sejer forced himself to be patient. "It would have been smarter if you'd told us this straightaway."

Gunwald wiped his brow.

"No-one must know that I told you this," he whispered.

"I can't promise that," Sejer said. "I understand your anxiety. However, like it or not, you're an important witness."

"You get frowned on here if you say anything. Look at poor Linda Carling. No-one talks to her now."

"If either Gøran or Einar or both of them have anything to do with this, don't you think people in this community would want them to get their just deserts?"

"Certainly. If it were them."

Sejer inhaled deeply and breathed slowly out. "We want to think the best of people we know. But we all know someone."

Gunwald nodded heavily. "So are you going over to bring him in?"

"He will have to give us a satisfactory explanation, won't he?"

"Jomann will have a heart attack. He buys his paper from Einar."

Skarre took a long look at Gunwald. "How old are you?" he asked gently.

"How old am I? I'm sixty-five."

"Will you be retiring soon?"

"Maybe," he said wearily. "But how else will I pass the time? It's just him and me." He pointed at the fat dog in the corner.

"The days will pass anyway," Sejer said. "I appreciate what you've told us. Even if you did take your time." He bowed politely. "You'll be hearing from us."

Gunwald followed them with his eyes. He heard the car start and turn right in the direction of the café. Then he shuffled over to the dog.

"Perhaps it is time to call it a day," he said, stroking the dog's dark head. "Then we could have a lie-in every morning. And go for walks several times a day. You might lose some weight."

He stared out of the window. Imagined Einar's face. A few more seconds before the shit hit the fan.

He walked to the front door and double-locked it. It was very quiet. It had actually been quite easy. "Come on," he said to the dog. "Come on, time we went home."

"Einar Emil Sunde?"

Einar squeezed a cloth between his hands.

"Yes?"

Two women were sitting there each with their coffee. They were staring openly. He had to support himself on the counter. Lillian was gone. Half the furniture was gone with her. The acoustics in the rooms were unfamiliar. Now the police stomping into the café. What would people say? Anger and fear came and went in the long face.

"You need to close up and come with us. There's something we want to talk to you about."

"And what might that be?" he said nervously. His voice failed him. Reduced to a mere squeak.

They drove in silence. The humiliation of having to ask the two women to leave had made him sweat.

"I'll come straight to the point," Sejer said.

They were sitting in his office.

"In the late evening of September 1st you were seen at Norevann. At the tip of the point. You were seen there holding a suitcase. You threw the suitcase into the lake and drove away in your green estate car. We retrieved the suitcase. It belonged to the deceased Poona Bai, who was murdered at Hvitemoen on August 20th."

Einar's head sank helplessly.

"We also know that she was with you, at your café. So the

225

question, Sunde, is: why were you in possession of Poona's suitcase?"

Einar underwent a terrible transformation. In a few minutes he was stripped bare, robbed of all dignity. It was not a pretty sight.

"I can explain it all," he whispered.

"I hope you can," Sejer said.

"That evening a woman came into my café. I already told you that." He hawked and coughed.

"Yes?"

"Just to make it absolutely clear . . . What I'm telling you now is the truth. I should have said it before. That's my only crime!"

"I'm waiting," Sejer said.

"She sat for a while with her tea. In the corner by the jukebox. I didn't see her clearly and besides, I was busy with other things. But I did hear her cough a few times. There was no-one else in the café then. Just the two of us."

Sejer nodded.

"Suddenly I heard a chair scraping and footsteps across the floor. Shortly afterwards the door slammed. I was emptying the dishwasher so it took a while before I went to the table to fetch the empty cup." He looked up. His eyes were flickering. "Then I saw the suitcase."

"She left it behind?"

"Yes. But the woman was gone. I stood for a while staring at it, thinking it seemed a bit odd, that you would forget something that big. She was really very upset. So I thought that perhaps she'd just gone outside to get some fresh air. That she'd be back in no time. She wasn't. So I took it and put it in the back room. There it stayed. Should I take it home with me or what? I assumed she would come back for it. It was at the café overnight. Then I put it in the cold storage room – it took up so much space."

"Go on," Sejer said.

"I remember hearing about the murder on the radio the next day, but I didn't hear all of it. Such as the woman being foreign. It took a long time before someone stopped by and told me that the victim might be Pakistani. Or Turkish. Eventually I thought it could be her.

And her suitcase was in the cold storage room. I realised the seriousness, given that she'd actually been in my café and we'd been alone. You could say that's when I started feeling nervous. Besides, I couldn't be sure it was her. But she hadn't come back asking for her suitcase. So I was worried. And the thing is that as time passed it got worse. Finally I knew it all. That she was Jomann's wife whom he'd met in India. And here I was with all her belongings! I thought, well, they'll catch the murderer anyway, with or without the suitcase. It wasn't going to be crucial to that investigation. So I decided to get rid of it. Who saw me?" he burst out.

Sejer tried to digest the story which he experienced as irritatingly plausible. For a long time he scrutinised Sunde's flushed face.

"Someone who wishes to remain anonymous."

"But it must be someone who knows me! I don't understand. It was quite dark. I didn't see a soul down there."

"Sunde," Sejer said, leaning forward, "I hope you realise the seriousness of this. If your story turns out to be true, you have withheld vital information in a murder investigation."

"If it's true?" Einar spat at him. "It's obviously true!"

"It's not obvious to us."

"Bloody wonderful! Now you know why I didn't call! I knew it would end up like this. You throw yourselves at every scrap you can get, just like I knew you would."

He spun round on his chair and turned his back on Sejer.

"Were you in touch with Gøran Seter during the day or the evening of the 20th?"

"We don't socialise. I'm nearly twice his age."

"But you shared something."

Bitterly Einar understood that he was referring to Lillian. "Not as far as I know," he said. "I've told you the truth. That's how it happened. I recognise now how stupid I've been, but I just didn't want to get involved."

"That's too late now," Sejer said. "You're very much involved. If you'd called straightaway we could have eliminated you a long time ago. As it is, we have now to look into a number of things. Such as your car and your house."

"No, damn it, no!" he screamed.

"Damn it, yes, Sunde. And in the meantime you'll wait here."

"You don't mean overnight?"

"As long as it takes."

"Hell no. I have kids and everything!"

"Then you'll have to tell them what you've just told me. The difference is that they'll forgive you. I won't."

He got up and left. Einar stayed sitting, in shock. Dear God, he thought. What have I done?

Four officers went to Einar Sunde's house. Skarre went straight to the bedroom. A large wardrobe contained linen and towels. It was plain that some part of the contents had been taken; the wardrobe was only half full. He sorted through the piles of sheets and soon found what he was looking for. Green duvet covers with water lilies. Monet's lilies. Perhaps Gøran was telling the truth, perhaps he was here on the evening of the 20th. Or he remembered the design from some other evening, so it wouldn't be an alibi after all. But it was disturbing. They towed Einar's car away for forensic tests. They went over it with a fine-tooth comb without making a significant find. How could a walking, talking, educated human being be so indescribably stupid? Was it not evidence of supreme arrogance? Skarre thought of the beautiful nightgown, the underwear and the sponge bag which Poona had bought in Gunder's honour. He had thrown it all into the lake. What sort of man *was* Einar Sunde?

"The worst thing is that I believe him," Sejer said later at the office. Skarre opened a window. He sat on the windowsill smoking.

"So you'll let him go?"

"Yes."

"Gøran is still our man?"

"I'm quite sure. But he has a strong survival instinct. His physical condition helps him."

"For my part, I don't trust Lillian Sunde," Skarre said, and told him about the green linen.

"OK. So she has a set like that. He was there once and noticed it.

I don't doubt that they were seeing each other. There are rumours that give it a certain credence. But he wasn't there *that* evening. When Ulla dumps him he leaves in a fury. He calls Lillian and she rejects him too. He still has the dumbbells in the car. Poona comes walking along the road alone. He stops and talks to her. Perhaps he offers to drive her to Jomann's house. Then he makes a pass at her and she gets frightened. His rage takes over. He never saw the suitcase. Now we know why. It was at the café. Then he kills her. He flees, panic-stricken, and changes his clothes. He simply puts back on the clothes he's worn at the gym. Comes home at 11 p.m. Tells his mother that he's been babysitting with Ulla. We know he hasn't been. The shape and weight of the dumbbells could have caused the injuries Poona sustained. The white powder is from the gym, we know of no other use for magnesium powder. He has no understanding of love. He has a woman or he hasn't. He's incapable of talking about his feelings. He is obsessed by sex and by having a woman he can show off to. He appears to be in a good mood, smiling and coping well in the circles he moves in, but I suspect that he is callous and very simple. Lacking in the ability to empathise with other people's feelings."

"You're saying he's a psychopath."

"That's your term, not mine, and by the way that's a concept I have never quite got to grips with."

"So you're going to go on wearing him down until you get a confession?"

"I'm trying to the best of my abilities to get him to a place where he understands that he has to make a confession. In order to move on."

"What if you don't get it? Do we have enough to go to court with as it stands?"

"Probably not. And that worries me."

"How is it possible to smash someone up the way the killer did without leaving any traces of himself?"

"It happens all the time."

"There are no traces of Poona in his car. Not a single fibre, not a single hair. Shouldn't we have found something?"

"She was wearing silk. It doesn't give off fibres like wool, for example. Her hair was tightly plaited."

"What did he do with the dumbbells?"

"I don't know. We found nothing on them. He has several sets. Perhaps he got rid of the ones he used to kill her. I want to talk to a number of people. Get hold of them and bring them in as soon as possible: Ulla Mørk, Linda Carling, Ole Gunwald, Anders Kolding, Kalle Moe. And Lillian Sunde." He looked at Skarre. "Anything else? Has Sara called?"

"Yes. Kollberg is still lying pretty much flat."

The dog looked up at him with sorrowful eyes when he appeared in the living room. It made a half-hearted attempt to stand, but gave up. Sejer remained standing, looking hopelessly at him. Sara came out of the kitchen.

"I suppose we have to force him a bit. As long as we keep feeding him he won't make an effort."

Together they tried lifting Kollberg to a standing position. Sara at the front and Sejer at the back. His paws skidded. But they kept supporting him. He began to whimper and collapsed. They lifted him again and the same thing happened. He was trying to please them so that they would leave him alone, but they weren't going to. They lifted him again and again. Sara found a scrap of carpet to stop him sliding. That worked. The dog's body shook as 50 kilos weighed down on its legs.

"He's supporting at least a fraction of his own weight," Sejer said brightly.

Sara wiped the sweat from her face. Her long fringe kept falling into her eyes and she began to laugh. "Come on, you fat lazy dog," she cried. Then they both laughed. Encouraged by all this good humour, Kollberg pushed himself off the ground and stood for a few seconds. Then they let go of him and he collapsed, barking cheerfully.

"Bloody brilliant!" Sara shouted. Sejer gave her a shocked look. "He's going to make it. We need more exercises for him to practise daily. We're not going to give up."

"I'll fetch a sausage," Sejer said happily and made for the fridge. Meanwhile Kollberg managed to paddle half a pace across the floor. Sejer came back with a whisky in one hand and a piece of sausage in the other. He stood over Kollberg and gave an uncharacteristically broad smile. Sara had a giggling fit.

"What's that for?" he said.

"You look like a big kid," she said. "And you haven't got a hand free so I can do with you what I like."

He was saved by the telephone. He threw Kollberg the sausage and answered it.

"They've all been contacted," Skarre said eagerly. "They'll be here tomorrow, one after the other. Except Anders Kolding."

"Explain."

"He's done a runner on his wife and everything. To Sweden, I think. Apparently he has a sister there. I wonder what this means?"

"The kid's got colic," Sejer said. "He can't take it any more."

"What a wimp! Are you saying we should let him go?"

"Absolutely not. Get hold of him."

He hung up and drained the whisky in one gulp.

"Good grief," Sara said. "That is the most indecent thing you've ever done." Sejer felt hot all over. "Dare I hope for more?" Sara smiled enticingly.

"Why would I want to be indecent?" he said bashfully.

"It can be very nice, you know." She moved closer to him. "You don't know how to do it," she said. "You've no idea what indecency is. And that's quite all right." She caressed his cheek quickly. "It really is quite all right."

CHAPTER 22

Linda was lying trembling in her bed when Jacob came out to discover the slashed tyres on his car. She could see it clearly. In her mind she was there comforting him. Later on she went a step further and bought a long-bladed hunting knife. The handle was made from alder. She put it in her bedside drawer and it became so important to her that she kept opening the drawer to look at it. Time and time again she admired the gleaming steel. She tried to picture the blade covered in Jacob's blood. The image was so strong it made her feel all flushed. When he collapsed at her feet and she held him tight she would close her eyes and shut herself off from the rest of the world and the rest of her life. Live only for the second when he drew his last breath. He would look up into her eyes and perhaps in this last second he would understand everything. He had made a terrible mistake. He should have accepted her. Linda held the knife in her hands, she was already comfortable handling it. She had not set a time, but she would wait for him in the hallway.

When at last he was dead she would call the police and tell them where he lay, anonymously of course. Not only would he belong to her forever, but the case would never be solved. Not until she herself had grown old without ever getting married. Then she would write down her story in a letter and send it to the newspapers. Thus would she become immortal. People would realise that they should never have underestimated her. She felt intoxicated by her own power and it struck her how strange it was that she had not realised until this moment how strong she was. Strong enough to stand alone against everyone else. She wasn't afraid of anything any more. If Gøran got out of prison and came to kill her, she would smile in the darkness. The accused man from Elvestad denies all charges, she read, sitting by the breakfast table with a cup of tea. She cut out the article and

232

put it in the plastic folder. Then her attention was drawn to another story, on page four: "Man (29) found stabbed in Oslo street. He died later from his injuries. The man was found bleeding in the street outside the Red Mill restaurant late last night. The victim had received several stab wounds and died later in hospital without regaining consciousness. There were no witnesses to the incident. The man has now been identified. The police, however, have no leads in the case." Her gaze wandered out of the window to the autumn sky. A paragraph such as this would appear in the paper when Jacob was dead. It was a sign. She started trembling. Cut out the paragraph. Put it in the folder with the others. Imagine, it being in the paper, just like that!

Suddenly an idea took shape in her head. She took the cutting out of the folder and found an envelope. Put the cutting in and licked the envelope. Wrote on it Jacob's address. It was like a declaration of love. Then it occurred to her that it could be traced. Her handwriting was distinctive, a little girl's handwriting with round letters. She opened the envelope and found another. Wrote the address again using rigid, unfamiliar letters quite unlike her own. She could post it in town. Better than if the postmark was Elvestad. No, she wasn't going to post it at all, but put it right into his letterbox. In his letterbox downstairs in the communal hallway. Oh boy, that would make him think! He would turn the cutting and the envelope over and over, put them down, pick them up again. Perhaps save it. Show it to his colleagues. Linda felt a genuine delight at her ingenuity. Sometimes life worked itself out, rolled itself out like a red carpet. She went to the bathroom. Looked in the mirror. Brushed her hair away from her forehead and gathered it up with a hair band. Now she looked older. Then she ran up to her room and opened her wardrobe. Chose a black jumper and black trousers. Her pale face seemed colourless in all the black: she looked dramatic. She took off all her jewellery. Earrings, necklace and rings. There was only her pale face with her scraped-back hair. She locked the front door behind her and walked to the bus stop. She stuck the envelope inside her bra. At first the paper felt cool against her skin, but it soon warmed up. Jacob's hands would touch the white envelope, which had been close to her heart. It was pounding now. She felt her nipples harden. Perhaps the envelope would smell of her. She felt the hairs on the back of her neck stand up, the ones she hadn't managed to catch with the hair band. The bus came. She sat down and started dreaming till she felt warm. No-one talked to her. If they had tried, she would have turned around and looked straight through them with glassy eyes.

"Hello, Marie," Gunder said. "There's something I haven't told you. That may be because I keep hoping you can hear, though I know better. The accident, Marie. The crash. The reason you're here. The other driver died, you see. He's been buried now and I went to the funeral. I stayed in the background, sitting on the last pew. Many people were crying. The service ended in the church, some people prefer that. I slipped out and went to my car. It seemed appropriate to be there, but I didn't want to prolong it; after all, I hadn't been invited. Then a woman came after me, she called out, quite gently, and I must admit that I jumped. It was his widow, Marie. She was about your age. I'm very sorry, she said, I know absolutely everyone in the church, but I've never seen you before. So I told her that I was your brother. I don't know what I'd expected. That she would get angry, or be embarrassed perhaps, but she wasn't. Her eyes brimmed with tears. How is your sister, she asked anxiously.

"I was very moved. I just don't know, I said. We don't know if she'll regain consciousness. Then she stroked my arm a few times and she smiled. People are much kinder than they are made out to be, Marie.

"But here's the most important bit. Poona was buried yesterday. It was very beautiful, you should have been there. Not very many people, true, and some came only out of curiosity, but no matter for that. Two police officers were there, too. But you should have seen the church! The vicar paled when he made his solemn entrance and saw the colourful coffin. I went to a florist in Oslo, a man who's a real artist with flowers. I thought that only the best was good enough. I didn't want what people usually order for funerals. Bouquets and so

234

on, in pink or blue. But huge garlands made from yellow and orange flowers. Something truly Indian, if you know what I mean. He was really excited and you should have seen the result. The temperature in the church rose by several degrees. It was like dancing flames on the dark mahogany coffin. We played Indian music. I think her brother really would have approved.

"We were six pallbearers and at first I was a little nervous. What if there wasn't going to be enough of us? But Karsten helped out, believe it or not, and Kalle and me and Bjørnsson from work. And two police officers. The last thing we did for Poona was to sing. Did you know that Kalle has a lovely voice?

"I didn't ask anyone back to the house. Thought Karsten might invite himself, but he left as quickly as he could. Oh, well. It's not easy for him. He's so scared of everything. I'm not afraid of anything any more. Not of God or the Devil or death. That's nice in a way. I will take each day as it comes.

"I'm back at work. That's why I'm so late. Young Bjørnsson is actually quite a nice chap. It was good to see them all again. At first they were a little awkward with me, didn't know quite what to say. But then they relaxed. I think they really respect me now. Everything that has happened has made them look at me in a new light. Svarstad even dropped by, probably sheer curiosity. But it was nice all the same. He's ever so pleased with the Quadrant. He's the only farmer in the district to have one.

"Today I bought a chicken. I've never been a very adventurous cook, but I went to an ethnic shop and asked for spices for the chicken. It didn't turn out red like Poona's chicken, but all the same it reminded me a little of the food in Tandel's Tandoori. Did you know that they colour their food? Here we think ourselves above that.

"It's extraordinary that you can survive on those few drops seeping into your veins. It looks like skimmed milk, but the doctor says it's sugar, fat and protein. Karsten is coming to visit you tomorrow. I know he's dreading it. But then I have no idea what he does when he sits here alone. Perhaps he talks the hind legs off a donkey? Though I doubt that. I have a strong suspicion that when you wake up they'll call me, even though he's your husband.

"I sleep quite well at night. There is a sadness in me, it feels as if I've gained some weight, but in fact I have lost a couple of kilos. But then I pull myself together and try to remember that after winter comes a new spring. Then I'll work miracles on Poona's grave. They don't give you much space, but God knows I'll make the most of it. I'm taking good care of her few belongings. The clothes in the suitcase, the little banana-shaped bag and the jewellery. The brooch she wore in the coffin and the same outfit as when we got married. It was like glacier lake water, deep turquoise. I remember her face. It's destroyed now, I know, because he smashed it with a stone. Or something like that, they aren't sure. But it doesn't upset me, I never saw it so I can't believe it either. I suppose that's a good thing, Marie. That people can believe what they want?"

Sejer read Skarre's report from the latest interviews. Anders Kolding had been tracked down in his sister's flat in Gothenburg, slightly drunk but still able to explain himself. He said he needed a break. He hadn't run away from anything. No, I couldn't have turned left, but it's true that I turned the light off. Didn't want to be flagged down and risk getting a fare in the wrong direction. I drove straight back to town, for Christ's sake! Ulla Mørk admitted that she had several times broken off her relationship with Gøran. She had always gone back to him, but she stated that this time it was final. Yes, he did sometimes keep dumbbells and other gym equipment in the car. If Adonis was packed then he didn't want to have to wait for the different machines. Lillian Sunde went on denying that she had had any dealings with the accused, yes, she knew the rumours, but that was the sort of place Elvestad was, a rumour mill. Someone had probably spotted them when they danced that time at the disco in town. Linda Carling repeated more or less word for word her earlier statement. A blond man in a white shirt running after a woman in dark clothes. "A red car stood parked in the roadside. It could have been a Golf." Karen Krantz, Linda's friend, was certain that they

236

could rely on Linda's statement. She was terrified of getting it wrong, she said. So what she's telling you is what she saw. Ole Gunwald was quite sure that he had twice heard the sound of a car starting up. Fifteen minutes apart. Why twice? Sejer wondered.

Day after day, hour after hour Gøran was questioned by Sejer. Gøran knew every last cut and scratch in the pale table. All the marks on the ceiling, every line on the walls. Exhaustion came over him in sudden jolts. A weariness which took his breath away. Eventually he grew to recognise the attacks in advance, the way they sneaked up on him. Then he would lean forward on to the table to rest. Sejer let him sit like that. Sometimes he would tell him stories. Gøran listened. The past and the future no longer existed, just that one day, August 20th. And the meadow at Hvitemoen, over and over. New ideas, new angles, sudden unpredictable leaps. I was with Lillian. He had said so many times, but now he no longer believed it himself. Lillian says no. Why is she saying that? August 20th. He was alone in the car driving along the road. Terrifying images leapt into his mind. Were they his own, were they real or imagined? Had they been planted there by this stubborn grey man? He groaned. His head felt heavy and wet.

"I can help you discover the truth," Sejer said. "But you have to want to do it."

"Leave me alone," Gøran said.

He felt something swell in his mouth together with an intuitive fear that he would let himself down if he opened up and spat out the words, once and for all.

"My dog's back on his feet," Sejer said. "He totters about and has started to eat a little. It was quite a relief. I feel invigorated."

This made Gøran groan even more. "I need to work out," he said. "I go crazy when I don't work out!"

"Later, Gøran, later. Then we'll deny you nothing. Gym. Fresh air. Visits. Newspapers and TV. Possibly even a PC. But we've got work to do first."

"I'm stuck," he sobbed. "I don't remember."

"It's a question of willingness. You need to cross a threshold. As long as you sit here hoping it was all a bad dream, you won't allow yourself to remember."

Gøran buried his head in his shirtsleeves and sniffled.

"But what if I didn't do it?" he whimpered.

"If it wasn't you, then we'll know, Gøran. From our findings. From what you're saying."

"Everything's a mess."

"Were you with someone?"

"No."

"Did you ask Einar to help you get rid of the suitcase?"

"She didn't have a suitcase!"

The words rang out in the room. Escaped involuntarily from his lips. Sejer felt a chill down his spine. He remembered it now, he was there in his mind. He saw her come walking.

She didn't have a suitcase!

"But the bag," he said calmly. "You do remember the bag."

"It was yellow," Gøran groaned. "It looked like a fucking banana."

"Yes," Sejer said. He said it softly, almost inaudibly. "There she comes walking. You see the yellow banana. Was she hitchhiking?"

"No. She was walking along the road. Then she heard the car and stopped. I wondered why and braked automatically. Thought she might ask for directions. But she asked about Jomann. If I knew him. I said no, but I know who he is. I can give you a lift. She got in. Sitting straight up in the passenger seat.

"'He's not at home.'

"'We can look,' I said. And asked what she was doing there."

Gøran was talking to the table. Sejer listened, not daring to breathe.

"'Is my husband,' she replied smiling. Squeezing the silly bag between her hands.

"'Bloody hell!' I laughed. 'That dirty old man!'

"She looked offended. 'Not polite to say so. You are not very polite,' she said.

"'No,' I said, 'I'm not very polite, sod it. Especially not today. And neither are women.'"

Gøran paused. Sejer felt a trembling in his body, which slipped away and was then replaced by unease. What he was witnessing was the actual story. It made him both relieved and sad. A cruelty he didn't want to see, but had become a part of. Forever, perhaps.

"I remember her plait," Gøran said. "I wanted to pull it right off."

"Why?" Sejer said.

"It was so long and thick and tempting.

"'You angry?' she asked, pretty cautiously, and I said, 'Yes, very angry. You women are so stingy.' Then she got a strange look on her face and shut her mouth.

"'Or maybe you're not stingy?' I said. 'Not if you're prepared to settle for old Gunder, and in that case I should be good enough for you.'

"She looked at me blankly. Started fiddling with the car door. I said, no, leave the fucking door, but she panicked and pulled and pushed like a maniac and I thought: she's one of those emotional women who don't know what they want. First she wants to get in the car, now she wants to get out. So I drove on. As we passed Gunder's house she gave me a really distressed look. Started screaming and shouting. So I slammed the brakes on. She wasn't wearing a seatbelt and went slap into the front window. Not that hard, but she started howling."

Gøran inhaled deeply. His breathing grew faster. Sejer imagined a car, askew on the road, and the agile woman, pale with fear, with her hand on her forehead.

Gøran's voice changed suddenly. It became lifeless, almost commentating. He straightened up and looked at Sejer.

"'Do Indian women have just as much room down there as Norwegian ones?' I asked her, and stuck my hand down between her thighs. She went off her rocker. Lost it completely. She got the door open and stumbled out. Ran out into the meadow, terrified."

And Linda, Sejer thought, is approaching on her bike, perhaps she is right around the bend. Any second now she'll see the car.

"I grabbed one of the dumbbells from the back seat and ran after her," Gøran said dully. "I'm in good shape. Running was easy, it turned me on, but she was fast too, she ran like a bloody rabbit through the grass. I caught up with her at the edge of the wood. It was weird, I saw a light flash in one of Gunwald's windows. But it didn't worry me."

"Did she scream?" Sejer said.

"No. She was busy running. All I heard was her feet through the grass and my own breathing."

"So you caught up with her. Then what did you do?"

"I don't remember any more."

"Of course you do. What were you feeling?"

"I felt incredibly strong. My body was on fire. Besides, she was pathetic."

"In what way?"

"Everything was pathetic. Her going to Jomann's. The way she looked. Her clothes and jewellery. All that tinsel. She wasn't young either."

"She was thirty-eight," Sejer said.

"I know. It said so in the paper."

"Why did you hit her?"

"Why? I was holding the dumbbell in my hand. She curled up with her hands over her head waiting for the blow."

"Couldn't you have turned round and left?"

"No."

"I need to know why."

"Because I'd reached a boiling point. I could hardly breathe."

"Did you hit her many times?"

"I don't think so."

"Could you breathe again once she collapsed?"

"Yes, I could breathe again."

"Did she get up again, Gøran?"

"What?"

"Did you toy with her?"

"No. I just wanted to finish the job."

"There were traces after you ran all over the meadow. We need to get this right."

"But I don't remember any more."

"Let's move on. What did you do when she finally lay still in the grass?"

"I drove to Norevann."

"What did you do with your clothes?"

"Threw them in the lake."

"You put on your gym clothes?"

"I must have."

"And the dumbbells?"

"I put them in the car. One of them was bloody."

"You had scratches to your face. Did she scratch you?"

"Not that I remember. She hit my chest with her fists."

"How long were you by the lake, Gøran?"

"Don't know."

"Do you remember what you were thinking as you got back in the car and drove home?"

"It's difficult. I drove to Lillian's."

"You're getting fact and fiction mixed up again."

"But I know that's how it was. I would see her in the rear-view mirror. She waved from the window, hidden slightly by the curtain."

"Why did you return to the crime scene?"

"Did I?"

"Had you lost something? Which you absolutely had to find?"

Gøran shook his head.

"No. I panicked. What if she was still alive and able to talk? So I got up and went back to the car. Got in and drove back. Then I spotted her. She was staggering around the meadow like a drunk. It was a nightmare. I couldn't believe that she was still alive."

"Go on."

"She was crying for help, but very feebly. She'd almost lost her voice. Then she spotted me. It was strange, but she raised her hand and called for help. She didn't recognise me."

"You'd changed your clothes," Sejer said.

"Yes. Of course."

He lost his concentration for a moment. "Then she collapsed in the grass. She was in a totally different place to where I'd left her. I grabbed one of the dumbbells and ran out into the meadow. Bent down and stared at her. That's when she recognised me. Her eyes at that moment, they were indescribable. Then she called – it seemed – for help, feebly, in a foreign language. Perhaps she was praying. Then I hit her many times. I remember thinking it was strange that there could be so much life in a person. But in the end she stopped moving."

"The dumbbell, Gøran? What did you do with it?"

"Don't remember. I might have thrown it in the lake."

"So you went back to Norevann?"

"No. Yes. I'm not sure."

"And afterwards?"

"I drove around for a bit."

"So you went home at last. Tell me what happened then."

"I chatted to my mum a bit and then I took a shower."

"And your clothes? Gym clothes?"

"I put them in the washing machine. Afterwards I threw them out. I couldn't get them clean."

"Think about the woman. Do you recall what she was wearing?"

"Something dark."

"Do you remember her hair?"

"She was Indian. I guess it was black."

"Was she wearing earrings? Do you recall them?"

"No."

"Her hands, which she hit you with."

"Brown," he said.

"With rings?"

"Don't know. Don't know any more," he mumbled.

He flopped on to the table.

"Do you confess to murdering this woman, Poona Bai? On August 20th at 9 p.m.?"

"Confess?" Gøran said, frightened. It was as if he suddenly woke up. "I don't know. You asked to see my images and that's what you got."

Sejer looked at him calmly.

"What shall I write in the report, Gøran? That these are your images of Poona's murder?"

"Something like that. If that's all right."

"It's not very clear," Sejer said slowly. "Do you consider this a confession?"

"Confession?"

Once again there was a frightened expression in Gøran's eyes.

"What do you think it looks like?"

"Don't know," Gøran said anxiously.

"You've given me some images. Can we call them memories?"

"I suppose we can."

"Your memories of August 20th. A genuine attempt to reconstruct what happened between you and Poona Bai?"

"Yes. I suppose so."

"So what have you in fact given me, Gøran?"

Gøran leaned across the table. In despair he sank his teeth into his shirtsleeve.

"A confession," he said. "I've given you a confession."

CHAPTER 23

Friis tried to keep himself under control.

"Do you understand what you have done?" he said hoarsely. "Do you understand the seriousness?"

"Yes," Gøran said. He lay dozing on the bunk. His body was entirely filled with serenity.

"You have confessed to the most serious crime of all, carrying the law's most severe penalty. Despite the fact that the police doesn't have a single conclusive piece of evidence. It is highly questionable whether they are able to bring a case on this weak basis at all. In addition they have to find a jury willing to convict you on postulations and hearsay."

He paced the floor angrily.

"Do you really understand what you've done?"

Gøran looked at Friis in surprise. "What if I did it?"

"*What if!* You said you were innocent. Have you changed your mind?"

"I don't care about that any longer. Perhaps I did do it. I've been sitting in that room for so many hours thinking so many thoughts. I don't know what the truth is any more. Everything is true, nothing is true. I don't get to work out. I feel like I'm drugged," he snuffled.

"They've put pressure on you," Friis said earnestly. "I'm asking you to please withdraw your confession."

"You could have sat in there with me! Like I asked you to! That's my right!"

"It's not a good strategy," Friis said. "It's best for us if I don't know what happened between the two of you. That way I can cast aspersions on Sejer's methods. Do you hear me? I want you to withdraw your confession!"

Gøran looked at him in amazement. "Isn't that a bit late?"

Friis started walking up and down the cell floor again.

"You've given Sejer the one thing he wanted. A confession."

"Are you looking for the truth?" Gøran said.

"I'm looking to save your skin!" he said sharply. "It's my job and I'm good at it. Heavens above, you're a young man! If they convict you, you'll be going down for a long time. The best years of your life. Think about it!"

Gøran turned towards the wall. "You can go now. To hell with it all."

Friis sat down next to him. "No," he said, "I'm not going. Under duress you have confessed to a crime you didn't commit. Sejer is older than you, an authority. He has exploited your youth. It's a miscarriage of justice. You're probably completely brainwashed. We will withdraw the confession and they'll just have to lump it. Now lie down and rest. Try to get some sleep. There's still a long way to go."

"You have to talk to my mum and dad," Gøran said.

The fact of the confession had barely been published when the papers had to inform their readers about its withdrawal. At Einar's Café people sat reading, their eyes wide. Those in doubt, who had maintained his innocence all along, felt tricked. In their heart of hearts they could not believe it. That a young man would confess to smashing a woman's head to a pulp in a meadow if he had not done it. They felt sick at the very thought. Gøran wasn't the person they thought he was. They could not relate to the legal and technical arguments or the article itself, which listed examples of people who had confessed to murders and much else besides which they had never committed. One newspaper reeled off several cases. They examined themselves and felt the resistance, felt that it had to be impossible. And that the people who would be on the jury one day would think as they did.

It was quiet at the café, no fresh debates, just people in doubt, wavering. Mode said, no, for fuck's sake, I'd never have believed it. Nudel was silent and Frank shook his heavy head in disbelief. What the hell were you supposed to think? Ole Gunwald was relieved. He had fingered Einar, but he had turned out to be innocent as the driven snow. True, that was what he had assumed about young Seter, but on reflection he did have sufficient imagination to accept the notion of a raging, over-fit young man who had just been cast off by his girlfriend. And then his mistress, so it was said. How had the papers put it? "A killer with brutal strength."

Gunder had twice come to the telephone to listen to Sejer's explanations. First that they had finally achieved a result, then just hours later this retreat, which didn't worry him, he said, the confession would weigh heavily in court, it needed explaining. We're hopeful that Gøran will be convicted, he said, sounding very persuasive. Gunder thanked him, but he didn't want to hear any more. He wanted it all to be over.

"How is your sister doing?" Sejer said.

"No change."

"Don't give up hope."

"I won't. I've got no-one else." Gunder thought for a while. There was something he wanted to mention. "By the way, I've received a letter. From Poona's brother. It's still in the drawer. A letter which Poona wrote to him after our wedding. In the letter she told him everything. He thought I'd like to have it."

"Did it make you happy?"

"It's in Indian," Gunder said. "In Marathi. That's no use to me."

"I can arrange to have it translated if you like."

"I would, yes please."

"Send it to me," Sejer said.

Robert Friis staunchly maintained that Gøran's confession was incomplete. That he had not in any way accounted for the murder. He didn't remember the woman's clothes, just that they were dark. There was no mention of gold sandals, likewise something as unusual as a Norwegian brooch on the woman's clothes. He had no opinion of the deceased's appearance, though everyone else who had had dealings with the victim had mentioned the protruding teeth. It's reconstruction, pure and simple, Friis thundered, volunteered in a moment of doubt and exhaustion. When questioned about where exactly in Norevann he had thrown the clothes, Gøran was unclear.

The initial confession was full of holes and unrelated detail. The later, subsequent reconstruction would reveal this. Friis ran into Sejer in the canteen and though the inspector stared resolutely at his prawn sandwich, Friis flopped down at his table. He was a gossip, but a real pro. Sejer was a man of few words, but equally sure of his ground.

"He's the right man and you know it," he said tersely, harpooning a prawn with his fork.

"Probably," Friis said immediately, "but he shouldn't be convicted on this basis."

Sejer wiped a trace of mayonnaise from his lips and looked at the defence lawyer.

"He'll be released back into the community sooner or later, but if he walks away from this, he'll still be ticking away like an unexploded bomb."

Friis smiled and started on his own sandwich. "You probably don't concern yourself with murders which have yet to be committed. You're busy enough as it is with the cases on your desk right now. So am I."

For a while they both ate.

"The worst thing is," Sejer said, "that Gøran felt at ease with himself for the first time in a long while. By withdrawing the confession he'll have to go through it all over again. It doesn't get him anywhere. He should have been spared this."

Friis slurped his coffee.

"He should never have been charged in the first place," he said. "You're an old hand at this, I'm surprised you took the risk."

"You know that I had to," Sejer said.

"And I know how you work, too," Friis said. "You're on his side. Buttering him up. Listening sympathetically, slapping him on the shoulder. Complimenting him. You're the only one who can get him out of that room and to some other place, irrespective of all his rights. They're the first thing you take away from him."

"I could shout and beat him up," Sejer said simply. "Would you have preferred that?"

Friis didn't answer. He chewed carefully for a long time. And then he said sharply: "You've planted an Indian woman in his consciousness. Like a scientist once planted a polar bear. An experiment, pure and simple."

"Really?" Sejer said.

"Play that game with me. If you know it."

"I think I do."

"Think about anything at all for a few seconds. Create an image of anything you like. Everything is allowed except this: that the image must not contain a polar bear. Apart from that, everything is allowed. But don't think about a polar bear. Do you get my drift?"

"Better than you think," Sejer said.

"So, start thinking."

Sejer thought, but he went on eating. An image came to him quickly. He remained sitting watching it.

"Well?" Friis said.

"I see a tropical beach," Sejer said. "With azure blue water and a single palm tree. And white foaming waves."

"And what comes padding along the beach?" Friis teased.

"The polar bear," Sejer admitted.

"Exactly. You escaped as far from the north of Norway as you could go, but that blasted bear followed you all the way to the tropics. Because I planted it there. Just as you planted Poona Bai in Gøran's mind."

"If you disapprove of my methods, you'll just have to accompany your clients to the interrogations."

"I've too many of them," Friis said.

"The video of the interrogation will be ready soon," Sejer said. "Then you'll have to change tack."

He went to his office and found Skarre there. Without a word Skarre handed him an envelope with a small newspaper cutting. Sejer read it.

"'Man (29) found stabbed in Oslo street. He died later from his injuries.' In your letterbox? No postmark?"

"That's right."

Sejer looked at him searchingly. "Does it worry you?"

Skarre messed up his curls nervously. "My tyres were slashed with a knife. We're talking about a knife here, too. Whoever it was has come right to my front door. Followed me. Wants something from me. I don't understand it."

"How about Linda Carling? Have you considered her?"

"I have, as a matter of fact, but this isn't a particularly feminine thing to do. Neither is slashing tyres."

"Perhaps she's not very feminine."

"I'm not quite sure what she is. I called her mother recently. She is very concerned about her. Says she's changed completely. Stopped going to college. Dresses differently and has become really withdrawn. Plus she's knocking back painkillers. One bottle after another. Then she said something really strange. That her voice had changed."

"What?"

"You remember her? The high-pitched voice, that distinctive chirping which teenage girls have?"

"Well?"

"It's gone. Her voice is deeper."

Sejer looked again at the cutting.

"Would you do me a favour and watch yourself?"

Skarre sighed. "She's sixteen years old. But, OK, I'll keep looking over my shoulder. However, I keep thinking about those pills."

"She's drugging herself," Sejer said.

"Or she's in pain," Skarre said. "From being attacked, perhaps."

Linda was sewing something on a white blouse. She sat very still beneath the lamp, sewing with a dedication and a meticulousness her mother had never seen in her. Didn't know where she'd got the blouse from either.

"Is it new? Where did you get the money?"

"I bought it from Fretex, 45 kroner."

"It's not like you to wear a white blouse."

Linda tilted her head. "It's for a special occasion."

249

Her mother liked the reply. She supposed it meant that there was a boy involved, which to some extent was true.

"Why are you swapping the buttons?"

"Gold buttons look silly," Linda said. "The tortoiseshell ones are better."

"Did you hear the news today?"

"No."

"They're going to put Gøran on trial. Even though he withdrew his confession."

"I see," Linda said.

"It'll come to court in three months. I can't believe he did it."

"I can," Linda said. "I wasn't sure at first, but now I am."

She kept on sewing. Her mother saw that her daughter was beautiful. Older. More quiet. Nevertheless she felt anxious about something.

"You never see Karen any more?"

"No."

"It's a shame. She's a nice girl."

"True," Linda said. "But dreadfully ignorant."

Her mother was taken aback. "Ignorant about what?"

Linda put down the blouse. "She's just a kid." Then she went on sewing. Looped the thread around the button and tied a knot.

"It's strange about Gøran," her mother said pensively. "Can they convict him solely on circumstantial evidence? The defence says there's not one shred of conclusive evidence." She was quoting from the newspaper.

"One shred of circumstantial evidence wouldn't mean much," Linda conceded. "But if there are enough of them that changes the character of the case."

"How so?" She looked at her daughter in amazement.

"Preponderance of evidence."

"Where on earth did you learn words like that?"

"The newspapers," Linda said. "He drove a car like the one I saw. He was dressed like the man I saw. He can't find the clothes he was wearing or his shoes. He can't account for where he was, he's told several lies to give himself an alibi, all of which have been repudiated.

His face was scratched the day after the murder. He kept something, which definitely could have been the murder weapon in his car. Traces of magnesium were found on the victim that probably came from Adonis, and he came straight from being there with his girlfriend right after she'd broken up with him. And last, but not least: during the interrogation he confessed to having murdered her. What more do you need?"

Her mother shook her head in confusion. "No, good God. I wouldn't know." She looked once more at the white blouse. "When will you be wearing it?"

"I'm meeting someone."

"Now, tonight?"

"Sooner or later."

"That's cryptic." Once again her mother felt uneasy. "You're strange these days. Well, I'm sorry, but I don't get you. Is everything all right?"

"I'm very happy," she said precociously.

"But what about college and everything? What about that?"

"I just need a break." She looked up, lost in thought. Held the white garment up against the light. In her mind she could clearly see the blouse red and sticky from Jacob's blood. She would save it forever and ever as a token of her love. Suddenly she had to laugh. She shook her head giddily. It was a long way from thinking something to actually doing it, this much she understood. However, she enjoyed the game. It made her feel alive. Take the bus into town. Hide in the stairwell with the knife behind her back. Suddenly she spots Jacob as he comes in from the street. In the light from the streetlamp his curls shine like gold. She springs out of the darkness. His voice filled with wonder. The last words he would ever say: Linda. Is that you?

CHAPTER 24

Sejer stood in the hallway listening out. The dog came tottering round the corner.

"How are you, old boy?"

He squatted down and scratched behind its ear. It had put on a little weight. Its coat was regaining some of its former shine.

"Come here," he said. "I bought hamburgers for you, but they need frying first."

The dog sat quietly by the cooker while Sejer clattered around with the frying pan and some butter.

"Seasoning?" he enquired politely. "Salt and pepper?"

"Woof," Kollberg said.

"You'll get draught beer today. Beer is nutritious. But only the one."

The dog showed that he was listening by raising his floppy ears. Gradually the smell of cooking filled the kitchen and he started slobbering.

"It's strange," Sejer said, looking at Kollberg. "Before, you'd be impossible by now. Jumping and dancing and barking and yelping and making a fearful racket. Now you're sitting there peacefully. Will you ever be the same?" he wondered, flipping the burgers over. "Not that it matters. I'll take you as you are."

Later Jacob turned up with a bottle. He spent a long time saying hello to Kollberg. Sejer fetched glasses and his own bottle of Famous Grouse. They sat down by the window looking out over the city, which was slowly settling down for the night. The dog rested by Sejer's feet, sated with food and beer. A faint rustling crept through the windows.

"Sara not coming?" Skarre said.

"No," Sejer said. "Should she?"

"Yes," Skarre said.

Sejer sipped his whisky. "She's with her father. He's poorly."

"What was wrong with him again? I've forgotten."

"MS," Sejer said. "New cortisone treatment. It's rough for him. He becomes difficult."

"I know all about difficult fathers," Skarre said. "And mine didn't even get the cortisone treatment. He just got high on the holy trinity."

His remark made Sejer look searchingly at his young colleague.

Skarre got up and rummaged around. Went through the CD stand. Hundreds of different artists, all female.

"Aren't men allowed to sing in here, Konrad?" he teased.

"Not in my house."

Skarre took something out of his pocket.

"Many happy returns, Konrad."

"How did you know about that?" He took the CD.

"You're fifty-one today."

Sejer studied the present and thanked him.

"Do you approve?" Skarre asked.

"Judy Garland. Heavens, yes."

"Speaking of presents," Skarre said. "I've had another greeting. No stamp. Someone's been to my flat again."

Sejer stared at the yellow envelope. It was sealed with a paper clip. Skarre tipped the contents on to the table.

"What are those?" Sejer said.

"Buttons," Skarre said. "Two heart-shaped gold buttons strung together with a piece of thread."

Sejer held them under the lamp. "Pretty buttons," he mused. "From an expensive garment. A blouse, perhaps?"

"But I don't care for it. When they lie there on the table in the light of the lamp they acquire some sort of significance. Which I don't understand."

"A proposal," Sejer said. "I bet the two buttons came from Linda." He smiled. "Don't read too much into it. People who call or send things are generally incapable of action."

He had a steady way of talking which calmed Skarre.

"Bin them," he said lifting his glass of red wine to his lips.

"The pretty buttons? Are you serious?"

"Throw them in the bin. I don't want them."

Sejer went out into the kitchen where he opened and then slammed a cupboard door and at the same time put the buttons in his pocket.

"They're garbage now," he said.

"Why did Gøran withdraw his confession?" Skarre said. "It really bothers me."

"Gøran's fighting for his life," Sejer said. "And it's his right. It will be a long time before this case is closed."

"Has Jomann been told?"

"Yes. He didn't say much. He is not a vindictive man."

Skarre smiled at the thought of Gunder. "Jomann is an oddball," he said. "Simple as a child."

His remark earned him a stern look from Sejer. "You should never equate eloquence with intelligence."

"I thought there was a link," Skarre muttered.

"Not in this case."

For a while they drank in silence. Skarre fished out his bag of jelly babies. He took a yellow one and dipped it in the red wine. Sejer shuddered. The whisky began to take effect. His shoulders relaxed and his body felt warm. Skarre's jelly baby turned orange.

"You can see only the tragedy here," Skarre said.

"What else is there to see?"

"Jomann has become a widower. Not the worst status for a man like him. In some way he seems so proud of her. Even though she's dead. Now he can live on this for the rest of his life. Wouldn't you agree?"

Sejer snatched the bag of jelly babies from his hand. "Your blood sugar's too high," he said.

Silence once more. The two men took turns raising their glasses.

"What are you thinking about?" Skarre said eventually.

"I'm thinking about how things happen," Sejer said. "Quite independently of one another. So that terrible events like this one can occur."

254

Skarre filled his glass and listened.

"Why did Poona die? Because Gøran murdered her. But also because Marie Jomann was a terrible driver. She had her accident and so Jomann didn't get to meet Poona at the airport. Or, she died because Kalle Moe didn't find her at Gardermoen. She died because Ulla broke up with Gøran. Because Lillian said no. There are so many elements. So many incidents which pave the way for evil."

"I'm thinking about Anders Kolding," Skarre said.

"He panicked and ran away to his sister's. But not because of a murder. He fled from a screaming kid and a marriage he probably wasn't ready for."

"The girl in the garage said he turned left."

"Everyone can make a mistake," Sejer said.

"Einar had her suitcase."

"He's a coward, plain and simple."

"I don't trust Lillian Sunde." Jacob looked his boss in the eyes. "I think she's lying to us."

"Absolutely. But not about that particular night."

Skarre bowed his head and looked down at his knees. Then he summoned up his last remaining courage. "To be honest, I'm not sure what I believe. Perhaps he's innocent. Did you hear about the letter Holthemann received?"

"Oh yes, I heard about it. An anonymous letter written with words cut from newspapers. 'You have got the wrong man.' I also heard about the woman caller who claimed to be a clairvoyant."

"She said the same thing," Skarre said.

"Precisely. And if the duty officer had half a brain he would have noted down her name and number."

"You wouldn't work with a clairvoyant, would you?"

"Not on her terms. She might not be a clairvoyant at all, but she might have known something vital about the murder. Soot thought she was a time-waster. I told him off," he said.

"You did indeed," Skarre said. "They heard you all the way down to the canteen."

"My own mother even wagged her finger at me." Sejer smiled wistfully.

"But your mother's dead?"

"That gives you some idea of how loud I shouted. I have apologised to Soot."

"What about Elise?" Skarre said. "Do you ever hear from her?"

Silence fell over Sejer's flat.

"Elise never scolds," he said at last.

It was late in the evening when Skarre got up to find his jacket. The dog padded after him to wish him goodbye. Its legs were weak, but they were growing stronger day by day. As they stood there saying their farewells, they were startled by the doorbell angrily buzzing. Sejer, puzzled, looked at the time: it was close to midnight. A woman was standing on the threshold. He stared at her for a while before he realised who she was.

"I am sorry for coming so late," she said. "But I won't keep you. I have only one important thing to say."

Sejer squeezed the door handle. The woman confronting him was Gøran's mother.

"Do you have children?" she said, staring hard at him. Her voice was trembling. He saw her chest rise and fall under her coat. Her face was white.

"Yes," Sejer said.

"I don't know how well you know them," she said, "but I know Gøran very well. I know him like my own body, and he didn't do this."

Sejer stared at her feet. She was wearing brown ankle boots.

"I would have known it," she said. "The dog scratched him. No-one would believe it, but I saw him that evening on the 20th. I was by the window, washing up, when he came through the gate. He was carrying his sports bag, and when he saw the dog, he dropped the bag and they started playing. He's fond of the dog and they play pretty roughly. Rolled around like kids. His face was scratched and there was blood on him when he came into the house. He took a shower then, and he was singing."

She said no more for a while. Sejer waited.

"It's God's honest truth," she said. "That's all I wanted to say." She spun round and started down the stairs.

Sejer stood for a while, recovering. Then he closed the door. Skarre looked at him in astonishment.

"He *sang* in the shower?"

The words seemed to hang in the hallway. Sejer went back into his living room and gazed out of the window. He watched Helga Seter cross the car park below the flats.

"Would someone sing in the shower having done a thing like that?"

"By all means. But not from joy, perhaps," Sejer said.

"What are you thinking?" Sejer asked him.

"Lots of things. Linda Carling, and who she is, what she did actually see, Gøran Seter, who is at the mercy of all these unreliable people."

"You want the loose ends neatly tied at the end," Sejer said. "You want every last piece of the jigsaw in place. Because people are like that. Reality is different. Just because some of the pieces don't fit doesn't mean that Gøran is innocent."

He turned his back to him.

"But it's bloody annoying, nevertheless." Skarre refused to back down.

"Yes," Sejer conceded. "It's bloody annoying."

"I'll tell you one thing," Skarre admitted. "If I were on that jury when the case comes to court, I would never dare convict him."

"You're not going to be on the jury," Sejer said. He breathed on the window. "And of course Gøran's a wonderful son to his mother. He's her only child."

"So what do you really think happened?" Skarre said, still in doubt.

Sejer sighed and turned around. "I think that Gøran drove around after the murder, in terrible despair. He'd already changed his clothes once and now the clothes he'd changed into were covered in blood. He had to get back into the house. Possibly he spotted his mother in the kitchen window. The blood on his clothes needed an explanation. So he throws himself at the dog. That way he could account for the scratches and the blood."

Suddenly he chuckled.

"What's funny?" Skarre said.

"I was reminded of something. Did you know that a rattlesnake can bite you long after it's head has been chopped off?"

Skarre watched his friend's broad silhouette by the window, waiting for enlightenment.

"Shall I call you a taxi?" Sejer continued without turning around.

"No, I'll walk."

"It's a long way," he said. "And black as night in that stairwell of yours."

"It's a lovely evening, and I need the fresh air."

"So you're not worried?" Sejer gave him an affectionate smile, but it was a serious question all the same.

Skarre gave him no answer. He left, and Sejer stood again by the window. Gold buttons, he thought, taking them from his shirt pocket. Slashed tyres. Newspaper cuttings about a young man found bleeding to death in the street. What did it mean? Then Jacob appeared in the streetlight. He walked with long, brisk steps away from the block of flats and out on the road. Then he was swallowed up by the darkness.

Two men sat together in Einar's Café. It was past closing time, everyone else had gone. Mode appeared calm, the hand holding his glass steady. Einar was smoking roll-ups. Faint music was coming from the radio. Einar had lost weight. He worked longer hours and ate less now that he was on his own. Mode was unchanged. Mode was in fact abnormally self-possessed, Einar thought, watching him covertly. So unchanged. He had closed up the petrol station for the night. From the window they could see the yellow shell light up the darkness.

"Why didn't they ever talk to you?" Einar demanded to know.

"They did."

Einar sniffed. "But they never checked your alibi and all that."

"They had no reason to either."

"But they checked everyone else's very carefully. Mine. Frank's. Not to mention Gøran's."

"Well, you did have the suitcase," Mode said. "Hardly any wonder they checked up on you."

"But you must've been driving home from bowling at Randskog around the time of the murder."

"What do you know about that?" Mode said, barely audibly.

"Been talking to people. You have to, if you want to keep yourself in the know. Tommy reckoned you left at 8.30 p.m."

"Ah," Mode said, smiling winningly. "So you take it upon yourself to go around checking people's alibis. But Gøran confessed. So I suppose this is just a joke, no?"

"But he withdrew it. And what if he's not convicted?" Einar said. "We'll have the murder hanging over us forever. We will always be suspecting each other."

"Will we?" Mode said, drinking his beer. He was very cool, was Mode.

"Tell me honestly," Einar said. "Do you think Gøran is guilty?"

"I've no idea," Mode said.

"Are people talking about me?" Einar wanted to know. "Have you heard any gossip?"

"I can't say that I haven't. But sod it. Gøran's locked up. We have to move on."

Einar stubbed his cigarette out in the ashtray. "There's too much that doesn't add up. It says in the paper that he threw his – presumably blood-stained – clothes and the dumbbells in Norevann. And yet they haven't found them."

"In all that mud," Mode said, "there would hardly be any point searching."

"Also there were problems with the reconstruction. The police interrogators probably coerced him. To get what they needed. That's how they do it."

"It's probably difficult to remember the details when you're stumbling around in a red mist of blood," Mode said.

"So you know what that's like? A mist of blood?"

Mode didn't flinch. "Imagine driving round with the dumbbells in his car," he said. "I suppose he goes cold turkey without them. That speaks volumes."

259

"People drive around with all sorts of stuff in their cars," Einar said, studying him. "You always drive around with your bowling ball. To and from Randskog all the time. How much does it weigh?"

"Ten kilos," Mode smiled.

"And you like those exotic women," Einar provoked him.

"Do I?" He smiled that smile again.

"You were seeing Thuan's eldest."

"We had a little fling. I've no regrets. They're different."

They fell silent once more, staring out of the black window, but they found only each other's faces in there and turned away.

Gunder went to the hospital as usual. He gathered up his strength to say a few words.

"Hello, Marie. It's coming to court now. If they convict him, he'll be jailed for many years. Afterwards they'll probably squabble about the sentence, Gøran and his defence lawyer. Say that it's too harsh. Because he's young. From my point of view he'll still be young when he's released. A man in his mid-thirties still has his life ahead of him. Poona hasn't.

"You don't look like your old self," he said heavily. "However, I recognise your nose. It looks bigger than usual because you're so thin. Imagine how long you've been lying here, I can hardly believe it. Has Karsten been here today? He promised to. He is such a stranger to me. Perhaps to you too. He was never around much, was he?"

Silence. He listened to his sister's faint breathing. The garish light from the ceiling made her look old.

"I've nothing more to tell you," Gunder said sadly. "I've talked so much." He bowed his head. Fixed his glance at the lifting mechanism on the bed, a pedal by the floor. Remained sitting, nudging it. "Tomorrow I'll bring a book. That way I can read to you. It'll be good for me to tell you about something other than myself. Which book should I bring? I'll have to look on the shelves. I could read *People of All Nations*, and we can travel the world, you and I. Africa and India."

His eyes brimmed with tears and he wiped them away with his knuckles. Raised his head and looked at his sister through a veil of tears. He was looking right into an alert eye. He froze when he saw the dark regard. She was staring at him from a place far away. Her eyes were filled with wonder.

Later, when the excitement had died down and the doctor had examined Marie, she slipped away again. Gunder could not tell if she had recognised him. She would probably regain consciousness and slip away several times before she regained consciousness altogether. He called Karsten. Heard a faint tremor of panic in his voice. Then he went to Poona's grave. Tended to the bushy Erica that could withstand everything, both frost and drought. Dug the cold soil with his fingers, caressing the little spot that belonged to Poona. Stroked the wooden crucifix and the letters which made up her pretty name. When he was done, he could not get up. His body was fixed in this position, he could not move his arms or his legs. Or raise his head. After a while he was cold and even stiffer. His back and knees started to ache. His head was empty, no grief, no fear, just an echoing void. He could stay like this till spring. There was no reason to get up. Ice and cold snow would soon cover everything. Gunder was a frozen sculpture as he knelt there with his white hands buried in the soil.

A shadow appeared in his field of vision. The vicar was standing beside him.

"Jomann," he said. "You must be cold on your knees here."

He said it so softly. The way vicars do, Gunder thought. But he could not move.

"Come inside where it's warm," Berg said.

Gunder tried to lift himself up, but his body wouldn't move.

Berg wasn't a big man, but he took hold of Gunder's arms and helped him. Patted him awkwardly on the shoulder. Nudged him gently in front of him to the vicarage. Got him inside and helped him to a chair. The fire was burning. Gunder slowly thawed.

"What have I done?" he said in tears.

Berg looked at him calmly. Gunder was having difficulty

breathing. "I tricked Poona into coming here, straight to her death," he lamented. "Put her in the cold ground even though she's a Hindu and should be somewhere else. With one of her own gods."

"But she wanted to come here to be with you," Berg said.

Gunder hid his face in his hands. "And I was going to give her the best of everything!"

"I think you have done," Berg said. "She has a beautiful place. If you had sent her back with her brother you might have regretted it. You had to choose between two desperate solutions. That happens sometimes. No-one could blame you for anything."

Gunder let these words sink in. Then he raised his head and looked at the vicar.

"I wonder what God's purpose was in all this," he said, subdued now. A flash of anger crossed his face.

Berg looked from the window at the treetops outside. The leaves were falling. "So do I," he said.

After a while Gunder pulled himself together. "In India the kids play football between the graves," he remembered. "It looked nice. As if it was natural."

Berg had to smile. "It would be nice. However, that's not for me to decide."

Gunder went home. Stood for a while at the foot of the staircase. Finally he made up his mind. He went upstairs and took out Poona's clothes, which were in a box. Slowly and filled with reverence he took out one garment after another and hung them in the wardrobe in the bedroom. The wardrobe, which up until now had been full of grey and black clothes, looked completely different. He put her shoes at the bottom of it. He carried her sponge bag to his bathroom. Put her brush next to the mirror. A little bottle of perfume found a place beside his own aftershave. Afterwards he sat at the kitchen table and looked out at the garden. The day had clouded over and everything was grey. He had hung a bird feeder outside the window. He must put food out first thing in the morning. His head was buzzing. What would life with Poona have been like? Was she looking forward to it as much as he was? Or was he just a well-off man and her key to a comfortable future? As his sister had said. Now he would never know if what they had done had meant anything to her. If she would have been a loving wife, a loyal companion. Or whether she was just happy at the thought of leaving poverty behind in Mumbai. How could he know for sure? His future, the one he was struggling to imagine, would be made up of guesswork and fantasies. Of how he had hoped it would be. And he had not even told her that he loved her. He had not dared. How he regretted that now. He wanted to shout it from the highest mountain so that everyone would hear: Beloved, beloved Poona!

What is love? His despairing thought. It was nothing but an ardent wish.

He rested his head on his arms and groaned. Trapped in enormous pain. What must Poona have been thinking when she could not find him at the airport? And then: where was Marie now? And what would she need?

The next morning, as he was making his coffee, he saw the postman's green van. It had stopped at Gunder's letterbox. He waited until the van was out of sight and then he wandered down the driveway. One letter. He went into the kitchen and opened it. It was Poona's letter to her brother. The original, in Indian, and a translation for him. Sejer had enclosed a note. He found his glasses, put them on and struggled to keep his hands steady. As he started reading, it brightened up outside. A cloud slowly unveiled the bright October sun. The grass glistened. There was a thin sheet of ice on the birdbath. A spotted woodpecker landed outside the window. It dug its claws into the bird feeder and started to hack away at the fat and the seeds which Gunder had put out not ten minutes since. A male, Gunder thought. The back of its head shone in the sunlight, red as blood. He read the letter slowly. Everything inside him felt still.

Dear brother Shiraz,

It is a long time since we saw each other. I am writing now on an important matter. And you must forgive me that I have not considered you.

I am a married woman. It happened yesterday. He is a good man, loving and decent. He carries me like you carry a child you want to help and protect. His name is Gunder Jomann.

Mr Jomann is big and strong and handsome. True he does not have much hair and he is not very fast when he acts or thinks. But his every step is well considered and his every thought is sincere. He has a house and a job in the country where he lives. With a garden and fruit trees and all sorts of things. It is cold there, he says, but I am not afraid. He has an aura of light and warmth. I want to be there forever. I am not afraid either of what you might say, dear brother, because I want this more than anything. I will travel to his country and live in his house. For the rest of my life. There is no man on earth who is better than Gunder Jomann. His hands are so strong and open. His eyes are blue like the sky. A quiet strength exudes from his strong broad body. Life with him will be good. Be happy for me!

Be as joyful as I am for everything that has happened.

Your sister, Poona